LAVISH AND LETHAL

THE DAVIA GLENN SERIES
BOOK FOUR

LAURA E. AKERS

ISBN 979-8-9873832-7-8 eBook

ISBN 979-8-9873832-8-5- Paperbacks

ISBN 979-8-9935909-0-5

ISBN 979-8-9935909-1-2

ISBN 979-8-9873832-9-2 Hardback

ISBN 979-8-9935909-3-6 Audible

THE DAVIA GLENN SERIES

DIOR OR DIE
KILLING WITH KINDNESS
POSH AND PERILOUS

PRAISE FOR THE
DAVIA GLENN SERIES

It's so fun to see Black Ops operative Davia navigate life among the frivolous filthy rich- Amazon Review of Posh and perilous

— AMAZON REVIEW

Akers is a true master of the crime thriller genre, and I'm so happy to have found this series!

— K PEARSON BRADLEY

This series keeps getting better and better with each book. Filled with mystery, romance, and a whole lotta action! Page turner until the end!

— S. CAMBRA

*To all survivors who have the
courage to seek justice*

If you know the enemy and know yourself,
you need not fear the results of a hundred battles
-Sun Tzu

Holding your pee is no way to live life
-Kendall Jenner

1

"Leave it to you to find matching Shetlands," I say to Adair Monroe, who holds the leads to two golden ponies with fluffy, flaxen manes.

"Twin girls, twin ponies, right?" he says to Evie and Emily. The six-year-olds sit tall in their English saddles, their blonde, curly hair peeking out from beneath helmets.

After last month's traumatic events, I'm thrilled their foster parent agreed to this outing. I'm seated on my black Quarter Horse, Ace, and Adair hands me the rope to Evie's mount. I wrap it around my saddle horn to avoid being trapped by his aquamarine eyes.

"Davia, I'll get my horse," he says. "Can you hold Emily for a sec?"

Adair's Thoroughbred is tied to a trailer at our meeting place, an English saddle already in place. When he mounts, I drag my gaze from his six-foot frame, the fitted breeches and tall boots drawing a fine line from hip to heel, and ask Evie, "Are you looking forward to getting out on the trails?"

"Yes! Your knight gave us lessons."

Is he my British billionaire in bespoke armor, or an unwanted complication?

Adair takes the lead to Emily's mount. "Ready?"

We proceed along a wide mulch path. Split-rail fencing borders a riot of multi-colored flowers on the forty miles of immaculate trails in Rancho Suprema, California. This landscape is surreal after surviving hellish missions with my Black Ops team, but I'm starting to see what Aunt Lilah had in mind, even if her plan to pamper me with a huge inheritance keeps getting derailed by dead bodies.

Adair and I ride next to each other, the girls on either side. He says, "I hope you're picturing our future where you're my wife and these are our kids."

I bite back a retort. Why ruin a nice day? Instead, I say, "We've been together a long time if our kids are six. Or perhaps we had children right away?"

"I'm going to want you all to myself for quite some time, so we've been married at least ten years."

"That also means my past hasn't caused more problems. Is Jason happy for us?"

"He smiles at you at least once every two years," Adair says about his right-hand man.

"That often?"

"Well…once every five. He likes our kids, though. They bring out the indulgent side he hid from MI6, and he sneaks them candy despite our protests."

"This is quite the idyllic fantasy you've got going. Do you write fiction?"

"Fiction? I play this as a movie in my mind every night before I go to sleep, although the details are much more, um," he draws closer, the word a low confession. "Erotic."

Before I can respond, a percussive beat of hooves drums the ground behind us. A man astride a brown Warmblood blows past at a full gallop. The ponies spook, heads spinning, and the girls grab for manes to stay seated.

Adair steps off his mount in a fluid movement. "Is everyone okay?"

I unwrap Evie's line and toss it to him.

"Davia, what are you—"

"You know what."

Cueing Ace into a jog, then a lope, I stand in my stirrups and smooch the air to encourage his pace. Ahead, a flowing tail disappears around a curve in the trail. Bending over my horse's neck, he flies across the ground at full speed.

Drawing level with the other rider, the outside of my leg bumps his. The man swivels, eyes widening, as I seize his horse's reins. Ace plants his rear, causing the Warmblood to wheel around and come to a stop. The abrupt movement catapults the rider off. He slams into the ground, and a dust cloud erupts.

When he gets to his feet, the flush from both the impact and anger mottles his neck.

"What the hell are you doing?" He grips a scraped and bleeding arm.

"Thinking about how I should have brought a whip today."

"A what?"

"A crop? A switch? Anything to beat some sense into you?"

The man bares his veneer-straight teeth. "How dare you—"

"Stop you for a chat?" I pull my black ballcap lower. "Think of this as a public service announcement for those who ignore trail etiquette. When you sped past us, my group members might have wound up like you, or worse. Two of them are only six years old."

"I, uh, I—"

"Want to tell me you're sorry and won't ever do anything like that again?"

He ignores this, his lower lip thrust out. "How am I supposed to remount without a block? My horse is too tall for me to put my foot in the stirrup."

"Should I care about this?"

"I doubt you do."

"I might have helped if you'd apologized." I gather my reins, wheel Ace around, and ride away.

———

"Did you catch the bad man?" Evie asks when I return. The twins' posture is rigid.

I should've let Ace trample him.

"Why don't we take this other branch of the trail?" Adair suggests. "I'm afraid if we run into whoever that maniac was, I'll wind up in another fistfight. Jason says I'm only allowed one per decade."

"Good idea."

After getting resituated, we turn our horses down a trail leading into a more secluded area. Trees line a wide dirt path, shading us. Sunlight filters through the leaves, and a hawk circles high overhead.

"I think this loops around and takes us past a corral where we can leave the horses and get a snack at the Golf Club's outdoor shack. Would you like some ice cream?" Adair says to the girls.

"You'll get us ice cream?" Emily says.

When he affirms he will, they brim with excitement. Adair uses this moment to hook his thumb into my belt loop, pull me close, and press a kiss on my cheek.

"What was that for?"

"Do I need a reason to kiss the woman I love, especially after she saved me the trouble of another black eye and busted lip?"

"I guess not."

Love? Our acquaintance is too new for such declarations, for me anyway, but this isn't the time to mention it. Again.

The grove ends, and the trail continues across an open pasture surrounded by sloping hills. The June heat casts a serene stillness over us, with no breeze to stir the untended field of dried grass.

"Evie, Emily, are you up for a trot?" Adair asks.

"You mean a jog," I correct.

"That's western rider terminology and doesn't apply to us, does it, girls?"

"Typical snooty English attitude," I tease.

We cue the horses into a steady pace, with the twins and Adair posting in time to their mounts' hoofbeats. Ace has a comfortable gait, so I relax.

A hum, wrong and electric, cuts through the wind of our movement. Craning my neck, I scan the area.

A metallic speck drops from the sky. A military-grade drone. Its murmur drills a cold wire of adrenaline down my spine.

"Look out!" I yell as the thing heads straight for us. It buzzes past the horses like an enraged hornet.

The ponies startle. The girls haul on the reins, fighting for control. The device swoops past Evie's mount, and the pony bolts sideways, tearing the lead from Adair's grip. The little steed flees, Evie's terrified cry trailing behind them.

"I'll get her," Adair promises and rides away in pursuit.

I knot Emily's line around my horn, dismount, and lift her off. Dropping my reins to the ground, Ace stands unmoving despite the pony whirling at his side.

"Come on." I throw an arm around Emily and hustle her forward. "Keep your head down." We sprint toward a nearby cluster of trees. After checking for rattlesnakes, I comb the horizon for the instigator of the attack, but no one's visible.

The drone circles Adair as he chases after Evie, then returns to swoop around Ace's head. Its whine screeches a taunting pitch. As a testament to Ace's training, he pins his ears but doesn't move. After a brief, unrelenting attack, the drone flits away.

Adair has caught Evie and is returning.

"You need to stay here and don't move," I say to Emily, who trembles beside me. "Adair and your sister are almost here."

She nods, eyes filled with unshed tears. I pull her into a brief hug, then run for Ace and mount. I unwrap the pony's line and let it fall to the ground. The Shetland's head raises, and the freed animal dashes off.

The drone veers away. I follow its path across the untended field, watching for gopher holes. With a sudden burst of acceleration, the gadget streaks up a steep incline like a missile locked on a target. Reaching the edge of the field and coming onto a steep dirt road, I dig my heels into my horse's sides, driving him into a flat-out run. We race upward, Ace's muscles taut as we close the distance with our mechanical prey.

When we crest the hill, a distant figure holds a controller near the passenger side of a dark SUV. The operator spies me as the drone folds its propellers and lands in an outstretched hand. Heart sinking, I drive Ace on, but the passenger door slams shut, and the engine roars to life. Tires spin, and the vehicle accelerates away down a rutted road, kicking up dust that fills my lungs and stings my eyes. Pulling on the reins, I ease Ace to a halt. The SUV disappears into a swirling cloud of fine sand.

Was that attack intended for Adair or me? The kids?

Coughing, I wipe the dust from my eyes and return to where Adair waits beside the girls and Evie's Shetland. I dismount, catching a tear on Emily's cheek with my thumb.

"You both kept cool heads," Adair says. "You should be proud of yourselves."

We retrieve the other animal, which crops some nearby grass. "Do you know who did it?" Adair asks me.

"No. I can only say it was two people in a dark SUV. The drone operator was too far away for me to tell if it was a man or a woman, and I couldn't make out the license."

Who were they targeting? Was it a prank or an ongoing problem? No matter. If anyone tries anything again, it will be their last mistake.

2

The twins lick ice cream cones topped with a swirl of chocolate mixed with vanilla, wearing as much of it as they're eating.

"Ice cream makes every day better, right?" Adair says to gooey grins.

We find them a shaded table, our horses tied in a nearby corral. Golfers pass, chatting as they make for the course while I pick apart the attack.

Expensive, specialized drone. Coordinated escape. Why us?

A woman with olive skin and shining brown hair approaches. "Adair? We retrieved the truck and trailer. Do you want us to load all the horses?"

"Davia, this is the manager of my equine interests, Julia Darrow. Given what happened, I thought it prudent not to ride to the trailer, so I asked her to collect it."

We exchange polite greetings, but her brown eyes slide over me and lock on Adair.

"Hi, Julia!" the twins call, and she waves at them.

"Julia helped me teach Evie and Emily to ride," Adair explains. "Do you want us to trailer Ace to your property?"

"No, I'll be okay."

"Can't you text José to expect your horse?" Adair says. "Jason's waiting in the parking lot to drive me and the girls to Stacey Templeton's, and your presence calms them."

"I'm fairly sure the ice cream did the trick," I say, but his down-turned mouth keeps me from protesting further. "Fine, but I want to call José and give him the full story."

As I move away, Julia steps into the space I vacated, and they begin to talk. I turn my back.

He's not my boyfriend.

After the call, I rejoin them and provide my address to Julia, who types the info into her phone.

"Thank you, Julia," Adair says, and she dips her head then departs.

"She's quite dedicated to her work."

"She's competent and professional, which is why she was hired. Are you sure you don't want an ice cream cone? The visual—" He lifts his eyebrows.

"You'll have to rely on your imagination."

"Drat." Adair gives a small laugh, and we settle at the table with Evie and Emily. "Girls, Julia's taking the horses, so Davia and I will go with Jason to take you home."

"Davia, you're coming, too?" Emily says with relief.

"Yes. Ace worked hard, so he deserves a ride instead of having to carry me back. Now, let me attempt to clean you up so Stacey doesn't scream when she sees you."

"She'll scream?" Evie says.

"She's exaggerating," Adair says, "although I think we should be safe and make sure you look presentable."

We clean them with paper napkins. While Adair wipes Evie's face, she says to him, "Where's your boss?"

"My boss? I don't—"

I silently curse the unpredictable avenues of children's minds. My operative team captain, James Warden, made a lasting impression on the twins when they met. All buff 6'3" of him, radiating authority like the concussive wave of a breaching charge. He had agreed with the girls' assessment that he was the boss of my other 'knights'—Adair included.

"She means Warden," I disclose with reluctance.

"Warden—" Adair almost spits the name.

"Knight Commander Warden told us you work for him," Emily interrupts.

"He did, did he?"

"He's way bigger than you!" Evie says.

Adair fixes me with a glacial look, and I stand. "We shouldn't keep Jason. Let's go."

The twins bound toward the parking lot, pausing to smell some pink and yellow roses blooming beside the path. We follow, Adair bending close to my ear. "You don't know he's bigger than me."

"What is it with you today? After what happened, why is your mind on—"

"The attack was another reminder to live life right now, Davia. How long do we have to—"

The appearance of Jason McCall stops his words. He's in his early forties and wears a suit despite the warm temperatures, his brown hair military short.

"Evie, Emily," Jason greets, squeezing the girls' shoulders.

"Jason," I acknowledge, and he grunts a response before he opens the rear door of a BMW SUV, helps the girls inside, and buckles them into their car seats. I ride in back with the twins, their chatter a distraction.

The drive to the property where the girls now reside with their foster parent, Stacey Templeton, takes less than ten minutes. We pass through open white gates emblazoned with the initials S and T, and fine gravel crunches under the tires as we glide past trees and flower beds lining the long drive. A statue of four brass turkeys in mid-flight dominates the front lawn before a sprawling Spanish Colonial Revival mansion. Two-story wings showcase a central three-story mass, a fortress of old money.

Evie and Emily unbuckle as Jason opens their door, and Stacey springs from the house like a jack-in-the-box powered by espresso. She's a brunette in her mid-fifties, sporting a lavender satin top hat adorned with mesh flowers, gems, pearls, and a plume of feathers. Beside her, a white male turkey wears a miniature version of the same hat.

"T5!" the girls cry and rush forward. Jason's eyes widen a fraction as he tracks Stacey with her turkey companion. I want to laugh at his loss of disciplined composure.

"The turkey's full name is Tiberius Torston Templeton the Fifth," I say, "Or Triple T5 for short. Wait until you see his elevator."

"His what?"

Adair claps him on the shoulder. "You've been in the realms of the rich a while now, so I don't understand why you're surprised. Remember when we were invited to an island retreat, and the hosts held an event labeled Jet Set Fetch?"

"Jet Set—what?" I say.

"Fetch. Everyone brought their pedigreed dogs, and their assistants played a game with drones carrying toys," Adair says. "Whichever pet caught the most toys won."

Jason's lips quirk at the memory. "There was a lot of high-stakes betting fueled by alcohol consumption."

"What was the prize?"

"A custom jet designed with the winning dog in mind," Adair says.

"A jet?" I exclaim. "You're making this up."

"Unfortunately, no," Adair says. "The pampered pet got a flying palace with a gourmet galley containing the most expensive dog food, an onboard spa with a grooming and massage station, and a selection of luxury pet care products."

Stacey runs past on the expansive grass lawn with the twins. T5 chases them, his wattles swinging with each stride.

"Adair. Come play!" the girls call, and he races after them, dodging around the turkey and taking Evie's extended hand.

When they reach a distant portion of the grounds, Jason says, "Care to tell me what happened today?"

I recount the drone attack, and his mild gray eyes turn sharp as razors. "Do you have any idea who might have done this?"

"I don't, and I'm unsure who the target was."

"My money's on you."

"You know jumping to conclusions is dangerous."

"Not if it's based on a consistent pattern. In the time you've lived here, you've taken on assassins, terrorists, human traffickers, and others, with Mr. Monroe in the middle almost every time. If he dies, you know I'll come for you."

"I expect nothing less."

———

Once home, I go to the barn to check on Ace. My property manager, José Valenzuela-Macias, is closing the door to his stall when I enter. "I gave him a bath and a snack for his hard work today."

"Thanks, he was stellar despite the dangers."

"As a reward, will you buy a fancy rig like Adair's? Ace enjoyed being conveyed in style."

"You only want one so you can drive around and show off."

"I recommend you hire Adair's horse manager to help me." Jose winks, running a hand through his dark hair.

"Did she seem interested in the position?"

"I'm afraid her boss will win no matter how *guapo* I am."

José is nearing twenty-five and isn't exaggerating about being handsome, but Adair's in another league. Even in Rancho Suprema's stable of beautiful people, he's a premium Thoroughbred.

"Do you think the drone operator was someone sent by Bradford Kensington?" José refers to a multi-billionaire whose hobby is revenge and destroying people, as casually as knocking over pawns in a chess game.

"Dunno. Could've been Rancho brats. Most teens here think consequences are something that happens to other people."

"Could be, but we both know Bradford has no loyalty to anyone but himself. Not even his own children."

"I agree. Be sure and stay on top of security and remain cautious."

We part company. The hike up the steep drive to my 7,500-square-foot home is brief but challenging because of my strained leg. The Spanish architecture features white stucco walls, a terracotta roof, and spectacular views from its prominent placement on the crest of a hill.

Stepping through the front door, I enter what's become a sanctuary. The open layout and natural light calm me, while the comfortable yet chic furniture and art, placed by my friend and interior designer Sherilyn Silvers, add to the tranquility.

If I recover from the nerve damage to my leg caused by a gunshot wound and return to my operative team, I hope someone will want to purchase this place fully furnished.

As if sensing my thoughts, my leg twinges like a blade stabs into my skin. It's not overwhelming, and I can ignore it for now. But what if it gets worse? What if I'm unable to recover?

A call diverts my thoughts.

"Davia? It's Brittany Guinn! Kennedy and I are starting a book club and want you to join."

Brittany and Kennedy...read? My mind implodes at the thought of these model-thin, perpetual selfie-takers doing anything that doesn't involve ring lights and camera angles.

"Uh..."

"When we visited Adair's property on the Ladies' League Home and Garden tour last month, we noticed his library. It reminded me of the one in *Beauty and the Beast*, you know, all those books floor to ceiling? So romantic! Kennedy and I decided that's probably where he seduces you. I mean, he's gorgeous, but we imagined him in there pulling down a big volume so you could talk books for hours."

Wondering how they concluded this is an entry to an endless rabbit hole, so I say, "What type of book club?"

"We'll meet monthly, and each member will take turns hosting and providing dinner, but all of us will bring wine. After we socialize, we'll discuss the book. Our first will be *To Kill a Mockingbird*. I'm sure it'll be a real page-turner! I mean, if it was banned, it must contain super grim content about some cruel murderer who leaves dead birds on his victims' bodies, right?"

"Something like that. How many members will you have?"

"Around eight, and a few have incredible homes. We're asking members to coordinate their outfits to match the colors of the book cover so the aesthetic will be on point."

A cold sweat pricks my palms. "Sounds...fun?"

Will they have complimentary Xanax with every glass of wine? My social anxiety is more manageable if Adair is along, or someone's trying to kill me at a party.

While Brittany babbles about details, I consider how many escape routes the average mansion contains. Could I convince my team to run an extraction drill during one of these meetings? For training purposes, of course. Nothing says, "Sorry, I have to leave early," like a tactical unit crashing through the windows.

Brittany brings me back to the now. "Francis Downs said she'll join. Isn't she on the Ladies' League board with you?"

"Yes, but do you mind if I think about it? I rode this morning and need to shower."

"Let me know soon because we're meeting next week. I won't be able to finish reading more than a few pages of our selection, but I'll look at the plot on Wikipedia. Don't tell anyone, okay?"

After promising and disconnecting, I stand still for a moment, overcome with incredulity.

How did I end up trading mission briefs for bestsellers with birdbrains?

Despite Aunt Lilah leaving me her fortune with conditions, the only story I want to read about is my triumphant return to my team and leaving Rancho Suprema and its lunacy far behind.

3

An alarm shreds the fog of fitful sleep. I peel open sticky eyes, tangled sheets clinging to my legs as I fumble for my clamoring phone.

Ladies League Board Meeting 11 a.m.

A groan escapes my lips. I got little sleep. First, I replayed the drone attack and details, but came up with nothing. Then, as I did every night, I thought about James Warden. A vivid slide show of memories played: the first time he threw back his head and laughed at something I said, his commanding presence taking charge of our team, his green eyes darkening with desire.

With a sigh, I drag myself into the bathroom and brush my teeth with more gusto than usual, thinking about Aunt Lilah's posthumous grip on my life. Per the trust, serving on a non-profit board fell under 'community involvement requirements.' The Ladies' League Vice Presidency isn't merely a time-consuming annoyance—it's another box ticked in her control-freak checklist.

After downing some yogurt, I don a blue linen pants set and low heels. Smoothing the few out-of-place strands of my long, blonde hair extensions, I swipe on some lip gloss and mascara and head out.

———

The Ladies' League building sits on the edge of Rancho Suprema's downtown, its elegant, understated Spanish-style architecture a testament to its historical significance. Lush gardens, artfully placed benches, and tinkling fountains surround the structure like a halo of self-importance.

A familiar figure slouches against an archway. It's Alex Gordon, my high-net-worth financial advisor. He's dressed in business casual, wearing dark jeans, a white polo shirt, and a khaki blazer, with his blond-red hair neatly combed.

"What brings you to this den of floral arrangements and passive aggression?" I greet.

He pushes off the pillar, all six feet of him uncoiling with a contained energy that's out of place amid the genteel surroundings. "Thought I'd increase my clientele. Or maybe I missed your company, LT."

I arch an eyebrow at his continued use of the 'Little Troublemaker' nickname he gave me. "Are you incognito? You've got the top of your shirt buttoned to hide the tattoos and removed your earrings."

He runs a hand over his left ear where the studs used to be. "Sometimes you need to blend in to stand out."

"That can't be the only reason."

"Got a call from Beatrice Gibbs asking if I'd take over the vacant Buildings and Grounds board position."

"And you said yes? It's hard for me to believe our club president could convince you to do anything."

Humor glints in his hazel eyes. "It's my civic duty."

"Leaving aside the difficult personalities running this organization, let me ask a more pressing question. Do you know anything about plants?"

"They need water and sunlight, right?"

"I think there's more to it."

"Fortunately for me, the gardening staff will take care of everything. God forbid a rosebush doesn't bloom, or a fountain stops gurgling for a microsecond. Half the members will resign."

"That's true. And the building maintenance?"

"I invest the money of some big developers. Pretty sure I could ask them to command their minions to help me if I get in a bind."

"I hope you won't regret trading spreadsheets for sprinklers."

We continue down a long hall decorated with oil paintings to a room set up for the meeting. Tables are covered with notepads, pens, and water bottles, but no one is there.

I check the time. "The meeting begins in five minutes." Rancho Suprema is a far cry from my old world, where a second's delay could mean a bullet to your head or a bomb ripping you apart. Here, punctuality is as foreign as a Walmart.

Alex makes straight for a beverage service set up on a side table. "Maybe they canceled and didn't tell us."

"We're not that lucky."

Moments later, Francis Downs floats in like a dandelion wisp blown on a breeze. A white visor covers her curly, ginger hair, and she wears a tennis outfit on her frail frame. "Where is everyone?"

"Maybe we've entered an alternate universe where clocks matter," Alex says, stirring cream into his coffee.

"Time is so troublesome," Francis says. "Davia, before I forget, you're joining Brittany and Kennedy's book club, right?"

Alex says, "Brittany and Kennedy are starting a book club?"

"We're going to read the classics," Francis says.

"Really?" Alex continues. "They'll think *Pride and Prejudice* is about beauty queens with attitudes."

Francis swats his shoulder. "Be nice. It'll be so much fun! Most of the hosts have ultra-luxury estates, ensuring a wonderful experience. You have to join, Davia!"

"You must," Alex says with a sly grin. "After each meeting, I'll want the play-by-play."

"I'll think about it."

Alex sets his coffee on the table, drops into a chair, and picks up the agenda. I take a seat beside him and do the same. Will I be stuck with any new responsibilities? In the three months I've lived in Rancho Suprema, I've helped with a silent auction, modeled in a fashion show, and headed up a home and garden tour. There's a charity event listed under new business. What's next? A carbon offset gala at a destination reached by private jets?

Before I can ask Francis for details, Beatrice Gibbs enters. In her sixties, the Ladies' League board president has sleek gray hair and wears Chanel like a suit of armor for the affluent. Fred Smith, the club's treasurer, is with her. A bald spot peeks out of a careful comb-over, and his fingers move like he's tapping out numbers on an invisible calculator.

"Margaux Fairfax won't be joining us today," Beatrice declares. "She's on vacation at her estate in Tuscany. Francis, please fill in as secretary. Send your notes to Evangaline afterward so she can do the newsletter."

"Of course." Francis picks up a pen, scribbling on a pad until the ink begins to flow.

"I'm so glad you've joined us, Alex." Beatrice favors him with a rare smile. "Losing Henry Adams left us in a precarious position. We can't have our reputation sullied by lack of oversight."

"Glad to be of service."

Beatrice appears not to notice his light, sarcastic tone. She doesn't bother greeting me, instead taking the seat at the head of the table like a dictator who considers democracy a failed experiment. "Fred, bring me some coffee and a scone."

He pushes the wire-rimmed glasses perched on his nose into a more secure setting and hurries to do her bidding.

Once everyone's settled, Beatrice calls the meeting to order and leads us through 'Old Business.' Fred provides the significant total raised by the Home and Garden tour the previous month, but I wonder if anyone will want to attend again after what occurred.

Under 'New Business,' we vote Alex onto the board, and he takes his oath of office. When we move to the Membership Committee report, Francis reads the names and qualifications of prospective members. The board's level of scrutiny seems more appropriate for a high-security clearance than a non-profit.

I whisper to Alex, "You realize you'll be forced to model in next year's fashion show because it's required of new officers, right?"

"It's time this community got a taste of real style. Don't blame me when everyone's wives start questioning their life choices."

We finally reach the dreaded charitable event item.

"And now, the most important question of the day," Beatrice says. "Who can ride a horse?"

I keep my hands in my lap and my face blank as heads turn to see if anyone responds in the affirmative.

Francis makes a little noise. "Davia, you know how to ride! I saw you out with Adair and those adorable twins the other day. I could picture you as a family and..."

"How well do you ride?" Beatrice asks, interrupting my thoughts of strangling Francis.

"Why?"

"We're coordinating a luxury barn tour with the Rancho Suprema Riding Club. The event will conclude with our community members performing alongside acrobats in a horse show. There'll also be a barbecue with dancing. They're bringing in Keith Urban to do the music, or someone else whose name escapes me. I understand he's a country singer."

"I only ride western," I protest. "Everyone in this area rides English."

"Since it appears you're the only board member with the necessary skills, you'll have to do, although," Beatrice sniffs, "I'm quite reluctant to have you represent us in any way after the last charity debacle."

Alex moves his hand to my shoulder. "You're made of tougher stuff than those Ascot types who consider a splash of champagne on their britches a genuine crisis."

"Yes, but…"

"Francis," Beatrice interrupts. "Provide Davia with the contact details so she can coordinate with whoever's running this at the riding club."

Fred says, "I won't be here the rest of this month and can't handle the finances."

Beatrice's attention moves to Alex. "Good thing you're a new board member. Can you take over?"

"I'll be in town."

After another vote to cede this matter to Alex, Beatrice adjourns the meeting and sweeps from the room like a glacier shedding ice.

Fred says, "Alex, I'll email you the contact information. I think it's someone named Elise, Elliot. Not sure."

"Won't I need access to the club's account?"

"I'll get you that information, too. Right now, I'm staying behind to reconcile the expense reports. There's a discrepancy of seventeen cents that cannot stand. I'll lock up." He trundles from the room.

Francis gathers her notes and rushes toward the door. "I'll email you the information, Davia. I booked a massage, and I might be late."

"As if that matters," Alex and I say in unison, but Francis is gone. We catch each other's eyes and laugh.

"Why bother having a board when Beatrice makes all the decisions?" Alex says as we leave.

"It's an unsolvable mystery. I hope you don't regret your new position and added financial duties."

"That's right in my wheelhouse, so it's no problem. Besides, things are turning out better than expected because we'll both be working on this charity event. And," He draws closer, "I hear riding requires strong thighs. If you need help with getting in shape, I'm happy to offer some private instruction. Maybe we should compare notes on our workout routines."

Warmth crawls up my neck, and I clear my throat. "I'm sure I can manage."

4

Gripping a shopping cart, I hesitate before the sliding glass doors of the Rancho Suprema Market. A simple trip to buy sparkling water shouldn't require this much mental preparation. The doors whoosh open, and the cool air conditioning battles the summer heat at my back. I force myself forward, half-expecting someone to drive through the front window in a Ferrari, then claim it was because they couldn't find valet parking.

Going straight to the beverage aisle, focused on my limited task, I collide with a crowd wearing overpriced athleisure. Their attention is fixed on a man in his mid-twenties who's commandeered an empty checkout counter. A banner across the register reads 'Blissful Beings Pop-up Enlightenment.' He wears flowing white linen pants and an unbuttoned shirt, revealing a chest as smooth as polished marble. A mane of tousled blond hair frames his serene face.

"Who's the AI ad?" I ask a woman with a cart full of kale and a tiny bottle that might contain unicorn tears.

She clutches a rose quartz pendant necklace. "That's Eathr Bliss! The life optimization guru? He's got millions of followers!"

"What does he know about..."

Eathr raises his arms, and the crowd falls silent. "Remember, my Blissful Beings, the secret to inner peace is curating your outer appearance."

Reverent murmurs erupt.

"The path to nirvana is paved with limited edition items," he continues.

Seriously? I maneuver past a woman in pink yoga attire who blocks the item I came for.

Eathr hops down from his check-out pedestal, bestowing hand-shakes as he moves through his throng of admirers. "Now, my loves, let's practice gratitude. Reach out and touch something you're grateful for!"

A Gucci-clad woman body-checks a silver-haired socialite to snatch the last jar of caviar-infused honey. Two men in golf clothes grapple over a wheel of aged cheese. A cluster of people descends on a display of saffron-infused water blessed by Tibetan monks. Near me, a man clasps a $1000 bottle of balsamic vinegar to his chest like it's his firstborn.

Taking advantage of the mayhem, I inch toward my goal, side-stepping a fistfight over the last package of Wagyu beef jerky.

Eathr floats by, trailing a scent of sandalwood. He halts, fixing me with electric blue eyes. "You, radiant soul! What wisdom can you share with us today?"

People halt their activities, all eyes on me.

"Remember to breathe?" I manage. "Because if you stop breath-ing, you...die. And dying is bad for your, um, chakras?"

Eathr gives several loud and deliberate claps. "Breathtaking insight. Breath. Taking. Get it? Behold, a natural sage walks among us!"

In an instant, I'm surrounded by women in compression tights and men with artisanal man buns and neat beards, clamoring for more of my impromptu wisdom. I back away, trying not to trip over a compact fridge filled with kombucha. Realizing my chances of a quiet shopping trip are dead, I abandon my cart and make for the exit.

Meanwhile, Eathr begins signing copies of his book, *The Art of Blissful Consumption*, which are stacked beside the register for a cool $100 apiece. He continues his pitch as I escape. "Remember, Blissful Beings, sign up for my private coaching to achieve further enlightenment."

I burst out of the store, gulping in air that doesn't smell like essential oils, freshly cut flowers, and pseudo-wisdom.

———

Francis texts me the details I don't want about my contact at the Rancho Suprema Riding Club. Her name is Samira Westbrook. When I click on the link provided, the club's website displays her polished headshot. Samira's brown hair frames flawless skin, complemented by subtle makeup that enhances her natural beauty. She wears a crisp white equestrian shirt with the collar turned up, and the edge of a navy blazer is visible, suggesting a complete riding outfit.

What do I have in my wardrobe that works for this event? Nothing. Does Bryce's Boutique carry English riding attire? Add it to the endless list of unforeseen social wardrobe needs.

With reluctance, I text the contact number on the screen.

Hi, this is Davia Glenn, Vice President of the Ladies' League. I'm your contact for the joint charity horse event. Let me know when you'll be able to meet.

I make a huffing sound, wanting to coordinate this as much as a condemned prisoner wants to try on a noose. After sending the text, I change clothes and reheat some fajitas left by my housekeeper, Ana Sanchez. As I stir the chicken with red and yellow bell peppers and onions, a delicious aroma of cumin, garlic, and chili powder wafts around me.

There's a forceful knock at the door. It's probably Sherilyn, who has my gate code, stopping to tell me I need to buy some expensive curtains woven from the silk of spiders fed on organic, fair-trade mangos.

Must be residual thoughts due to Eathr exposure.

James Warden's six-three frame of honed muscle fills the doorway. His green eyes, usually calm and assessing in the field, are dark and intense, and his posture is stiff.

"Warden? I thought you were in Virginia."

"They gave me more time off."

He steps inside, and I close the door behind him.

"You've got a slight limp," I say.

"Noticed that, did you?"

"You'd be disappointed if I didn't."

We're less than a foot apart. His brown hair is longer than regulation, and a hint of stubble shadows his jaw. The scar through his eyebrow stands out, and a puckered line from a recent bullet mars a bicep.

"Aren't you able to return to work?"

Warden catches my hand, his calloused fingers engulfing mine. "I'm fine. Remember what you said when I got shot?"

"It's a long way from your heart?" The coppery scent of blood and the feel of his leg, hot and slick beneath my pressing hands, is a sharp memory.

"It's us I'm worried about. I know we're on a break, but I want to do whatever it takes to resolve this. I told you how sorry I was, but..."

"I've thought about this a lot as well. What you did was understandable, but I expected you to be right beside me. Warden, you're the one person I trust when the world goes wrong."

"I know, but seeing you and that Brit—I mean Adair— on national TV looking at each other with..."

"I'm not going to explain again."

"I'm not asking you to."

Before I can respond, he pulls me to him, one hand cupping my chin while the other slides around my waist. His lips collide with mine, hungry and demanding. I melt into him, longing and frustration pouring into our kiss.

Our embrace is like a flash bang, white-hot and explosive. Warden rests his forehead against mine, his thumb tracing my cheekbone. "I've missed you," he murmurs.

His words unlock something in me, and I pull him down for another kiss, reveling in his warmth. There's only Warden, his strong arms around me, and the promise of a renewed future.

His head goes up. "Is something burning?"

"Oh no." I rush to the kitchen, turn off the gas flames beneath my now-ruined lunch, and fill the pan with water.

Warden trails behind me and gives a low laugh. "At least you didn't set off the smoke alarm."

I stretch to kiss him. "Want to see if we can trigger the one in my bedroom?"

5

The Rancho Suprema Riding Club is situated down a long drive, marked by bronze signs at discreet intervals: *Speed Limit 5 mph*, *Horses Have the Right of Way*, and *All Visitors Must Check in at the Main Office*. This pretentious lead-up has the feel of "If you're uncomfortable, you don't belong here." I half-expect the next sign to read, "Net Worth Verification Required."

Member vehicles hog the covered parking, but I wedge my Land Rover beneath a sturdy tree. Expensive placards designate spots for "Bitsy Aldrich-Cavendish," "The Montclair-Worthington-Cross Family," and others. I imagine a committee saying, "We're sorry, Ms. Glenn, but you lack the weighty ancestral heritage and medieval titles required for membership. We cannot approve you."

Evergreen shrubs manicured to resemble two rearing horses frame a walkway leading toward Samira's office. The few people who pass me wear starched blouses, riding breeches, and polished knee-high boots. My worn Western boots, jeans, and button-up blouse feel like a declaration of war against this pristine perfection.

A dark wood stable lies before me. It contains around forty stalls with solid oak dividers, brass fittings, and automatic waterers. The central aisle is wide enough for four horses to pass, and windows in cathedral ceilings showcase the sleek coats of costly animals standing in shavings. Staff fork manure into wheeled carts.

A mid-forties woman with chestnut hair pulled into a sleek chignon stops beside me. Her nose scrunches in a brief show of disgust as she takes in my problematic footwear. "Are you here about the stable hand opening?"

"No. I'm Davia Glenn, Vice President of the Ladies' League. I'm here to meet Samira Westbrook."

"I see. I'm Marilyn Voss, the riding club's event coordinator for fifteen years—until *Samira* took over management, that is."

How do I negotiate this minefield?

Before I can respond, she says, "Do you know how to ride?"

"Yes. I—"

"Marilyn!" calls a man entering the barn. "Want to have lunch at the club?"

"That sounds lovely," Marilyn beams at him. "Davia, this is Jeremy Maxwell-Price. I'm sure you won't know this, but he was a member of Team USA at the Rio 2016 Olympics."

Jeremy studies me, then recognition clicks. "You're the woman who caused me to fall off my horse a few days ago."

"Actually, your lack of seat caused that. Oh, and your lack of manners."

"How dare—" He balls up his fists, his features almost as red as when he hit the ground.

"Lack of seat?" Marilyn echoes, mouth falling open. "He's a grand prix jumper."

More like a grand prix prima donna.

"I'm late for my meeting. Excuse me."

Hurrying away, I duck into a narrow walkway beside the barn— and slam into someone.

"I'm sorry, I—"

"No problem, princess." A tall blond man with model features leers at me. He doesn't move, and the space is too confined for me to pass.

Should I shove him into the hedge?

"I'm Chase Matthews," he says, then waits for...what? Is this another person I'm supposed to recognize?

"I'm Davia Glenn."

He gives me a once-over. "You don't ride English?"

"I don't."

"How about you take some private lessons with me? I'm the Longines World Number One rider. First Yank to knock the Euros off the throne since '18."

"Uh..." Longines is a...?

Chase gets closer. "Trust me—my rhythm's flawless, and my stamina's built for the jump-off."

"Are you friends with Jeremy Maxwell-Price? You both have the same style."

He recoils. "That hack? He got lucky on his one Olympic alternate rider qual."

A pretty young woman in riding attire enters the path behind Chase. "Hey, Mr. Double-Clear," she purrs. "If I buy you a coffee, will you ride my mare over the practice oxer? She needs a tune-up—and so do I."

Chase changes his position to scrutinize the newcomer, and I slip past.

"Who's that?" the woman says as I move away.

"A prospective student."

Suppressing an inner snarl, my footsteps are loud as I pound up the stairs to the manager's office. Samira meets me at the door, dark hair spilling over a shirt with the Rancho Riding Club logo embroidered on its pocket.

"Sorry, I'm late," I say.

"That's okay, we're just getting settled." Her focus moves past me to Chase and the young lady, who hover inches apart, and her lips press flat. "Let's go in. I'll introduce you to the women who'll be assisting us."

The office has picture windows with views of an arena where a rider schools a bay horse over a series of obstacles. A mahogany desk commands the center, flanked by shelves lined with trophies and color-coded event binders. Two women rise from chairs in a spacious sitting area.

"Davia Glenn, I'd like you to meet Vivienne Reese and Elise Harrington," Samira says. "They'll be our partners to help ensure this charity event is successful."

Vivienne steps forward first, her brown hair shifting shades in the light. Her fitted suit and confident handshake radiate professionalism. "Wonderful to meet you, Davia. I'm coordinating the equipment and hiring the talent. I understand you'll be representing the Ladies' League."

I nod, noting she's scrutinizing every detail of my appearance like everyone else I met today. Should I have shown up in a pastel polo shirt, hairnet, and used an accent borrowed from Downton Abbey?

Elise gives me a gentle smile, her honey-blonde bob framing a freckled face. "I manage the financial aspects," she says, fidgeting with her wedding ring. "It's quite an undertaking, but so worthwhile for the cause."

The cause. I wonder if any of them know what charity this will benefit, or if it's another excuse for Rancho Suprema to throw an expensive party and call it philanthropy. Wait. Do *I* know who gets the proceeds?

"Remind me, who are we raising money for?"

Elise brightens. "It's for Reins of Hope, an equine therapy program for veterans with PTSD."

"We've decided to name the event, 'Hoofbeats for Heroes,'" Vivienne says. "It will be spectacular."

"Please, sit," Samira says. "We should go over the details."

As we settle, Vivienne pulls out a tablet. "I've sent requests to the best equestrian entertainers. They're adaptable, but I'll need to know your skill level, Davia, to have Talia design an outfit and routine that showcases both your abilities and theirs."

"I only ride Western. I'm not sure how well that's going to mesh with whatever you've planned."

A brief silence follows. Vivienne's professional demeanor doesn't waver, but something flickers in her eyes. Elise stops fiddling with her ring, and Samira clears her throat.

"Western," Vivienne repeats, as if I announced I planned to perform naked. "Well. That's unexpected."

"I'm happy to bow out. Surely someone else in the community can take my place."

Please. Please let someone else do this.

Samira frowns. "Beatrice says no one else on the Ladies' League board rides."

"Is it in a rule book or something that a board member is required to ride?" I persist. Whoever wrote these societal strictures needs to be flogged.

Vivienne ignores my question. "You date Adair Monroe, don't you? He must have someone on staff who could give you lessons."

And I'm back in my usual dilemma of telling them we aren't dating, which isn't believed, or coming up with something else. "I'm not going to bother him."

"Ooh, Samira. What about Chase?" Elise says. "You could ask him to give her a few lessons."

Samira's expression hardens. "We split up."

"But I thought you were engaged?" Elise persists.

"Let's move on to a more productive discussion, shall we?" Samira says, and Elise's cheeks flush as she drops her head and whispers, "Sorry."

"I'll figure it out," I say. "I've ridden my whole life and have advanced skills. Unless you have me jumping eight-foot fences, I'm sure I'll be fine."

"All right, then. We'll also need to schedule a day for a walk-through of all the barns on the tour, Davia," Samira says. "Victor Hayes won't sign off until we've witnessed his equine Taj Mahal since a recent upgrade. He's one of our biggest donors, so we need to cater to his ego."

I appreciate Samira's candor. "Sounds like this shouldn't be too difficult."

"And speaking of Adair Monroe, his barn is also on the tour," she says, and my enthusiasm dims once more.

We spend the next hour discussing the event, which includes a tour of three elite barns with transportation for guests in custom vans, followed by an evening barbecue, concert, and horse show at the Rancho Riding Club.

"I'm still negotiating with Keith Urban's people," Vivienne says. "We might have to settle for Chris Stapleton. But, we'll end with a big equestrian finale in a customized tent."

"Isn't this going to cost a lot of money? I mean, how will we make a profit?" I say.

"We have donors lined up, including Victor Hayes, as Samira mentioned earlier," Elise says. "And tickets will start at $500 for general admission and $5,000 for the VIP experience."

Five thousand dollars to enjoy barbecue, music, and watch people ride horses?

"The goal is to raise significant money, maybe a few hundred thousand or more," Elise says. "I'm confident we'll generate a lot of enthusiasm and meet that with ease."

"I'll email you copies of the timeline and expectations leading up to the event," Vivienne says. "I always stay on top of the bookings and report as we go, so there are no surprises. Oh, and Samira and Davia, you'll need to wear something suitable for the barbecue and concert, then change into costumes for the horse finale. We'll schedule a rehearsal before the actual. I'll need your measurements."

"I've got them on my phone. I'll send them," I say, grateful for once that Kincaid Foxx sent them to me after I modeled at the Ladies' League fashion show.

When we finish, Samira and I set up a date to do the barn inspections and say our farewells. As I return to my car, I ponder what might exclude a barn from the tour. Perhaps using gold-plated feed buckets instead of solid gold ones?

Who knew?

———

"What was the threat level on your charity op?" Warden says from where he's sprawled on the couch, reading.

"I encountered multiple hostiles. Two alpha males marking territory, one bitter ex-management female, and a recently single female with trust issues."

Warden sets his book on the coffee table. "Were any of them armed?"

"Only with unified disapproval of my wardrobe."

He sits up to give me room beside him.

"They didn't like what you wore?"

"My pre-mission briefings never cover appropriate Rancho camouflage."

He pulls me to him, and his hand slips under my shirt. "You should ditch this offensive outfit, then."

Desire spreads through me. "Are you sure you're prepared for close-quarters engagement? You never win."

"That suits my objective."

6

"You sure have a lot on your calendar," Warden remarks as I dress for the book club meeting. "And you have to coordinate your clothes with the book cover? Good thing you developed your attention to detail skills with our team."

"They texted a photo of the correct cover, so we get it right." I scowl at my reflection in the full-length mirror. "At least I didn't have to buy a new outfit. What are you going to do while I'm gone?"

"Go for a swim in your pool, take advantage of your home theater, or practice small talk about hedge funds to fit in with your neighbors."

"Ha. Better study up on yacht maintenance while you're at it."

"Wouldn't I have people for that?"

"Good catch."

As I pick up my tote and keys, Warden reels me in and plants a kiss on my forehead. "Can't wait for the debrief."

"Me either. That means I'll be home and the event is over."

———

GPS directs me to Kennedy Conner's residence on the southern edge of the community. The wrought-iron gates stand open, revealing a cobblestone drive lined with shade trees at perfect intervals. At the top is an expansive motor court and I slide my Maserati MC20 into a slot beside some other luxury vehicles.

As I exit, I take a moment to appreciate the multi-tiered fountain outside the front entrance, whose oscillating water jets change colors with LED lighting. Three women in their twenties, whom I don't recognize, have paused for a group shot before the feature. They strike a pose with ease, and I'm confident this is a recurring routine.

Brittany and Kennedy appear at the top of some stairs outside the front door of a Mediterranean-style manor, its honey-colored stucco and terracotta roof bathed in low, amber light as the sun descends. The entryway is framed with towering palm trees and birds of paradise in decorative pots, their orange blooms adding pops of color.

Kennedy rushes down the steps, her sleek dark bob and crisp dark brown mini dress paired with towering platform sandals. Behind her, Brittany flounces down in a fitted emerald mini with cutout details, her long, platinum blonde hair in a sleek ponytail, designer sunglasses perched on her head.

"Oh my GOD!" Brittany's statement carries across the courtyard at a frequency that could shatter glass. "Davia! You're on fleek. I'm obsessed with your outfit!"

Kennedy nears me first, arms outstretched. She wraps me in a hug, her frame so skeletal, it's like being embraced by a life-sized Praying Mantis. The three women by the fountain pivot toward us, their antennae tuned to detect fresh social opportunities.

"Ladies!" Kennedy calls. "Come and meet our dear friend Davia!"

Dear friend? We've exchanged maybe fifty words total in the whole of our acquaintance.

They approach with synchronized enthusiasm, their whitened smiles so bright they could power the fountain's light system. Each carries a wine bottle like an accessory, while I grip my bottle of Chardonnay tight and admonish myself not to memorize the number of steps it takes to my car.

"I'm Crystalle—with two L's!" announces a blonde, extending a hand adorned with so many bejeweled rings it's a miracle she can lift it. "I have to say, your energy is *sooo* magnetic!"

"And I'm Brynlee!" The woman bounces like a spring on leather sneakers, her golden tresses swinging. "Kennedy, your home couldn't be more ideal for content."

The third woman, a brunette with dramatic winged eyeliner sharp enough to cut glass, looks me up and down before she removes a vape pen from her mouth. "I'm Tiffaney, spelled with an E-Y. It's an honor to meet you."

"Thank you. What do you—" I begin.

"You're dating Adair Monroe, right?" Tiffaney says. "You need to tell me everything. How many homes he owns, his favorite foods, the size of his—"

"Davia, since you don't know the others, I'll catch you up," Kennedy interrupts. "Crystalle is a luxury lifestyle influencer like me and Brit, and she's closing in on a million followers, Brynlee has an athleisure collection, and her content is all about fitness, while Tiffaney is beauty and gossip focused."

"I'll get you some of my clothing if you'll agree to wear and promote it on your platforms," Brynlee says.

"I'm not on social media," I say.

The group gapes.

Crystalle finally speaks. "You're not?"

"You should check my tutorials on makeup," Tiffaney says, her voice husky, perhaps from her constant vaping. "You've got those big blue eyes and sharp cheekbones, which will draw in all kinds of followers."

"And fill her inbox with DMs from men all over the planet offering to give her money," Kennedy says.

"They send all sorts of unsolicited dick pics, too, though." Brittany pretends to vomit. The women all nod, noses wrinkled.

"And don't even get me started on the sugar daddy offers," Tiffaney says, rolling her eyes. "Like, some guy saying he'll give me a ten grand a month allowance when I make fifty times that as an OF model."

"Right?" Crystalle laughs. "They think that's life-changing money when it wouldn't even cover my skincare routine."

"The audacity is what kills me," Brynlee adds. "I spend more than that on a weekend in Cabo."

"Anyway, Davia. We'll have to set a date for you to guest on my 'Tea Time with Tiffaney' podcast so you can share the latest gossip about Adair," Tiffaney says.

The intrusive questions, the imagined horror of posting about myself, and the thought of being on a program make me curl my toes inside my shoes, my body coiled for an exit.

"You have a lovely property," I say to Kennedy to force a change in the subject.

"Doesn't she?" Crystalle sweeps her arm toward the water feature. "We were saying how this fountain is serving major ancient Rome vibes."

Yes, Rome was overrun with LED décor.

Brynlee points at the pink sky. "We should totally do a group shot! The lighting is perfect right now. It's golden hour magic!"

"Can we talk about how we all nailed the color palette?" Kennedy surveys everyone with approval. "I mean, we're a living *To Kill a Mockingbird* cover!"

She's right. Each woman has interpreted the book in her own way, incorporating rust, black, white, and green into their outfits and jewelry. Looking down at my own rust-colored top and black pants, I realize I somehow managed to blend into their coordinated fashion parade.

After I fake-smile my way through a series of shots, Kennedy says, "Let's go in!"

The group spills through the double doors and into a soaring two-story area. A staircase has steps that appear to float without visible support, and its glass railing catches the light like a glistening jewel. A contemporary chandelier lights the room, showcasing walls of pink with rose gold accents and a marble floor in blush tones.

"I love this, Kennedy!" Crystalle gushes. "It's like stepping into one of your YouTube videos."

"Thank you. I ensured that every part of my home serves as a suitable backdrop for my content creation. Remind me to show you my media room later."

"Will you?" Crystalle exclaims, and when Kennedy affirms her intention, a collective "Whoa" escapes the group as they lower the phones they were using to capture the immediate space.

"For now, come through to the kitchen," Kennedy says. "Everyone brought such attractive bottles; we'll set up a display."

"Kennedy, you go on," Brittany says. "The others are parking, and I'll bring them."

We follow Kennedy across an open-concept great room stretching at least fifty feet, its windows offering canyon views. A white sectional sofa, large enough to seat twenty, dominates the space with oversized ottoman cubes in dusty rose velvet surrounding it. The outline of a person is under a luxury throw on the edge of the couch. Did another guest arrive early and decide to take a nap?

The kitchen has an island the size of a car, topped with rose quartz counters and surrounded by bar seating for twelve. Custom cabinetry, high-end appliances, organized rows of aesthetically pleasing containers, and a walk-in pantry large enough to hold a film crew complete the space. Of particular note is a blush pink refrigerator covered with Swarovski crystals.

Kennedy notes me looking at it and says, "That's where I fridgescape."

"What's that?"

"Let me show you." She marches over and opens the door. "Ta-da!"

Inside are pink vases holding flowers, pink crystal pitchers containing milk and juices, baskets of vegetables and fruit arranged to maximize their aesthetics, and pink crystal picture frames of Kennedy in various poses. Nestled among porcelain dishes painted with pink roses are miniature sculptures of Greek gods.

"Um, that's pretty," I manage. How did she find anything to eat? I imagined myself knocking over gods and vases in a quest for an apple.

The others gather behind me and make impressed sounds, with Brynlee saying, "I'm making notes on my phone. You've given me so many ideas!"

Kennedy closes the fridge's door, its ornamented surface glittering, and we place the bottles on the island next to the evening's food. A placard states "A Michelin-Star Experience Curated by Chef Martinel." Gold-edged cards identify the content of plates, which hold microscopic offerings. One selection is labeled "Grilled Pea Canapé with Egg Yolk Jam and Ossetra Garnish." Each portion consists of one pea, one drop of jam, and two caviar pearls arranged on what appears to be a piece of volcanic rock. The card helpfully notes, "Please consume in a single bite for optimal flavor profile integration."

Another culinary option appears to be a sandbox. It's labeled "California Foraging Experience," and is filled with edible soil made from dehydrated mushrooms. There are tweezers for guests to "harvest" hidden truffles.

While I mourn the absence of cheese and crackers, everyone ignores the elegant food, as if consuming it would break an unspoken covenant. Only Crystalle approaches, positioning her phone for a photoshoot of food she'll never eat.

I step into the great room to give myself a moment to breathe and glimpse someone tossing aside the couch throw and running from the room.

Kennedy comes up beside me, rolling her eyes. "I tell my staff not to be seen, but do they listen?"

"Finding good help is such a trial," Crystalle agrees.

Before this common Rancho lamentation continues, Brittany enters, accompanied by Samira, Francis, and Marilyn. After introductions, the newcomers place their wine beside the other bottles, with Kennedy realigning them so all the labels face the same way.

"I didn't have time to redecorate the house to fit the theme," Kennedy says, "but I did put together a photo station outside on the deck."

While Kennedy and Brittany coordinate the inside shot, Francis gives me a hug and whispers, "I'm thrilled you decided to come."

After group shots behind the display, we go out through double doors onto a large veranda. A backdrop of flowing white linen drapes has been erected against its stone railing. Cascading eucalyptus garlands, rust-colored Moroccan lanterns at varying heights, and oversized floor pillows in forest green velvet and rust linen surround a vintage wooden bench.

It's like Pinterest exploded all over the patio.

The women pose, their placement harmonized by Brittany and Kennedy. Videos and photos are taken by one of the staff members, who must have received special permission to be seen.

"Everyone, let's go in for food and drinks. We can discuss the book in about twenty, okay?" Kennedy says, to murmured agreement.

"Davia! I didn't know you'd be here," Samira says. "What a nice surprise." She's in an elegant, deep green wrap-dress, more feminine than her riding club manager attire.

"It's good to see you as well. Is there anything we need to address about the upcoming charity event?"

"Yes, Samira. Is everything going to be ready?" Marilyn says. She wears a crisp white blouse paired with pearls, camel-colored slacks, and loafers. "I know from experience how difficult coordinating all the details can be."

"We have it under control," Samira says, and Marilyn's lip curls for a fraction of a second.

To stop a verbal war, I say, "How long have you two been involved with the Rancho Riding Club?"

"My grandfather was one of the founding members," Marilyn says, her shoulders straightening. "He built Voss Industries after his engineering degree at Stanford. He established our family foundation and focused on philanthropic efforts. I grew up riding ponies at the club, and competed in dressage and show jumping."

Samira says, "I joined a few years ago, but recently took over management, so I'm still learning from everyone."

"How refreshing," Marilyn says. "It must be quite an adjustment, managing something so steeped in tradition. Where did you grow up, dear? I don't think you've ever mentioned."

"East County. My father worked construction."

"How...industrious," Marilyn says, the pause between her words stretching a beat too long.

"When did you learn to ride?" I ask Samira.

"Recently. I always wanted to, and worked as a groom at the club, which gave me an opportunity to be around horses."

"If I recall correctly, Chase Matthews introduced you to all the ins and outs," Marilyn says, examining her wine. "But it seems he's moved on to other pursuits now, hasn't he?"

"Chase and I decided we wanted different things."

"You mean different *people*." Marilyn's sly expression is saccharine. "Well, I'm sure you'll find someone more suitable to your upbringing. Excuse me, I need to refill my glass." She gives Samira's arm a condescending pat before gliding away.

"Sorry about that," Samira says. "Marilyn's still adjusting to the management transition."

"That's one way to put it. How long ago did you take over her position?"

"Eight months. Marilyn was the club's manager for fifteen years, but," Samira pauses. "The club needed a fresh perspective. Some of the vendors hadn't been paid, and we were hemorrhaging members due to outdated policies."

"That sounds like a mess to inherit."

And similar to the Ladies' League.

"It was a fight," Samira admits. "But worth it. We've increased membership by twenty percent, and I made our youth program accessible to families of all socioeconomic backgrounds. We have so many people working for homeowners in Rancho, but their children can't afford to participate. I grew up that way, desiring more opportunities and feeling left out. Now, I can rectify some of the inequities."

"Did you get any grief over that? From what I've seen since moving here, mixing income levels is frowned upon."

"Many weren't thrilled, but I pitched it as an opportunity for giving back to the less fortunate."

"Allowing people to believe they're Mother Theresa is a smart approach."

"Yes, but enough about my work. How do you know Kennedy and Brittany?'

"We met when we took a limo up to Kincaid Foxx's showroom in LA for a fitting before the Ladies' League Fashion Show a few months ago. You?"

"They did an episode of their podcast, *Living Luxe,* about the riding club. They interviewed me, but I was surprised when I received an invitation to their book club. I mentioned I read in my free time, and am surprised they logged that away."

"I'm fairly sure it was a struggle to come up with many in their set who read classic literature."

Samira's eyes twinkle. "Can't wait to listen to their analysis."

7

Kennedy summons everyone inside, and the women make a last-minute dive for the decanters before the discussion about the book. As Samira and I enter, I notice the tips of shoes poking out from under the silk brocade curtains in the great room.

"Kennedy." I catch her elbow. "Are we having a hide-and-seek game?"

"Hide and seek?"

I point to the concealed figures.

"I told you, I can't tolerate my staff being seen! They didn't make it out of the room before I came back in, so they'll have to stand there."

"I—"

"Kennedy!" Brittany calls. "Should I bring the dessert out now?"

"Yes! Everyone! We're having goat milk mousse with chocolate truffles served on a meringue."

And none of you will touch it.

I take a seat on the couch and pull a copy of the book from my tote.

Tiffaney settles beside me and takes a long drag from her vape. "What's that about? If you tell me, I'll let Brynlee and Crystalle know."

"You didn't read it?" The words escape before I can stop them.

"*Pssh*. We came to boost our engagement. Brittany and Kennedy have millions of devoted followers, so this will give us all a spike."

Crystalle sits near us, holding her refilled glass. "I didn't have time to read this one, because I was trying to finish *Captivating Sofia*."

"Oh, me too!" Brittany says, joining us. "I couldn't put it down. It was *soooo* addictive."

The other women sink into their seats, and Francis says, "Did I hear you mention that dark romance by CC Jennings? It's so exciting!"

Before this continues, Kennedy comes in and claps her hands. "It's time to begin tonight's first Rancho Book Club meeting. How many of you finished *To Kill a Mockingbird*?"

Samira and I are the only ones who raise our hands.

"New show of hands! How many of you have read *Captivating Sofia?*" Brittany says.

Everyone puts up their hand, except for me and Samira, and I notice the curtains rustle with movement as the invisible staff also raise theirs.

"Majority rules, then," Brittany says. "We should discuss *Captivating*."

"That plot was intoxicating!" Brynlee gushes.

"Davia and Samira haven't read it," Tiffaney says. "We need to fill them in on the plot."

"I'll do it!" Brittany says. "Sofia Sinclair, a virgin in her early twenties, is driving alone at night in a rural mountain area. A man suddenly appears in the middle of the road, and she slams on her brakes. He taps on her window and asks for help to find his lost dog."

"Men don't usually need help," I say. "Is this a Ted Bundy thing?"

Brittany blows a puff of air that disturbs her bangs. "No! He's a hottie and seems desperate to get his dog back, which melts Sofia's heart because she volunteers at an animal rescue. Anyway, she parks her car on the side of the road...and ten masked men appear out of the woods."

"This is a romance novel?" Samira says.

"Just listen," Crystalle says. "Sofia tries to get back to her car, but they grab her and take her keys."

"Then they explain the rules to her," Kennedy says.

"In menacing, but deliciously deep voices," Tiffaney inserts, shivering.

"Sofia's told she'll get a twenty-minute head start. If she makes it to the boundary line, which is some old barn on the other side of the woods, she wins her freedom," Brittany says. "But if any of the men catch her..."

"She becomes his, and then their shared prize," Marilyn finishes with a sigh. "I mean, the description of their chiseled abs, sculpted shoulders, and bulging packages made it difficult to choose who I'd want to catch me."

"And the way they called out to her in the darkness!" Tiffaney clutches her glass. "Taunting her, telling her exactly what they'd do when they caught her... all I could think was how lucky she was."

"She runs through the dark, and trips over tree roots and rocks, but she enjoys the experience in the end," Brittany says, tracing the rim of her glass. "She realizes even though she was terrified at first, she wanted to be caught all along. The theme is about discovering your deepest shadow desires."

Crystalle nods. "The author truly understands female psychology. We all have dark fantasies of being completely overwhelmed by powerful men, right?"

Images of sunken, dark-circled eyes, sallow complexions, and facial bruises unspool from when my team rescued women who had been raped and trafficked. "Non-consensual sex is an act of violence," I say, voice flat.

Marilyn waves a dismissive hand. "It's consensual non-consent. Sofia wanted it, even if she didn't know it."

"But she was hunted like prey," Samira protests. "How is that romantic?"

The only sound is a delicate clink as Crystalle sets her glass on a marble coaster.

Kennedy bolts to her feet. "Should we open more wine?"

"Yes, let's!" the others chime, and the group flocks to the kitchen, leaving Samira and me staring at each other, eyebrows at our hairlines.

"I could go for something stronger right now," she says.

"That was..." I shake my head and stand. "I'm going to attempt to eat something so I can distract myself. You?"

"Good idea."

We fill small plates with a few of the selections, to disapproving glances that make it clear we've committed a social sin. I eat a spoonful of the goat's milk mousse.

"This has a rich, unique taste," I tell Samira.

"The mushroom harvest truffle bites are also a treat, despite the odd concept," she says. "But it doesn't cut the bad taste left by that conversation."

"I hear you."

By the time the women drift back to the great room, glasses replenished, the topic has moved on. Kennedy says, "Since Samira and Davia read tonight's selection, maybe they could share the highlights?"

We do, but I can tell by the way their eyes skate away from ours and the long swallows from their drinks that the group's not interested. When we finish, most thank us, but Tiffaney says, "That has so many triggering themes! Racial prejudice, good and evil, social justice... I need to get my aura cleansed."

"Speaking of cleansing, did you know Eathr Bliss is in town?" Brittany says. "I hear he's working with private clients, but he got booked up before I could get a spot."

"He's such a divine soul," Marilyn says.

As they continue their chorus of admiration for the guru, my attention shifts to how the staff managed a well-timed exit from their curtain-hiding spots after the women flocked to the kitchen. They would make excellent partners in escape rooms.

"Won't you join us, Davia?" Kennedy says.

"Um, sorry. I didn't catch what you said."

"Although Eathr's unavailable, there's going to be a special program at the Serenity Springs Wellness Resort in two weeks," Brittany says. "It's supposed to be an utterly transformative experience, with forest bathing, molecular nutrition, and anti-aging therapy.

"That's my surprise for tonight!" Kennedy says. "I reserved rooms and paid for us all to go. My treat!"

Brynlee puts her hand on Kennedy's arm. "You did?"

"Yes. I told them we'll give them glowing reviews afterwards, although phones or cameras aren't allowed during the experience."

Francis sighs. "Digital detoxing is so fashionable."

I scramble for an excuse. I barely made it through a few hours with this group. Except for Samira, I can't imagine a whole weekend. "What are the dates? I have out-of-town company."

"Davia," Francis says. "I know you recently moved to Rancho and might not be familiar with the area, but Serenity Springs books out almost a year in advance. That Kennedy got us in as a group is unprecedented."

"Adair might even pick out a book for you to bring along," Brittany says.

"Yes, I'm sure Adair will love showing you the rarest parts of his library before you go." Francis gives me a wink.

"Then it's settled," Kennedy says. "I'll text everyone the specifics."

After another round of chatter about the 'once-in-a-lifetime' and 'priceless' trip, the evening concludes. Samira joins me as we leave the residence. "I'll see you tomorrow for our meeting with the barn owners, except Adair, who doesn't require that. I'm sure his property will be of the highest quality anyway."

"Your office, nine a.m., right?"

"Yes. I'm so glad you're part of this group. We can watch out for each other at the retreat," Samira says.

We exchange a look that promises a pact of mutual defense, and I head for my car.

The rear tire is flat.

Crouching to examine it, I find a clean puncture in the sidewall.

"What happened?" Samira asks.

"Someone slashed it."

"God! Who would do such a thing? And to your supercar!" Brynlee cries. "What a disaster!"

I stand and dust off my hands. "I'll need to call a tow company. This model doesn't have a traditional spare."

Excusing myself, I go back into the house to find Kennedy and explain the situation. "Do you have security cameras?"

"Of course! I have so many valuable possessions, how can I not? But the system's been glitchy lately." She finds her phone, pursing her lips as she mutters, "I have so many apps, and did not expect to have to deal with this right now...wait. Here it is." She shows me the security feed.

The front view of her house is black.

"How long have you been having problems?" I ask, mind on the drone attack. Did someone know I'd be here and plan this?

"A few days, I think. I don't know. My focus isn't on handling maintenance." She says this last word like it's a contagious disease. "Sorry about your car. I can give you a ride home."

"That's okay, thank you." I make arrangements for a tow and text Warden.

Twenty minutes later, headlights sweep into the driveway, and a man loads the vehicle onto a flatbed truck. He's finishing when Warden pulls in, driving my Rover. He gets out, checks the flat, and then scans the dark lawn and tree line.

"Someone either tampered with your car, or you drove over something on your way in, and it was a slow leak," he says.

"I didn't hit anything," I say as we get in the Rover and follow the tow truck back down the long drive. "I wonder if it's low-level mischief by Bradford."

"That mansion has security cameras galore."

"I checked, but the host said her system's having issues. The feed for that part of her property didn't work."

"Maybe Bradford hired someone in your book club to assist with your downfall," Warden teases.

"He might have. After tonight's discussion, I'm not sure what they're capable of."

8

Warden and I are almost done with a workout in my home gym early the next day when my phone notifies me that Kyle Kavanagh is calling.

"Are you leaving your South Dakota farm behind and coming out to play golf?" I greet.

"It's still in the eighties, so I'll plan a visit for July or August when the outdoor furnace is set on high. What's new?"

"Warden's here."

"Oh? Does this mean I've lost my Adair golfing buddy privileges?"

"I'm sure he won't hold it against you."

"But he might hold it against you. Is everything else quiet?"

Detailing the drone attack and flat tire to my former Delta Force mentor, I conclude by saying, "I'm not sure if it's Bradford, but it fits his MO."

"Guy struck me as someone who'd pay people to make your life annoying for his amusement, so it might be. But scaring horses with the twins present is unacceptable. Are they okay?"

"They were shaken, but a little ice cream shifted their attention.

Mostly, anyway. Stacey Templeton has a new turkey, T5, that they enjoy playing with. It's only been a few weeks since what happened, and you know it'll take time."

"Kids are resilient, but still."

"Have you seen my parents lately?" I say. "I talked to Dad a couple of days ago, and he said he and Mom might come out next month. Maybe you guys could book a flight together."

"They'll quiz me about Rancho Suprema the whole time."

"I thought they stopped their inquisition."

"No. I still get questions when we have dinner together. I leave out the murders and other problems you've been caught up in, but there's something about California and a high-end community that gives them pause."

"They've always been too smart for their own good."

Kyle chuckles. "Indeed. Keep me posted on what's happening. And say hello to Captain America for me."

When the call concludes, I relay his greeting to Warden.

"Maybe he's decided to like me." He doesn't pause his bicep curls with fifty-pound dumbbells. "I think he still pictures you as a kid and wants to protect you."

"He knows my capabilities since he's the one who trained me."

"He's still your watchdog."

"He wants me to be happy."

Warden stops. "And, are you?"

I bite my lower lip as I take in the sweat glistening on his bare upper torso. "I think I will be. Ready for a shower?"

———

A few hours later, I drive to the Rancho Riding Club for my meeting with Samira. My thoughts are on how happy I am to have Warden here. I've never been one to fantasize about domestic life, but a sense of contentment catches me by surprise. Is this what it would be like if we lived together?

After parking, I take the path along the barn. The air smells of dust, horses, and fresh hay, and a few stable hands nod at me as they go about their chores. There aren't many people around, and I think it will be nice to have some time to get to know Samira better. When I reach the landing outside her office, a man's watch with a broken band lies in the center of the space, and I pick it up. The clock face of the accessory bears the Longines name, positioned directly below the number twelve.

"Longines, Longines," I mutter, then connect the name with Chase Matthews. Did he drop this? Did I even want to mention him to Samira?

Tucking the item into my pants pocket, I decide to find him and return it after our meeting.

And if he hits on me, I will push him into a hedge this time.

Knocking on the door frame, I enter. The lights are off, but sunlight streams through the windows, illuminating a figure slumped before a desk, a shining liquid spreading across the surface.

"Samira?" I rush forward and tap her on both shoulders. "Can you hear me?"

She doesn't move.

Examining her, I find that the source of the blood is a hole in the right side of her neck. A jugular vein strike. I place a finger under her nose to check for breath.

There's none.

Past experience tells me she's dead, but I lift an eyelid. Her pupil is fixed and dilated.

Who did this? Why?

Shut down your feelings.

Stepping away from Samira's body, I call 9-1-1 and report the murder. Unsure if Detective Ricardo Montoya's team at Sheriff's Homicide will be assigned, I spend a few minutes debating, then decide to contact him.

"Davia? I can't talk right now. I got called into a murder investigation in Rancho."

"I reported it."

"Of course you did. Be there soon."

Samira's right arm hangs by her side, her hand covered in blood, like she placed it over the wound and tried to stop the bleeding. There's no visible weapon near her, so I bend to look beneath the desk. On the floor are a set of keys, which I leave in place. Her computer and the coffee pot are off, and the chairs in front of the desk and the sitting area are undisturbed. Her clothing isn't disarrayed, and there are no other apparent injuries besides the neck wound.

Someone got close but didn't alarm her. Did she know her killer?

Backing out with care, I nudge open the door with my foot and exit. There's a bench built into the landing area, but I decide to wait at the bottom of the stairs. Soon, I hear sirens. The first to arrive is a Rancho Patrol officer, a man with a steady demeanor, around five-ten with a medium build and short-cropped brown hair.

"I reported this." I introduce myself and give him the details. "No one's gone in since I found the body. I'm sure you know that a team from Sheriff's Homicide is on the way, but I spoke with Detective Montoya and—"

"Yes, I'm Officer Darren Bradley," he interrupts. "Wait here." He runs up the stairs, checks inside, then returns to secure the area with crime scene tape. "I want you to wait over there." He points to where some riding club members hover at the barn entrance, whispering. Behind them, a few of the stable workers hold rakes and stare.

I position myself far enough away from the group that I won't have to answer questions, but Marilyn appears and strides toward me.

"Davia! What's happened?" she says. "Why is Ranch Patrol here?"

"Samira died."

"What?"

Chase Matthews pushes his way through the people near the barn. "What's going on?"

"Samira—" I begin.

The color drains from Chase's face. "She-she's...dead?"

When I nod, he explodes toward the tape. I don't think—I act, planting myself in his path and hooking my arm through his, using his own momentum to unbalance him. At the same time, Officer Bradley slams into his other side. We deflect him, turning his charge into a stumbling lurch.

"You need to calm down, sir," Bradley says, but Chase continues to struggle against us, screaming, "No, no, no! This can't be true."

Two other officers come into view and rush forward, tackling him to the ground.

They tell him that if he doesn't cooperate, he'll be placed under arrest. After a final, raw struggle against their hold, the fight seems to drain out of him. He goes limp on the ground, his screams dissolving into ragged sobs. Only then do the officers release him. He pushes himself up from the dirt, his body shuddering, but remains on his knees.

"This is all my fault, Samira! I'm sorry, so, so sorry!" he cries, tear-streaked face upturned toward the office.

Marilyn watches him, then approaches me again. "Did you find her body?"

"Yes."

She keeps her attention on the office landing, then asks in a nonchalant tone. "Did you see anyone else?"

Did I see you, maybe?

"Aren't there cameras?"

"Yes, but none are directed toward this area. They're focused more on the perimeter and the barn where the valuable animals and riding equipment are kept."

"You might need to show the homicide team where they're placed and any footage."

"Of course."

Jeremy emerges from the barn leading a saddled chestnut mare, then stops. "What the hell is going on?"

Officer Bradley steps forward. "Sir, you need to secure your horse and wait with the others."

"Wait for what? I reserved arena time that begins in five minutes." Jeremy's eyes dart to the taped-off staircase.

"Sir, please secure your horse," Bradley repeats. "You won't be able to leave until you make a statement."

"A statement?" Jeremy's pitch rises. "I haven't done anything wrong, but the way people here overreact, the next thing you know, I'll be in handcuffs."

"Jeremy, calm down," Marilyn says. "No one's accusing you of anything."

"Yet. Samira had it out for me! You know what will happen."

"Sir," Officer Bradley interrupts, his tone more forceful. "I need you to return your horse to its stall and remain available for questioning. If I have to tell you again, you'll wait in my squad car."

Jeremy turns on his heel and yanks the horse's reins, leading it back into the barn. When he's gone, we lapse into silence, me wondering what his problem is. Sadness for a good woman lost weighs on me. I push the feeling down and keep my attention on the people around me. Is one of them the killer?

Chase continues to cry, hands covering his face. Dust now covers his polished boots. I notice he doesn't wear the watch he wore when I met him. Is the one in my pocket his?

"I'll probably be asked to take over Samira's position," Marilyn says with a note of satisfaction too bright for the circumstances. "The charity event's coming up soon, and we won't have time to hire someone unfamiliar with the process."

The Ranch Patrol officers instruct everyone at the scene to wait to be interviewed and close off the facility to newcomers. Soon, Detective Montoya stalks along the side of the barn with other members of the homicide team. His brown hair is messy, his suit rumpled, but he takes in every detail as he nears. Beside him is Detective Worth, a highly competent female I encountered at other crime scenes.

A Latina woman in her forties with graying black hair pulled into a practical bun turns to the team. "While we wait for forensics, let's interview witnesses, okay?"

Montoya comes straight for me and asks Marilyn to step away. "Davia, tell me everything."

I give him details, then say, "Do you have an evidence bag?"

"Of course."

Removing the watch from my pocket, I explain where I found it. "My prints are on it, but I think it belongs to Chase Matthews, the deceased woman's ex-fiancé. He was here when the forensics team arrived and appeared distraught. I don't see him now, though."

Montoya finishes marking the evidence bag and makes a note on his pad. "Anyone else suspicious?"

"Marilyn Voss, the woman who was next to me when you arrived, is the former manager. Samira took over her position, and there's no love lost between them."

"That it?"

"I've only been here once before, for a preliminary meeting to coordinate a charity event between the Ladies' League and the Riding Club, so I don't know these people that well. Samira and Marilyn were both at a book club meeting I attended last night. Marilyn made some catty remarks, but this community trends that way, so I didn't think much of it."

"You're in charge of a charity event *and* a member of a book club?" Montoya's eyes fill with mirth. "I should add you to the suspect list. You might have killed the victim because you needed some excitement."

"There's been a little." I fill him in on the drone attack, the flat tire, and my suspicions about Bradford Kensington, and his amused look fades.

"Tell me if anything else happens. After what Sherilyn—"

Four people come into view. They wear white Tyvek suits and carry equipment. They speak to the homicide team leader, are let into the cordoned-off scene, and go up the stairs. Outside the office door, they put on gloves and booties.

"New supervisor?" I say to Montoya.

"Yes, that's Detective Sergeant Maria Santiago. She's sharp and possesses integrity, unlike our last boss."

"Should I stay? Warden's out for a visit."

"I know how to find you. Give the big guy my regards."

There's nothing more I can do, so I decide to leave.

"Are you going to Crown Point?" Marilyn says as I pass her. "You don't want to miss the appointments Samira scheduled."

"Now?"

"The charity event is almost upon us, so yes. Victor Hayes is the priority, of course. Crown Point Farms is the premier facility on the barn tour, and he gave a generous donation to the event. Thornfield Equestrian is the next, with Adair Monroe's private barn finishing out the participants. I have the addresses and contact information if you don't."

"Did Samira keep you in the loop or something?"

"Not officially, but I make it my business to keep tabs on anything that might reflect poorly on the club. Let me make a call. I'll let Victor know you'll be there soon."

She steps away, and I quell my outrage to text Warden.

Going to be later than expected.

I don't go into details, deciding to let him enjoy the day. He responds with a thumbs up and a photo with his legs stretched out on one of the lounge chairs by the pool.

Marilyn rejoins me. "Victor says he'll expect you soon. Davia, you need to keep him on board for this. Do whatever you have to make him happy."

"What does that mean?"

"Stroke his ego."

As long as that's all he expects me to stroke.

Marilyn texts me the addresses and contact info, and I return to my Rover. A Ranch Patrol officer checks with the homicide team to ensure I've been released, then pulls a barricade aside to allow me to exit.

———

On the way to my destination, I replay the morning. Did I miss anything? A heaviness fills me, and my emotions bounce between sadness and anger.

Montoya will solve the case, but it won't bring Samira back.

I turn into the cobbled entry to Crown Point Farms, and grip the wheel tighter. Does a charity barn tour really take precedence over a death?

Halting before carved wooden gates, I hit a button and identify myself. When they open, I drive past mature shade trees toward an immense barn made of stucco with a red-tiled roof. In the distance, sunlight glints off a lake.

I park, and a man comes toward me. He's around fifty, with salt-and-pepper hair and broad shoulders above a slight paunch.

"I'm Victor Hayes."

I introduce myself.

"I can't believe what happened to Samira," he says without preamble. "I spoke to her early this morning, checking to see if she got extra liability insurance to cover anyone getting hurt here during the tour. One twisted ankle, and I'll get hit with lawyers and lawsuits, so I wanted to emphasize the importance."

"What time did you call her?"

"I don't know, I guess around six-thirty? She's usually at work by six to get a head start on the day before members show up."

"Was she at the club when you spoke?"

"She didn't say." He frowns. "I'm shocked she's dead."

"Was there anything unusual about your call?"

"No, it was all business. With the money and time I've put into this place..." Victor stares into the distance, then says, "Marilyn told me the event is going forward, and even though that doesn't seem like the right decision, I'd best show you around. Crown Point sits on eighty acres."

We pass an outdoor water trough long enough to service thirty horses at the same time, then enter the structure. Natural light streams through windows set in a twenty-foot-high wood ceiling, and wrought iron chandeliers are at intervals in the long breezeway. Horses hang their heads out of slots, and one gives a soft knicker.

"The stall doors are made from bamboo. It's hard and durable," Victor says. "Each stall has a fan, and the whole barn has an anti-fly spray system."

We continue, and he pauses before an interior wash stall. "Got fourteen of these inside, with four on the exterior, so there's no wait-ing. In the wing over there," he waves in its direction, "is a treadmill and a hydrotherapy setup that was completed a few months ago. An outside partnership with Meridian Equine Technologies, based in England, made it feasible. They wanted their name associated with a cutting-edge facility like mine."

"I didn't know horses had treadmills."

"You're not a horse person?"

"Not at this level. I grew up in South Dakota on a farm."

"Then Rancho is a whole new world."

You have no idea.

Victor directs me toward a door. Inside is a lounge with couches and chairs, a kitchen, and a wall-mounted television. "This is an area for riders to take a break. It has air conditioning because, even though we're blessed with nice weather here, it can get pretty warm in the summer, especially after a ride."

The cool air is a welcome respite from the rising temperatures. "It's inviting," I say. "Did you know Samira well?"

"I met her when she began dating Chase Matthews. They came to a grand prix event I hosted, and they seemed smitten. When I heard they were engaged, I wasn't surprised. The man couldn't take his eyes off her."

My mind flashes to his anguish this morning after hearing Samira had died. Had his grief been real?

"Guess Samira broke it off recently," Victor continues. "Chase was a real player, so perhaps he returned to his old habits. That boy never deserved her. All flash, no substance. She was too smart for him, but sometimes smart women make foolish choices about good-looking men."

I recall how Samira reacted when she saw Chase with the pretty girl at the stables on the first day I visited. She seemed both angry and hurt.

He leads me next to a plush tack room with rows of polished saddles and bridles, Saltillo tile flooring, and a granite sink.

"The equipment and horses are expensive, so I invested in a top-level security system. Let's go upstairs," Victor says.

After we ascend, we enter a large room with furnishings crafted from carved wood and leather. Horse paintings adorn the walls, and a desk is situated at the far end. "This is my foreman's office space, but we also use it for parties."

French doors lead to a patio overlooking a one-acre flat arena and an eighty-foot round pen. A green grass pasture is beyond, and a herd of horses grazes, their tails moving lazily. Bougainvillea with pink-red blooms cling to the wrought iron railing of the terrace, and there's a fireplace and comfortable seating outside.

"I had a shelf added along this banister so people could set down their drinks and watch the riders," Victor says, then points at the arena. "That's a European surface."

"What's it made of?"

"The Euros thought of it before us, but it's high-quality sand mixed with polyester geotextiles. It provides a stable, cushioned base, reducing the impact on horses' bones and joints, especially when jumping. Riders take tumbles, so I prefer bruised pride to broken bones."

I recall I'm supposed to flatter him. "It seems you've thought of everything."

He stands a little straighter. "It's taken a lot of sacrifice, but Crown Point Farms remains the West Coast's premier facility." Victor checks his watch. "If you'll excuse me, I need to make a few calls. I realize you've been thrown into the forefront now Samira's dead, but will you let me know about the insurance as soon as you can?"

"Of course." I thank him for his generous donation and time. Back in the quiet of my car, I plot a course to the next property.

10

Cassie Whitman, the manager at Thornfield Equestrian Center, is my tour guide. She's mid-thirties and speaks with a cultivated accent.

"Our facility features an indoor arena with a viewing room designed like a theater for the comfort of observers," she says as we step into the barn. I note that it lacks the chandeliers and other luxury touches that Crown Point has. *What is wrong with me?* My barn at home has one stall and is also used to store farm equipment, with a few cats being its most unique feature.

We pass a blonde woman who examines her long, painted fingernails next to a man grooming a black Warmblood. Cassie says, "Giselle, I found your Hermés hoof pick pouch the other day and put it in your tack bin."

Giselle slaps the groom's back. "You need to be more careful with my things, Rafael."

He pauses his task. "Ms. Giselle, you had it last. You showed it to Ms. Chelsea."

She heaves a put-upon sigh. "I thought about ordering a replacement, but the goods can take *weeks* to arrive. Given their prices, they should have next-day delivery. That pick alone cost over $300! I bought the whole set of grooming tools so I'd get a discount."

"Everyone loves a bargain," Cassie says.

Giselle resumes examining her nails, while I process the idea of someone spending hundreds of dollars on an item to clean dirt and rocks out of a horse's hooves.

As we walk on, Cassie mentions "summering in the Cotswolds" and some rider names I don't recognize. At my blank expression, she explains they're all Olympic-level equestrians.

"Do you know Chase Matthews?" I say.

"You aren't up on the gossip, are you?"

"Probably not."

"He was engaged to Samira Westbrook, but she caught him with one of his students, who I think was nineteen or something? I'll never understand why he thought it was a good idea to seduce someone at the riding club in an empty stall. Couldn't he at least spring for a hotel or take her home?"

"I'm sure that was a shock for Samira."

And now she's dead, and he's grieving.

"I heard through the grapevine she's been having a rough time since the breakup. Chase still trains at her club, and they've had a few public shouting matches." Cassie adjusts her blazer. "Though between you and me, I think she's better off without him. Chase's the type who'll never change."

I don't break the news about Samira's death, but make a mental note to call Montoya and share this with him.

———

As I start my car, my phone vibrates with a text from Vivienne Reese.

Went by the riding club and found out about Samira. Can you meet?

Twenty minutes later, I sit across from Vivienne and Elise at Naked Café in Encinitas. We place orders, but remain quiet until after the waitperson brings our drinks.

Vivienne takes a sip of her coffee, shaking so much she spills a little. "I can't believe this happened. I've already signed some vendor contracts, and we'll forfeit a sizable amount in penalties if this event doesn't go forward."

Elise picks up her chai latte, but doesn't take a drink. "That's not important right now, Viv. Samira's dead, and she was truly a kind person."

"She was. This is dreadful. How did she die?" Vivienne asks me.

"I'd rather not say. I think it's up to the sheriff to release any information."

"That makes sense, but we recently received a huge donation to the event," she continues. "Bradford Kensington gave—"

"Who did you say?" I interrupt.

"Bradford Kensington. You might not know him, but he's a multi-billionaire."

Setting down my tea with a little too much force, I say, "I met him last month when his property was on the Ladies' League Home and Garden Tour."

"You were there?" Elise says. "I heard—"

"Yes," I interrupt again, not wishing to review the past. "How much money did he donate?"

"Four hundred thousand," Vivienne says. "He told me to use it to pay for expenses, so more could go to Reins of Hope. Coupled with Victor Hayes' donation, Elise thinks we'll be able to surpass our fundraising goal."

Elise nods, but her mouth droops. "If only Samira were here. She was so enthusiastic about the cause. Her father was an Army veteran, I think."

Our food arrives, and I force myself to eat. "I toured two of the barns today," I say. "Victor Hayes seemed concerned about some extra liability insurance Samira was going to obtain. Do either of you know if she did?"

"No," Elise says. "I'm not even sure how to check her records since her office is a crime scene."

"I have a contact with Sheriff's Homicide who might be able to tell me when we can get in," I say. "What else do we have to do?"

"There's some money being contributed from the Ladies' League, but I don't know who's in charge of that. Do you, Davia?" Elise says.

"Our finance chair is on vacation, and Alex Gordon is taking over his role. I'll tell him what happened and give him your contact information."

When we finish eating, Vivienne says, "This has been a difficult death to process, but I guess we'll move forward as best we can."

"Maybe we should put *In Memory of Samira Westbrook* on the advertising and programs. What do you think?" Elise says.

"I'll make sure to do that," Viv says.

———

Driving home, I call Alex.

"Are you calling to spill the tea on the book club meeting?" he says.

"I wish. I have some bad news. Samira Westbrook, the manager at the Riding Club, was murdered."

"What happened?"

I fill him in.

"Is the charity event going to be canceled or postponed, then?"

"Doesn't look like it. Marilyn Voss, the former manager of the club, pressed me to visit two of the barns slated for the tour today."

"That's a woman with some misplaced priorities."

"And I've got more bad news."

"Worse than a murder?"

"Bradford Kensington has made a significant donation to offset costs."

Alex releases a low whistle. "That reeks of revenge to me. He probably got wind you're involved and is trying to force you to show him gratitude."

"That will never happen." I go on to tell him about the drone, the flat tire, and my suspicions that Bradford is behind it.

"Sounds like he's made a game out of messing with you, then."

"That's what Kyle said. Warden's here, and he agrees."

"How long is he staying?"

"Not sure."

"I know you're capable, LT, but I feel better when he's around. Although Lord Byron won't appreciate his presence."

"Adair's barn is part of the tour, so..."

"I can picture his perfect pout now."

"Getting back to the event, Samira hired two women to help with coordinating the show and the finances." I give him Elise's contact, explaining her role. "And Victor Hayes at Crown Point Farms seemed more distressed about extra liability insurance than Samira being dead."

"Without access to Samira's computer or notes, it'll be difficult to get the full picture."

"I'll talk to Detective Montoya and see when we can go into her office."

"I'm glad a familiar face is on the case. I'll touch base with this Elise person, see what she knows, and how we can proceed."

11

"You can't be serious," Warden says after I tell him about the morning's events. "You get more action here than on our missions."

"I didn't expect crime in Rancho except maybe someone demanding their personal chef be arrested for using white instead of black truffles." My chest tightens as an image of Samira's blood-soaked blouse comes unbidden to my mind. "She was so authentic, you know? Trying to help others."

"Is there anything I can do?"

"Distract me."

"I thought I did this morning before you left. A few times," he says, but pulls me into a hug.

"I haven't forgotten." I snuggle into his big frame and lay my cheek against his chest.

"I shouldn't joke," he says, stroking my hair. "I can tell you liked Samira, and I'm sure it's difficult."

"She could have become a good friend."

With Warden here, I can exhale, let him lend me his strength.

After a few minutes, I look up. "I forgot to mention it, but our newest donor to the horse event is Bradford Kensington."

Warden releases me, making a disgusted noise. "Thought he'd still be busy cleaning the blood out of his estate."

"His property manager is mega efficient. She probably put Hazelton in order by that evening. Besides, he owns so many homes around the globe; it's rumored he hasn't visited some of them."

"Then he should pick one on the opposite side of the planet and stay away."

I go into the kitchen for some iced tea. "Bradford has the money to hire a small army, a top-level assassin, or a team of them. For now, I'll take him being a nuisance."

"Do you have a plan to stay safe?"

"Other than living by our usual awareness? No. Bradford lets others do his dirty work, so even if he's at functions, he'll be limited to veiled threats while holding a glass filled with premium liquor."

"You said your leg's better, so maybe you can cut your losses and return to the team early?"

"I said it's better, but not one-hundred-percent. Nerve damage is unpredictable."

Warden stares at the view over the valley, where multi-million dollar estates cling to the hills. I recognize the expression he wears, the one that appears when he's absorbed in mulling all the possibilities.

"What's on your mind?" I say.

"How different it is to have time off, to not push ourselves to the limit training every day.

"Or be gone on a high-threat mission."

Warden retrieves a can of beer from the fridge. "Remember that time we did a joint op with the Raiders in Somalia?"

"You mean the ship boarding operation that went sideways? Of course." We head to the outdoor patio to sit. "Are you trying to put today's homicide into perspective?"

"Maybe."

The memory is clear and brutal. Eight-foot swells pounded our craft for six endless hours. A pitch-black night, a ship trying to evade us. The boats heaved, every surface slick with salt spray, and our heavy gear threatened to pull us overboard. Then Ned slipped off the caving ladder during our initial boarding and plunged into the roiling waters.

"When Ned fell, K went in after him without hesitation," Warden says.

"I remember. K saved his life, but nearly drowned himself in the process."

"Point is, we trained for that scenario, knew the risks, had contingency plans. But when it came down to it, instinct kicked in. K didn't think; he acted. That's what you do for your team." Warden grows sombre. "Today, you walked into something completely different. No backup, no intel, no tactical planning. You and a dead woman in an office."

"So you're saying I should appreciate the simplicity of a straight-forward murder investigation? Isn't that a little cold?"

"Out here, you're alone. The threats don't come with an action plan or a warning. They come in a cardigan like Bradford, or as a fake smile in a stable."

"That's still bleak."

"Davia, you've got to look at your situation. When I return to Virginia, you're left out here injured and alone. If Bradford decides to escalate his revenge, you'll be vulnerable."

"What options do I have?"

"Which brings us to the worn topic of how we remain together," Warden says. "I think we've rehashed our ideas so many times we can recite them from memory."

To change the futile subject, I say, "Want to go with me to Bryce's tomorrow?"

"Who's Bryce?"

"The owner of a clothing boutique. I need his advice on what to wear for the charity event. I don't have any English riding gear, and I doubt he supplies that, but he'll point me in the right direction."

"Your days seem to be made up of meaningless social events, clothing choices, and the occasional murder."

"That's a succinct summary of my new life."

———

Bryce's Boutique is located in downtown Rancho Suprema, situated in a cottage at the end of a jasmine-covered trellised walkway, where the sweet smell of the blooms adds to the quaint aesthetic. The bell tinkles as Warden opens the door into a crowded shop filled with racks and shelves packed with the latest designer clothing. Half a dozen women browse, but conversations halt mid-sentence as heads turn toward Warden.

"Davia!" Bryce cries, rushing forward to kiss each of my cheeks. His dark hair is styled in the latest fashion, and he's dressed in a fitted black shirt and jeans. He gives a little gasp when he spies Warden beside me. "And I *finally* get to meet this mysterious man! He's even more gorgeous up close, *non*?"

"Bryce, this is James Warden," I introduce.

He circles Warden like an artist studying a sculpture. "*Mon dieu*, such shoulders! And those eyes—like emeralds, *oui*?"

I check to ensure those eyes aren't narrowed, but Warden wears a bemused expression.

"I'm in charge of a joint charity event between the Ladies' League and the Rancho Riding Club, so I need something to wear," I tell Bryce.

He points at a flyer on a display board near his register. It proclaims "Hoofbeats for Heroes" in red, white, and blue lettering, with a horse and rider jumping over an American flag. "Someone brought that by a little while ago. It says in memory of Samira West-brook. I was shocked."

It's only been a day, but why let murder get in the way of photo ops and donor tax deductions?

"Did you know Samira?" I say.

"She came in often and was so organized and intelligent. And her style! She didn't have an unlimited budget, but possessed impeccable taste, unlike many who think money equals fashion sense." He winces as a customer holds up a clashing outfit. "*Pardonnez-moi*, I must intervene before someone commits a crime against couture." Bryce moves off with the speed of a firework shot into the sky.

"He's a lot," Warden says.

"Do you recall the blue gown I wore to the gala when I first moved here? He chose it for me."

Warden's face softens, and he gives me a devastating half-smile. "I'll never forget how you looked—both in and out of it."

Bryce overhears this as he zips back. "And you can thank me for the lingerie."

"I'm in your debt," Warden tells him, then bends close. "I might need to get some fresh air."

With that, he exits. Everyone in the shop watches him until the door closes.

Bryce fans his face. "Now I understand why you've been so reluctant to let Adair Monroe pursue you. Your man should come with a warning label."

"For many reasons."

"What are you looking for today?"

I explain about the pre-event barbecue and concert. "Then I have to put on a costume and ride English in the grand finale."

"At least you won't be in five-inch heels or clad in a Kincaid Foxx creation."

"That is an upside. Do you have anything?"

"I have a pair of Lucchese boots in your size. They're a hand-stained Alligator in red and blue. They're an iconic brand, although I also have some Miron Crosby boots, but...wait here." Bryce dashes off and is back faster than Usain Bolt in a dead heat. He shoves a pile of garments at me. "Use Room One. I put the boots in there."

I slip into a pair of faux-leather butter-soft black pants, pair them with an old-fashioned cowboy shirt with pearl buttons, and pull on the boots. When I step out, Bryce says, "One moment. You need something else." He brings me a lightweight, red suede jacket with fringe. "In case of a chill."

"It's summer," I protest.

"And the nights can grow crisp. If you don't use it, bring it back."

When I learned to be prepared in Girl Scouts, I don't think they meant buying a two-thousand-dollar coat in case of cold weather.

While Bryce totals my purchases, he lifts his chin at the flyer. "*Pauvre petite*, you're stuck coordinating this now, aren't you?"

"Marilyn will probably step into her old role as the Riding Club's manager, and Samira hired two professionals for additional support. I toured Crown Point Farms and Thornfield Equestrian yesterday so we can keep on schedule."

"What a mess," Bryce says as he folds my items. "Marilyn was in here last week with some brute. He seemed angry, muttering about Samira threatening to ban him from the club."

"For what?"

Bryce gives an eloquent shrug. "Not sure. Marilyn noticed other shoppers giving him disapproving looks, and they left."

"Probably Jeremy Maxwell-Price." I describe him.

"*Oui.* Is he going to ride, too?"

"Not so far, but I'm not in charge of the finale. I had hoped to tag along with Samira and stay in the background."

"How was Crown Point?"

"I don't have a lot to compare it to, but it seemed top-notch." I tap my card on his machine, trying not to wince at the total.

"Rumor has it Victor Hayes let half his staff go due to money troubles. Someone mentioned he's been meeting with investors about 'restructuring.' All that luxury doesn't come cheap, especially when the money stops flowing."

"Now that I think about it, there weren't many people at the facility when I was there. He showed me the foreman's room, but it was unmanned, and there were no grooms or stable hands."

"Half my clients are leveraged to their eyeballs. For many, the appearance of wealth can be smoke and mirrors."

"Victor said he partnered with Meridian, a British corporation, to do some upgrades. Perhaps he's recovered."

"Could be." Bryce gives me my bags.

"Tell Ramon hello," I say, referencing his hair stylist partner.

"Book your hair appointment for the horse event now. You know the Salon Divine drill."

"Unfortunately, I do."

Stepping out into the sun, I scan the area for Warden.

He comes toward me, but isn't alone.

Adair strolls along beside him.

12

They approach at an unhurried pace, engaging in easy conversation, neither rushing to reach me. Warden moves with the controlled menace of a panther, Adair with the grace of his ballet training.

"Picked up a stray," Warden says.

"At least I'm house-trained." Adair brushes his lips against my cheek. When he straightens, Warden's eyes carry a dangerous glint.

"Allow me." Warden takes my bags, and I laugh at his weaponized politeness.

"Careful," Adair says. "The last time I assisted Davia near Bryce's, she threw me halfway across a sidewalk."

"Why only halfway, Davia?"

"I can't with you two. Adair, I'm stuck coordinating a charity tour of your barn and others, and have a favor to ask."

"Anything for you."

"I have to ride English in the horse extravaganza finale. I'm sure it won't be a problem, but I'd like to sit in an English saddle and test how it affects my seat."

And see if the angle exacerbates my injured leg.

"Julia keeps the facility and horses in top condition, and I'll have her pick out a suitable saddle and mount for a trial run."

"Thank you. By the way, what are you doing in town? And..." I check behind him. "Where are your bodyguards?"

Adair's cheekbones tinge pink while Warden's lips twitch with amusement.

"I don't need them on local errands."

"Don't let pride kill you," Warden says. "You're not bulletproof."

The two men study each other, and Adair's eyes drop to Warden's injured leg.

"Fair enough."

Footsteps cause us to turn, and Alex enters the path from a rear parking lot. He halts beside me.

"I didn't expect to find you handling a diplomatic crisis," Alex says to me.

"Warden, you remember Alex Gordon?" I say. "He's on the Ladies' League board now."

Warden says, "Are you running numbers for them?"

"Only for the upcoming horse charity shindig because our treasurer is on vacation. I'll oversee the building and grounds maintenance otherwise." He gestures to the bags emblazoned with Bryce's logo that Warden holds. "Did you find something fetching to wear?"

"They don't carry my size, but the owner could probably dig up something for you and this scrawny Brit."

A trio of women exiting Bryce's interrupts any response, and we make room on the sidewalk to allow them to pass. They take in the men with interest before continuing.

"I'm glad to have run into you, Davia, saved me a call," Alex says. "Have you heard when Samira's office will be open? The documents Fred sent me are minimal. I'm not sure how to get into her computer, but perhaps she had other notes."

"Did you talk to Elise?"

"Yes, but she was a wreck. Unlike you, some people have emotional reactions to tragic events."

"I—"

"Kidding, LT," Alex says.

"LT?" Warden questions. "Did you get promoted and not tell me?"

"It's not short for lieutenant. It means Little Troublemaker," Alex explains.

"I see," Warden says. "I'll have to let our, um, friends know they have two options now."

"Two?" Alex says.

"To our friend group, she's Bombshell."

"And not because she's blonde, I bet," Alex says.

Warden grins. "Correct."

Ignoring this, I say, "I'll find out from Detective Montoya when the office will be available. It'll give him a chance to laugh at my priorities."

"Be sure and tell him Beatrice Gibbs won't understand if a pesky little murder delays her social calendar," Alex says.

Adair checks his platinum watch, whose intricate features display multiple time zones. "My apologies, but I must dash. Davia, I texted Julia to prepare for your lesson. Let me know when and we'll be ready."

"Thank you, Adair," I say, and he pulls me close for a farewell hug before he hurries away.

"Sometimes I forget that walking magazine cover runs international enterprises," Alex says.

"And ignores boundaries," Warden says.

"It astonishes me someone like you would feel threatened," Alex says. "Davia doesn't want her own money, let alone his."

"I'm not threatened. I'm observant."

"Observing Adair's ridiculous perfection is annoying," Alex says. "It'd help if he were more of a...what's that British term? Wanker."

———

After Alex excuses himself to meet a client at his nearby office, Warden says, "What next?"

"Are you hungry?"

"Yes."

"Probably from the exertion of carrying my shopping bags."

"I try to be a gentleman, but all I get is grief."

When the purchases are stowed in my car, we make our way along the Spanish-style buildings containing the downtown businesses. Warden stops before a realtor's office to read some of the flyers displayed in their window. "I think you skimped. You should've bought this 10,000 square foot, twenty-nine million dollar five-bedroom, eight bath home with..." he squints, "a Kalamazoo grill and Afyon white marble countertops. Whatever that is."

I join him and point at a different home. "This one has more bang for the buck. For around the same price, I'd get a 31,000 square foot home with nineteen bedrooms and twenty-three bathrooms *plus* a private, organic orchard and lake view."

"If you want me to live out here, please upgrade."

We walk hand in hand to the location of the former Chateau Rouge French restaurant, now under new ownership and renamed Le Jardin Blanc. The auburn-haired hostess, Sarah, has retained her position and greets me by name, although she shoots a questioning look at Warden. I'm sure he doesn't miss this and has put it together that she's used to seeing me ith Adair.

"Would you like to dine inside or out?" she asks. "Our patio has a wait today."

"Inside's fine," I say.

Sarah leads us through a transformed interior. Gone is the dark leather and wood décor, replaced by a soft lavender and cream palette, featuring limestone floors and wrought iron details. She seats us at a cream leather booth and provides us menus. "Your server will be with you in a moment. *Bon appetít*," she says, then returns to her station.

"This place looks like a hotel lobby in Cannes now," a woman seated at the next booth says to her male companion.

"Where's the intimacy? It's so bright," the man says.

"At least the menu still has the same favorites, but look!" She lifts a napkin folded over some bread in a basket. "They've changed the proper *pain de campagne* to these industrial baguette slices. And the butter isn't even room temperature. How gauche."

We review the menus, and I'm pleased to see the lobster salad with grapefruit and mangos remains. Am I becoming set in my ways like some of the people of this community?

Warden leans back. "I'm going for the prime fillet with grilled asparagus, but I'm not sure what the side of *pommes Robuchon* is. I'll call it mystery potatoes for now."

When we place our order, the server explains that the dish is named after the famed French chef Joël Robuchon and is made with potatoes, butter, milk, and salt.

"So, essentially mashed potatoes," Warden says when he's gone.

"It doesn't have the same flair."

The restaurant continues to fill as we wait for our meals, consuming the inadequate bread and butter. I'm taking a sip of my iced tea when peals of laughter draw my attention to Chase Matthews, now occupying a corner booth on the opposite side of the room. With him are four attractive women in their late teens and early twenties. He's holding court, relating a story about one of his many championship rides, and his expansive gestures enact the near-toppling of an upper rail.

"It wobbled for a few heart-rending moments, but it stayed up."

A brunette is filled with concern, "What happened?"

Chase gives her a cocky smile. "I won, of course."

The others in his group applaud with delight, and Warden says, "Is that Adair's fair-haired cousin? Same movie-star looks and coterie of admirers."

"That's the former fiancé of the woman who was murdered, Samira Westbrook."

Warden takes in Chase and his conspicuous good spirits. "His mourning period was rather short."

The server places our meals before us, while I recall Chase's display of grief the day Samira died. Had it been a performance? Or was this his way of trying to return to normalcy?

Warden and I are only a few bites into our food when Marilyn and Jeremy enter and pause before Chase's table.

"Enjoying yourself, Chase?" Marilyn's question silences the group. "Samira's funeral arrangements aren't even finalized."

Chase's arrogant attitude fades as his admirers shift, uncomfortable. "I—"

"You what? Thought you'd celebrate your freedom?" Jeremy says. "At least I don't have to worry about her trying to bar me from the club anymore, but you were the one she had true emotional leverage over."

"That's enough," Chase snaps. "Samira's death had nothing to do with—"

"With what? Your wandering eye?" Marilyn crosses her arms, her disdain unmistakable.

"You wanted your old job back," Chase says. "I've overheard your insults and watched you undermine her at every turn. You tried, and failed, to get rid of her. Perhaps you resorted to murder?"

Marilyn's mouth falls open. "How dare you!"

She launches forward to slap Chase, but Jeremy takes hold of her scrawny arm, stopping her. He gives a bitter laugh. "She had dirt on all of us."

A chilling silence descends. The women with Chase look between the three like spectators at a tennis match. When the conversation continues, the trio lowers their volume, but their tight features and furious stares remain.

"Are you taking notes for Montoya?" Warden says. "At this point, he should put you on retainer."

"I know we're both trained in behavior observation, but I can't tell if those three have murderous motives or are simply voicing petty concerns.”

Warden cuts another piece of his steak, considering the group. “You said Samira was kind and intelligent. I can't imagine she enjoyed any of those people's company.”

“I think she truly did love Chase, but I don't think she liked the other two. I've only known them briefly, but if I never speak to them again, it will be too soon. Unfortunately, the woman, that's Marilyn Voss, will be on the resort getaway.”

“Fun times.”

Our plates are cleared, we decline dessert, and are waiting for the bill when a crowd exits a private dining room to our left. Leading the way is Eathr Bliss, his highlighted blond hair flowing over a vibrant, burnt-orange top adorned with mystical symbols, which he's paired with crinkled white linen pants and sandals. The shirt is unbuttoned low enough to display his hairless chest, and his face is a picture of tranquility.

“Should I even ask?” Warden says.

“Now you know why I struggle to live here. Today's lunch has given you a condensed version of life in the Ranch.”

“At least there's no gunfire. At the moment, anyway.”

As the parade of Blissful Beings continues past us, Eathr's vivid blue eyes light on me. He shakes off his entourage to approach our booth.

“It's the radiant soul I met during my pop-up enlightenment session at the Rancho Suprema Market!” He beams at me. “The universe has orchestrated our reunion.”

“Has it?” I say. If so, I'd have words with it later.

Eathr puts a finger to his temple and surveys Warden. “The masculine energy beside you radiates a desperate need for in-depth shadow work to undo his multi-layered, toxic trauma.” Warden turns stony-faced, but Eathr doesn't pause. “I'm sensing you're an alpha used to being in control, but you hold such incredible tension in your body. Cookie-cutter therapy might work for suburban soccer dads, but your unique brand of damage calls for a customized regimen of healing. Tell me, what truths have you learned from all your exquisite suffering?"

"What I've learned is problems get solved when talking ends."

Eathr claps. "Your wisdom is both true and insightful. Silence is highly valued and underutilized. Your sage observation has elevated us all."

Around him, his groupies murmur with excitement. Our server threads his way past them with a black leather folio containing our bill, which Warden takes. He stands, and Eathr's surprised gaze travels upward.

"Such a sublime specimen, reminiscent of Ares, the Greek God of War. You have to attend my exclusive retreat this weekend. I call it 'Titans Unleashed: A Sacred Brotherhood for Exceptional Men.' It's for CEOs, athletes, and others who operate at an apex frequency. We do deep ancestral trauma work, primal roar therapy, and indulge in luxury sweat lodge rituals."

In response, Warden turns to help me exit the booth. "If you'll excuse us—"

"Wait! You're the perfect specimen for my men to witness. Your stoic magnificence could unlock breakthrough moments for the entire brotherhood." Eathr begins to talk faster. "And at only thirty thousand, the return on investment for your emotional ascendance will be exponential."

Warden steps to within inches of the guru. "I have a brotherhood. Forged in ways you don't practice."

"Shall we compare? I'm always eager to learn about other methodologies."

"No." Warden removes some bills from his wallet and stuffs them into the folio. "Shall we?"

Eathr wheels around and addresses his followers. "My sacred tribe, you've just witnessed how high-vibrational beings recognize one another. That man's aura was absolutely in sync with my frequency. True power is a match for true power."

As we step out of the building, Warden says, "Next time, I'm having lunch delivered."

13

We lie entwined in bed, enveloped by the darkness of night and quiet peace. I place my fingers near the top of Warden's forehead and rub soothing circles.

"Am I helping release some of your exquisite suffering?" I say and kiss him softly on his cheek. He turns his head and puts his lips to mine, then pulls me closer.

"If I say yes, will I have to pay you thirty grand?"

"I'm more expensive than that."

"There goes my down payment on a house. At least a house that's not in this zip code."

The feel of our naked bodies pressed together fills me with something deeper than desire. A brief memory flashes, a mission where an extraction from Kandahar went sideways. Wrong landing zone, comms down, hostiles closing in, but Warden adapted in real time, even with mortar rounds shaking the ground around our team. I can trust him with my life, but how do I convince him to stay?

Instead of bringing up the impossible scenario of us being together full-time, I say, "Warden. I love you."

He raises his head. "Davia—"

"I should have told you sooner, when you said it to me. It's just, I don't want to take you away from a job you—"

The house alarm cuts through my words, and we sit up.

"What is that?" Warden says.

"Perimeter." I'm off the bed and pick up my phone, scrolling through the exterior camera feed.

Warden pulls on his pants. "Do you see anything?"

"No. For some reason, a few of the grids are black. Here." I give him my .45 from a bedside drawer.

"Most women keep other types of toys in their nightstands," Warden says as he checks the magazine.

"Those are in a different drawer." I dress in dark sweats and pick up my 9mm, along with a pair of compact night vision binoculars. "The alarm's from the top driveway area. José has alerts in his residence and will probably check this, so..."

"Don't worry, I won't shoot him."

Without further discussion, I go out the front door and across to the courtyard gate while Warden goes into the backyard. Our footfalls are trained to be soft, our movements fluid, and our training drills have taught us to utilize shadows and concealment without thought.

My gates are all well-oiled, so we can move throughout the estate in silence. The property is equipped with ground vibration sensors, thermal imaging cameras, and electromagnetic pulse detection systems. Did Bradford hire a professional team capable of disabling it all?

Concealed against the courtyard wall, I crouch to check my phone's feed, but still see no one. Sliding past the gate, I stay low and scan the alarm area with the binoculars. The only movement I detect is José moving along the driveway and Warden emerging from the gate near the pool house.

We search in silence, and I push the possibility of a high-powered rifle scope trained on us from my thoughts. Am I naïve to think Bradford won't have someone assassinate me from afar?

After twenty minutes, we've combed the whole property, but we've only discovered two cameras destroyed by gunfire. There are no casings, tire tracks, or footprints.

We regroup in the courtyard.

"Someone was here, and knew how to take out your cameras, but why stop at two?" Warden says. "Your alarm isn't audible outside, is it?"

"It isn't," I confirm. "Same with José's."

"I got outside fast, but triggered a motion light at the barn. Maybe that threw them off?" José says. He wears jeans, but is barefoot and shirtless, evidence that he wasted no time tracking the intruder.

"Did you hear any gunfire, José?" I say.

"No."

"Maybe they used a suppressor. It took a pro to bullseye those cameras in the dark," Warden says.

"Let's do a more thorough search when it's morning," I say. "I'm confident something spooked them."

Inside, I reset the security system. "This seems futile."

Warden wanders toward the kitchen, places the weapon on the counter, and retrieves a bottle of water. "I'm more focused on the bad timing. You finally tell me you love me, and we're interrupted by an event that required clothes and weapons."

I lay my gun and binoculars down, then wrap my arms around his waist. "It's given me time to reconsider my feelings for you. What was I thinking?"

Warden faces me. "What you're thinking is how you'll take me to your bedroom so we can explore what's in your other secret drawer."

———

We conduct a thorough search in the morning but find no additional clues about who tried to penetrate the property.

"The skill it took to find those tiny cameras at night and disable them makes me rule out local kids or burglars," Warden says as his phone vibrates. "Hang on, it's Streeter."

Warden steps away. Colonel Streeter is in charge of our team, and I hope this isn't news that someone has been hurt or killed. The conversation doesn't last long, but when Warden returns, his mouth is set in a hard line.

"Is everything okay?"

"Streeter needs me at work."

"But, your leg…"

Warden hesitates. "It's intel analysis only, but he can't say much on an unsecure line other than my expertise is urgently needed."

"When are you leaving?"

"This afternoon. The timing can't be worse after the breach on your property last night."

"I can take care of myself."

"Of course you can, but I want to be here for you, not enact another scene of unwanted goodbyes. Searching for a positive, it's only been four months since you left the team, and we've seen each other more than people whose loved ones are deployed. This isn't the worst case."

"True, but do you think you'll be able to come back?"

"Can't say. Streeter was terse."

I picture our wiry commander, his gray hair regulation short and his attitude all-business. "When isn't he?"

"We should go in so I can book a flight and pack."

Warden gathers his belongings with the efficient movements I remember so well. Soon he'll be in Virginia with the team—our medic Hodge spouting Texas expressions no one understands while patching our injuries, Savant analyzing intel with his razor-sharp mind, Ned cracking jokes to lighten the mood, and K handling explosives with his quiet expertise. Even Craig Kilburn, who took my place while I'm on leave, will lurk around the edges, all scarred intensity, unpredictable menace, and extreme competence.

I miss the camaraderie, the bond between us, and the feeling of belonging. I push away the ache.

Warden checks his watch. "I'm done. Now we'll have at least an hour to give ourselves more reasons to miss each other."

14

When I drop Warden at the airport, he gives me a kiss and says, "I'll text you when I arrive." He closes the door, moving with his usual confident stride toward the building. I watch until he disappears, then pull the Rover into the hectic traffic, where I'm forced to wait at a red light for people dragging luggage across the busy road.

It's the same drill. He leaves, I stay. We both pretend it's manageable.

The light changes, and I maneuver to an exit that takes me along a harbor filled with sailboats, past the skyscrapers of downtown San Diego, and to the freeway. A call from Sherilyn brings me out of my misery.

"Davia! What are you doing? We haven't talked in a while and—"

"I just took Warden to the airport. He came in for a few days but got called to Virginia."

"Girlfriend, this is a big yikes event that's set on repeat! It's like a movie where the two leads are madly in love, but life keeps separating them. Think *Romeo and Juliet* without the poison and *Titanic* without the iceberg. But with Adair thrown into the mix, it could be an updated love triangle where both guys are worth choosing. I should write a treatment to pitch to Hollywood based on your life! I know someone who knows someone who works with a producer who did that Netflix series about the billionaire and the dog walker, which wasn't great, but it got picked up for three seasons, so clearly the bar isn't that high, and I think your story has way more potential because you have skills and there will be a criminal element and—"

Sherilyn continues her rapid-fire commentary on her dramatic rendition of my life, and I let her prattle wash over me like background noise. My body relaxes, and I begrudgingly recognize that sometimes her endless yammering is exactly what I need.

"Davia? Are you doing that thing again where you pretend to listen, but you're replaying your time with Warden, thinking about how your guns need cleaning, or are plotting the takedown of some dictator?"

"Sorry."

"You need to learn to say *um-hm* or *uh-huh* at intervals or make some other noise. Think of it as a skill to trick people or something. Anyway, how about we meet up? There's a new chocolate shop on Cedros in Solana Beach, and what crisis can't be solved with chocolate? And don't get literal and say chocolate can't solve world problems. I'll take a gooey ganache over a grenade any day, and don't you dare criticize my strategy. Sometimes the best weapon against sadness is small-batch chocolate paired with champagne."

"I'm not upset enough to go down the day drinking road."

Sherilyn makes an exasperated noise. "There you go doing that literal thing again. The name of the place is O'Keeffe Chocolates. See you soon."

———

My petite blonde friend is inside the shop perusing a display case laden with temptations when I manage to get around a line that's half a block long and enter.

The sophisticated space features exposed brick walls, copper accents, and glass display cases, with the scent of cocoa and vanilla filling the air. Staff members bustle behind the counter, taking orders, and a man emerges from the kitchen area, wiping his hands on a black apron. His shirt has its sleeves rolled up, revealing powerful forearms, and his raven-black hair contrasts with his striking blue eyes.

"Davia!" Sherilyn exclaims. "Come meet Kyran O'Keeffe, the owner. I was his interior designer, so I called to let him know we were coming, and he reserved a table for us. I mean, it's summer, and look at the line! Not that there isn't always a line, but when kids are out of school and people are on vacation, it's madness."

Kyran listens with a resigned look on his excessively handsome face. He isn't what I imagined a chocolate maker would look like, but had it ever crossed my mind?

"Welcome in," he says, his Irish accent making him even more attractive. "Whether it's a celebration or commiseration, I've got what you need."

"Commiseration," Sherilyn says. "Davia's man jetted out, but I'm sure chocolate therapy is exactly what's needed to soothe her woes."

"Fortunately, I haven't experienced relationship turmoil in some time," Kyran says. "I'm recently engaged."

"Congratulations!" Sherilyn shrieks while I repress the urge to throttle her for oversharing about my life. "I've met his fiancée, Davia, and she's a food stylist who's ironically allergic to chocolate— but at least she's not allergic to *him*."

Kyran laughs. "I've developed a line of flavored caramels because of Candace, so meeting her led to the expansion of my menu. Now, ladies, what would you like?"

I take in the trays of artful, painted candies. Heart-shaped choco- lates are adorned with tiny painted flowers, rose-shaped pieces bloom in pink and coral, and square chocolates showcase designs from Celtic spirals to abstract art in metallic paints. "It's a difficult decision when everything looks so tempting."

"I've got a solution!" Sherilyn says. "We'll take an assortment of your most ordered items with some sparkling water."

"Sarah, can you put together a selection box with the salted caramel with Achill Island sea salt, strawberry ganache, honey dark chocolate, hazelnut praline, and peppermint cream? And also bring two sparkling waters to table four."

"Of course," Sarah says, and begins placing items on a tray.

"I'll check on you," Kyran says.

"You've given us enough of your time, Kyran," Sherilyn says. "If you don't return to your kitchens, you'll sell out of inventory in an hour!"

"I'm scarlet from your praise. Please let my staff know before you leave, and I'll come out to say goodbye."

We settle at the table and soon have our order arranged before us.

"These look too exquisite to eat," I say.

"Taste one, and you'll get over that notion fast." Sherilyn selects a piece, takes a bite, and gives a satisfied moan of pleasure.

I try the peppermint cream, and the cool, clean flavor cuts through the lingering bitterness of watching Warden walk away. Perhaps chocolate can't solve all my worries, but I have to admit my friend's onto something.

"Now," Sherilyn says. "Catch me up on everything. Ric told me you discovered another dead person, this time at the Rancho Riding Club. I swear, Davia, you need to take a vacation, cleanse your aura to stop attracting darkness, or something."

"Montoya's on my speed dial," I say about her detective boyfriend. "And as for aura cleansing, I've been force-invited to a free weekend at the Serenity Springs Wellness Center with other members of Brittany Guinn and Kennedy Conner's book club. Samira Westbrook, the murdered woman, was the only club member I could tolerate. Francis Downs isn't bad, but we don't truly connect."

"I know a lot of them, and those women think falling social

media engagement rates are a national emergency," Sherilyn says. "I can't imagine how you can be around them."

"It's not easy."

"But Serenity Springs? Do you have a clue how exclusive that place is? We're talking about a resort that makes most others seem like budget motels. I know the cost is insane, but their meditation gardens were designed by the same landscape architect who created those Japanese gardens at the Met. Their spa treatments utilize ingredients flown in from Switzerland, Tibet, and possibly a remote mountain in Bhutan where monks bless the water. The wellness treatments are run by over fifty physicians, and their anti-aging program can take your cell health and immune function back to infancy!"

"Maybe I should skip out and book a session with TikTok guru Eathr Bliss," I joke, filling Sherilyn in on his encounter with Warden. When I finish relating the tale, tears of laughter fill her eyes.

"I can picture Warden now, running a full tactical assessment in his head. Ignore the nuisance? Or deploy one of those terrifyingly efficient takedowns he never talks about? The internal debate must have been epic."

"He settled on icy disdain, so Montoya didn't have to work another homicide."

There are four or five remaining chocolates, but my head is fuzzy from the sugar rush. I sip the sparkling water while Sherilyn updates me on her booming interior design business and budding relationship with Montoya.

When I insist on paying for the meal plus some boxes we order to go, I blink twice at the total. With a tip, this is more than most people's weekly grocery bill, but today I feel less guilty about an indulgence, recalling what Alex said last month about my inheritance.

"Decide what this money might bring that's a positive, rather than focusing on the negatives."

As we prepare to leave, a willowy woman with curly strawberry-blonde hair pushes through the front door, avoiding the line of customers with practiced ease.

"Hey, Candy," one of the staff members calls out with a wave.

She returns the greeting as she slips past the display cases. Kyran emerges from the kitchen area, and he lights up when he spies her.

"There's my girl." He pulls her into an embrace despite the cocoa dust on his apron.

Candy brushes at the dark spots now decorating her green blouse. "My dry cleaning bills are getting out of control."

"I'll add it to my expense account." He kisses her forehead before glancing our way. "Davia, this is Candace, my fiancée."

While we exchange greetings, I notice the easy intimacy between them, the way she wipes a chocolate smudge from his cheek, and how he keeps a hand on her lower back even as they talk. Something twists in my chest. Will I ever have this daily normalcy with Warden?

After we say farewell and go outside, Sherilyn considers me. "Your mood has shifted downward again. What happened? Should we open one of these to-go boxes right here?"

"Not unless you want to watch me heave. I'm full to the eyes with sugar. But don't worry, it's me wishing for a more stable life with Warden."

Sherilyn pats my arm. "Davia, I hate to be the one to tell you this, but I'm pretty sure neither of you would be happy if your lives weren't in jeopardy at least twice a month."

15

The estate gates swing open. I navigate a long drive lined with Jacaranda trees, past Adair's English-style manor house that's big enough to be a hotel, and head for the barn. I bought the outfit I have on—breeches, tall boots, fitted shirt —at a local tack shop. To surprise Adair? Or so his barn manager has no excuse to sneer? Maybe both.

I park, but Adair doesn't come out. The old Adair would have been at my door before I killed the engine, pulling me into an intoxicating embrace. Even after my recent time with Warden, his absence deflates me.

He appears in the barn doorway but stays there, leaning against the frame, arms crossed. "You look perfect in that," he says, waiting for me to come to him. "Finally on the correct side of the equestrian world."

"It helps me blend in."

"Where's Warden? I figured he'd tag along to protect your virtue."

"Work called, and he left."

A ghost of a smile touches his mouth, then vanishes. "I had Julia prepare a mount for you."

Inside, the barn smells of oiled leather, cedar, and horse. The walls are lined with rich wood paneling, and the floor is covered in rubber matting in an intricate pattern. Tied to a stall is a tall, sorrel stallion with a shiny coat. Julia adjusts the English saddle's cinch as we approach.

"Davia, you remember Julia Darrow?"

Julia's eyes flit to Adair. A common reaction, but it still sparks a twinge of inexplicable possessiveness.

"This is Wellington," Adair says. "Named for the Duke."

"He's been going beautifully since we adjusted his program." Julia strokes the horse's neck, not looking at me.

Adair nods. "Morrison's thoughts on his schedule?"

"Thermal in February, then the circuit. George says he's ready for the grand prix if his form holds." Her tone is intimate. "We'll see how he handles the Hermès footing before Europe."

"Very good. Here you are, Davia." Adair hands me a helmet.

I strap it on while Julia says, "Wellington's book is nearly full for next season." She checks the girth with practiced efficiency. "We had three inquiries after Spruce Meadows alone. That Hanoverian mare from the German syndicate would be an interesting cross."

"The one with the Cornet Obolensky dam line?"

"Exactly. Her movement is exceptional, and the temperament match would be ideal." Julia finally glances at me with pity, or a good imitation. "Don't worry, Davia. Wellington's gentle, unlike those western horses that spook at everything."

"Horses are unpredictable," I say. "The discipline doesn't matter."

"I set up some low rails in case you feel like trying," she says.

"Let me see how it goes, and I might." At home, I jumped my pony across fallen logs and took plenty of risks when I rode. Would the lack of a saddle horn make that much difference?

Julia leads the horse to a mounting block. She adjusts the stirrups once I'm seated. Pushing my heels down, I check for any pain in my injured leg, but there's none. Will this change when I put Wellington into a trot and be required to post?

The outdoor arena is neatly groomed, featuring six jumps of varying heights arranged in the center. The highest is a daunting six feet, nothing I want to go near. When Julia latches the gate closed behind me, she and Adair stand close together, forearms propped on the rails as they watch. She says something to him, and he gives a low laugh.

Taking my mount to the rail, I make a circuit of the enclosure at a walk before cuing him into a trot. My leg remains unaffected when I post, and a sense of relief fills me.

"Not bad for a newbie," Adair comments when I pass.

"There are poles on the ground to practice going over obstacles, or you can attempt those low jumps on the end," Julia calls.

Putting Wellington into a canter, I approach the first jump. It's around two feet, and he sails over with no effort.

"Brava!" Adair calls as I turn away from the next jump and return to the rail. I flash him a smile, pulling the reins to circle the horse.

Wellington gives an abrupt, hard shake of his head. The crown piece slips over his ears.

The bridle falls.

His nostrils flare when he realizes he's free, and he erupts into a mad charge. The English reins form a single continuous loop, preventing the bridle from falling. I consider tossing them over his head. Too risky. Gathering them tight, I pull the failed equipment snug against his chest.

Wellington runs full tilt. He almost slams into the railing, but spins at the last moment, and it takes everything for me not to go sailing off. Adair vaults the fence, arms wide, trying to cut the arena in half. Julia mirrors him on the opposite side.

Spying them, my mount wheels around—and goes straight for the six-foot jump.

Catastrophe looms. My stirrups aren't set for extreme jumping. All I can do is try to keep him from tangling in the bridle and breaking a leg. The jump rushes at us.

I pray we make it.

16

In two short strides, Wellington tucks his front legs and launches.

Stay focused. Fearless.

I hold my breath, lift from the saddle, and crouch forward. High in the air, suspended, I feel his power. Then the descent throws me off-center.

Wellington's back legs clip the rails.

We crash down sideways.

My horse folds his legs and rolls, pitching me off. I tumble across the dirt, winding up on my side.

"Davia!" Adair runs toward me while Julia rushes to take hold of the horse. He drops to the ground beside me. "Are you okay?"

"Got my breath knocked out," I gasp. "Nothing's broken."

"Oh, thank god."

"Give me a sec."

Once I can sit up, Adair pulls me against him. "You were brilliant. Your first time out, but when a catastrophe struck, you handled it like a pro."

My heart thuds with adrenaline. "Western riders can't be beat."

He sits back, but keeps hold of my shoulders. "Only you would joke at a time like this."

"You're not admitting English riders are in second place, then?" I undo the chin strap and remove the helmet.

Julia has the reins tight around Wellington's neck. He prances, still excited from his escape, but she leads him to the gate. Four other members of Adair's barn crew are there, and one holds a halter, which she puts on the runaway.

Adair helps me stand, but doesn't release me once I'm up. "Are you sure you're okay?"

"I might have a few bruises tomorrow, but I'm fine."

Julia hurries over, her focus on Adair. "I don't know how that happened. I'll check the equipment. I had Manuel call the vet for Wellington."

"Thank you." Adair gives her my helmet and loops a protective arm over my shoulders. "But if anything happened to Davia, there'd be no excuse."

Julia stiffens.

"It was an accident, Adair," I say. "You both know that if you ride a lot, it's not a matter of if, but when something will go wrong. Don't be so hard on Julia."

Adair's eyes stay on me. "You're right, but that was terrifying to watch." He turns to Julia. "My apologies."

"High-powered horses are more problematic than most," I say to her. "It's not your fault."

"I'll update you if anything's wrong with Wellington, but I'm sure he's fine," she says. "Is there anything else you need?"

"Have someone bring a golf cart to the gate. I'm going to take Davia up to the house."

Julia's gaze lingers on his features, searching. Then she hurries off.

"I'm fine, truly," I tell Adair, but his arm stays around my shoulders as we leave the arena. A worker brings a golf cart. We drive past acres of flowers and vegetable gardens to the rear of the house.

Before I can protest, Adair leaps out, picks me up, and carries me toward a rear door.

"I wasn't knocked senseless or something," I say, placing my arms around his neck.

"This is chivalry. It doesn't question your capabilities."

"Is this a lesson in embracing my feminine side?"

"Someday you'll have to. Baby steps."

Adair opens the door and takes me to a sitting room with elegant yet comfortable furnishings and warm lighting. He sets me on a couch.

"I think that's you." I point at an oil painting above the fireplace. It's of a boy with Adair's sandy brown hair and aquamarine eyes dressed in a blue velvet outfit with ornate silver trim and a cascading white lace cravat.

"Only if I'm a vampire. That painting is hundreds of years old."

Footsteps sound in the hall, and Jason appears in the doorway. "My staff informed me there was a disturbance at the stable, Mr. Monroe. Are you—"

"Davia took a spill," Adair says. "Wellington threw his head and slipped his bridle."

"And I didn't break my neck," I say, thinking Jason might have preferred that outcome.

"Did someone tamper with the equipment?"

"It was a freak thing," Adair says, "And no, I won't sell my horses and encase myself in bubble wrap."

Jason's gray eyes close to near slits, but he says, "Do either of you need any first aid supplies?"

"That's not necessary," I say.

Adair comes to sit beside me. "Let's enjoy a snack to give you time to recover. Food pairs well with trauma."

"I don't—"

"I'm sure Alain is bored. Jason, tell him to keep whatever he prepares light and refreshing since it's so hot outside today."

"Absolutely not," Jason says. "I'm not stating the obvious to him.

His sensitive soul will perceive it as an insult, and he'll start muttering in French about *idiots anglais*. We'll get stuck eating cold lamb for weeks."

"True. He'd rather intuit our needs," Adair says with a laugh, and Jason departs.

"Point me to the closest bathroom," I say. "I don't want to get dirt marks on the Louis XIV furniture, or whatever priceless antique you've put me on."

When I return, Adair leads me to an elevator and we go up to his private suite.

"It'll be quieter up here," he says. "I told you my dining room could comfortably host a gathering of the U.N., and it's too warm to go out on the patio."

He indicates a sitting area, and I settle, ignoring memories of his fevered kisses when I was stretched out beside him only a few weeks ago in a downstairs bedchamber.

"Let me get you some water." He retrieves some from his private kitchen.

"You seem different," I say when he returns.

He sits in a chair opposite. "How?"

"More..."

"Reserved? Restrained?"

"That's it." His careful distance should be exactly what I want, so why did it leave me unsettled?

"Davia, my feelings haven't changed. I'm giving you space instead of forcing the issue."

"I've always told you, I love Warden."

He goes still. "Love? You've never used that word before. Did his last visit bring you clarity?"

Alain knocks at the door, interrupting us. He carries an elegant silver tray loaded with delicate offerings.

"Thank you, Alain. I appreciate all your hard work," Adair says, and I add my gratitude.

The chef sets the tray on a table, gives a terse bow, and departs.

Our conversation is general as we eat, Adair regaling me with stories about his recent business exploits. Listening to him reminds me of how fun and easy it is to be in his company, how a part of me feels lighter around him.

After our meal, Adair says, "Let me drive you to your car."

This is how it should be. He's respecting my relationship with Warden.

Inside the elevator, his hand brushes mine. He pulls it away like he's been scorched, and the restraint shows how hard he's fighting himself. I am, too.

At my car, he opens the door. I get in. He wheels away and is gone.

17

The next day, I'm a little stiff, and electric pain shoots down my leg, nerve damage's calling card. I spend time in my sauna and tell myself the twinges will subside with some rest and stretching.

This isn't a setback. The fall made this act up, nothing more.

Am I being delusional? I refuse to believe I won't recover, not yet.

But dwelling on it won't help, and I have responsibilities. The charity event can't fall apart because of my personal problems, but if my leg doesn't improve enough for me to ride, I'll consider it a win.

A meeting with Montoya, Marilyn, and Alex at the Rancho Riding Club is set for ten a.m. I park next to Alex, who gets out of a red Porsche, its enormous rear wing and bodywork suggesting it escaped from a racetrack.

"It's not even noon, and it's starting to swelter," Alex says.

"It's not truly hot 'til you hit 130."

"Have you experienced that?"

"In the Middle East. Nice wheels."

"Thanks. I've got a weakness for cars that were designed to break lap records, not obey speed limits."

He's shed his toned-down Ladies' League look, tattoos highlighted by his fitted V-neck black T-shirt paired with jeans. I keep my attention on the sleek frames of his sunglasses.

"Those shades look good on you."

"They're Akoni Sprint-A. When you drop a grand on sunglasses, you've got to get some mileage out of them."

"Pretty flashy for this meeting. Montoya let a cleaning crew in, but I doubt they can counteract the odor left by blood in a closed, hot room."

"You sure know how to kill the mood."

A few people are in the barn, grooming horses or preparing to ride. A girl of around eleven stands beside a saddled pony with her arms crossed.

"I'm not riding this nag," she declares.

"Your father paid over $300,000 for this animal because you said you didn't like the other one you have. And now you're refusing to ride?" a woman scolds.

"But, Mom," the girl whines. "I said I wanted a buckskin, not a palomino!"

"Do you even know the difference?" her mom says.

"Do you?" the girls spits.

When we're far enough away, I say, "You told me my inheritance is something I should appreciate, but I'll never get used to how disconnected from reality most people here are."

"When you've never had to choose between paying rent or buying groceries, a three-hundred-thousand-dollar mistake is another Tuesday. I manage money for people who think a 'budget crisis' means they can only afford two vacation homes that year. Or their life is ruined because their private pilot canceled on a planned birthday flight for their three-year-old and ten of her friends to enjoy a private princess party at Euro Disney outside Paris."

"By comparison, your expensive sunglasses are a dollar store purchase."

"Exactly."

Detective Montoya stands outside the office door with Marilyn.

"When will I get my keys back?" she says to him. "I'm taking over Samira's position, so..."

"You said you let her borrow them the day she died because she lost hers, right?" Montoya says.

"That's right."

"We found her keys in her purse. Are you sure she asked you for them?"

"Yes. Wait. Are you saying I'm a suspect?"

"I'm only stating facts."

"But, but, I..." she stammers.

San Diego Sherlock strikes again.

"Let's go in," Montoya says. "I cracked the windows and kept the door open since I got here, but it won't be pleasant."

The stench hits us as soon as we enter—lingering putrid decomposition that even the cleaning crew and ozone generators haven't eliminated. Alex and I don't flinch, Montoya breathes through his nose like it's just another day, but Marilyn pinches her nose closed.

"Oh god," she gags. "How can you stand it?"

Montoya switches on the lights. The room is once more a typical office, and even the desk is clean and tidy. "Davia, does being here bring back anything you might have forgotten to tell me?"

I scroll up the memory of finding Samira. "Nothing new comes to mind."

Marilyn continues to hover right inside the door. "How are we supposed to work in here?"

"Do you know if she kept a file on the computer about the event?" Alex asks her."I gave the sheriff's homicide team the passcode, but I obviously haven't checked."

"We got a warrant and went through it," Montoya says. "I wasn't the person who did the examination, but there wasn't anything obvious like threats or evidence of blackmail."

"Here," Alex retrieves a pen and a notepad and gives them to Marilyn. "Write the login info down for me, and I'll look."

She does, then says, "I'll wait outside."

While Alex boots the computer, I say to Montoya, "Did you check the security footage?"

"Yes. Problem is, the cameras are focused on the inside of the barns, tack rooms, and outdoor riding areas for liability and theft-prevention reasons. The office and its access points don't have footage. Someone who knows the riding club could easily skirt them."

"What about the watch I found on the landing?"

"It belongs to Chase Matthews, like you thought. Said he and Samira argued when she got off work the night before her death, and it likely came off then."

"What, like a physical altercation?"

"No, he said it was an exchange of words about their broken engagement, and he might have banged the watch on something around the horses, weakened the band, and it fell off."

"Wouldn't Samira have noticed it and picked it up?"

"Difficult to speculate on that. Maybe she had had enough of him and decided to leave it."

"Did you believe he didn't hurt her when they argued?"

"The only injury to the victim was the neck wound, no other scrapes or bruises, so it doesn't discredit his statement that their argument was only verbal."

While Alex examines the computer files, I fill Montoya in on what I heard from Cassie Whitman at Thornfield Equestrian about the couple's public fights, and what was said at Le Jardin Blanc between Chase, Marilyn, and Jeremy.

"Sounds like lots of motives, but we don't have any specifics. Here, look at this." Montoya pulls up a photo on his phone. "This is from a notepad that was on the desk beneath the victim's body."

The pad has a splatter of blood on one edge, but is legible. There's a handwritten note that reads, "VH donation, Crown Point. Problem? Meridian."

"Do you know what that means?" Montoya says.

I peer at the photo. "Meridian is a UK company that invested in Crown Point's operation recently." I fill him in on Victor Hayes and his rumored financial issues. "But he's a big donor for the charity event, so perhaps he got things in order."

"So this can possibly be interpreted as Samira being concerned about the donation, but maybe making a note to ask Victor Hayes if Meridian had solved his financial woes," Montoya says.

"Yes, and I haven't had a chance to tell you, but Bradford Kensington is also a donor."

Montoya's head jerks up. "Does he have a connection to either organization putting on this event?"

"He had his home on the Ladies' League tour last month, but it's hard to say."

Alex continues to type, but says, "I still think he's playing games with you, Davia."

"Perhaps it's his way to remind you there'll be payback," Montoya says.

"And he's willing to spend almost half a million on a donation to get my attention?" I say.

"He probably paid with coins he found in the couch cushions," Alex says.

Montoya gives a grim laugh. "Did you find the file?"

Alex nods. "I conducted a preliminary review and found some late vendor payments and a few cash flow inconsistencies, but I'll need more time. I copied the club's accounting file into my Dropbox account, and I'll set up a meeting with Elise Harrington."

When we exit, Marilyn is seated on the landing, arms wrapped around herself despite the warm air. She stands. "Find anything?"

"I located the accounting file, sent a copy to myself, and will set up a meeting with Elise," Alex says, though Marilyn watches Montoya.

"You're free to use this space now," Montoya tells her.

"How long will it take for the smell to leave?"

"Hard to say when it'll be tolerable for you."

We head for the stairs when Marilyn says, "Davia, Alex, while you were in there, I got a message from Vivienne. She's set up a donor thank-you party at the Rancho Country Club. You'll need to attend."

"Won't a party like that cost us more money?" I say.

"It's standard. The cost is a fraction of what we've been given to cover most of the expenses." Marilyn uses the snide tone of someone explaining the obvious to an outsider. "I'll text you the details."

Marilyn takes the key from Montoya and goes to lock up.

"So we're spending donor money to throw a party thanking donors for giving us money?" I say as we descend the stairs.

"It's the circle of life, Rancho style," Alex says.

Montoya gives a dry laugh. "I'll stick with solving homicides."

18

The donor party is in an opulent room of the Rancho Country Club. Dark wood paneling surrounds arched windows overlooking a portion of the golf course. The bell-sleeved dress I wear is made of ivory and blue cotton, with a neckline that plunges lower than I prefer and side slits high enough to reveal some serious leg. But it's a donor thank-you party, and as co-chair, I need to look the part. If my stomach didn't feel upset, I might pull off the wealthy socialite act.

"You look glorious, LT," Alex greets when I enter, surveying me with a wolfish grin. "That dress might give some of these old-money donors heart palpitations. Want me to get you a glass of wine?"

I follow him to the bar, where he orders our drinks. His cream linen blazer, worn over a navy polo and chinos, highlights his broad shoulders and causes more than a few women to pause their conversations. Within moments, three women descend on him like designer vultures.

"Oh my god, you're so tall!" Crystalle squeals, angling her phone for a selfie with Alex in the background. "And I see some tattoos peeking out at your collar. So naughty!"

"I love your whole aesthetic," Brynlee gushes, running a finger along his forearm. "Such edgy vibes."

"Wait, aren't you that financial guy?" Tiffaney vapes between questions. "I need someone to manage my revenue streams."

"I handle sophisticated portfolios, hedge funds, private equity, and crypto. Probably not quite what you're looking for."

"What kind of car do you drive?" Crystalle says. "I'm doing a series on successful men and their rides."

"That's a lengthy discussion—"

"Davia!" Brynlee interrupts, spotting me behind Alex. "Come here! You're slaying tonight. That dress is everything!"

Tiffaney exhales vanilla-scented vapor, and nods at Alex. "Will you introduce us?"

After I do, Crystalle snaps a photo of me beside him. "You two make a perfect couple. Are you dating?"

The bartender slides our glasses across the bar, and Alex hands me one. "Ladies, if you'll excuse us..." he says.

"Wait!" Brynlee calls as we move away. "Alex, what's your sign? I'm doing a whole athleisure line inspired by astrology..."

Alex doesn't answer, moving us toward a more quiet corner.

"It seems you attract a lot of admirers," I say after we're a distance away.

"Who were they?"

"Some of the other members of Brittany and Kennedy's book club. Actually, more like hangers-on. They want their followers to skyrocket by pretending to read."

"Please tell me you left early."

I give him details about the upcoming retreat at Serenity Springs.

"A weekend trapped with that group doing wellness activities? That's not self-care, that's torture."

"I'll probably have to listen to them rhapsodize about your good looks. You're as much of a female magnet as Adair."

Alex takes a sip of his wine. "It's difficult for me to believe you didn't notice every man in here straighten their shoulders, suck in their stomachs, and try not to stare at you. What happened to your instincts?"

"Put me in a room full of people, and anxiety dulls my situational awareness."

"You didn't seem that way when I first met you."

"That was different. You came up behind me and grabbed my arm, triggering my self-defense training. I'd rather handle a physical threat than make small talk at a party. That's when my radar goes haywire."

"Interesting. So you're saying if I display some physical affection, you'll snap back to normal?"

Before I can respond, Marilyn approaches. "Davia, Alex. This is much more pleasant than our last encounter."

"The smell's improved," Alex says.

"I was talking to Victor Hayes," she nods to where he chats with Tiffaney, Crystalle, and Brynlee, the trio appearing to hang on his every word. "He asked about the event insurance. Did you see anything when you looked at that file, Alex?"

"I wasn't focused on insurance, but I'll check."

"I'll also go through the details when I can tolerate being in the office. I should test how long I can hold my breath and try to send everything to my home computer. With the date almost upon us, we can't afford any glitches. Oh, there's Jeremy. Talk later."

She turns on her heel to join him.

"Is she related to Beatrice Gibbs?" Alex says. "You know, the give orders and go type."

"They both probably took the same course of indifference to anything but their social power. You mentioned some account irregularities. Did you figure out any specifics?"

"Not yet. Had some urgent meetings with nervous private clients to allay concerns about economic fluctuations, as if they haven't happened since time began. I'll do a full examination soon."

"Vivienne and Elise have arrived," I say. "Let's catch them now to deflect a future scolding from Marilyn."

After I introduce Alex, Vivienne says, "When Samira died, ticket sales soared. The VIP experience is completely sold out!"

"Coupled with the generous donations, we should exceed our goal for Reins of Hope," Elise says.

"Do either of you know if Samira obtained the additional insurance Victor wanted for Crown Point?" I say.

The women shake their heads.

"We weren't even that far along with planning when she was murdered," Elise says. "Alex, Marilyn told us you were able to access the accounting file?"

"I did, and noted a few minor discrepancies, but..."

"Discrepancies?" Vivienne interrupts. "What do you mean?"

"Nothing big, but like I told Davia, private business has kept me from a deep dive."

Alex begins a side discussion with Elise about sharing information and coordinating the finances between the Ladies' League and the Riding Club. Vivienne says, "Davia, because Samira's dead, I've combined her role with yours in the grand finale. I'm still working out details with the professional acrobats and equestrians, but you'll have a larger part to play."

"What will that entail?"

"I'm not entirely sure. We'll have the rehearsal a few days beforehand, and the other entertainers are experienced. I wouldn't worry too much."

"Vivienne, Elise!" Marilyn calls, motioning them over to her group, which contains Jeremy, Victor, and some others.

"I'll text you the rehearsal date," Vivienne says to me, and the pair moves away.

A passing server takes our empty wine glasses.

"Want some more?" Alex says.

"Yes, but I'll have to drive home."

"There's always Uber, you know."

A stir at the door draws our attention. Adair enters, creating a palpable shift in the room's energy—conversations die mid-sentence, and whispers begin. His trio of bodyguards blends into the crowd. Unaware of the ripple effect he creates, Adair pauses, and Julia enters, placing a proprietary hand on his arm. She's in a form-fitting navy cocktail dress that highlights her curves, the perfect foil for his gray pinstriped blazer with a hint of navy at the turned cuffs, paired with a dark green shirt and navy chinos.

"Who's his date?" Alex says.

I tell him, explaining, "That's the manager of his equine interests."

His eyebrow arches as his gaze lingers on Julia. "Lucky horses."

Crystalle, Tiffaney, and Brynlee have been filming with their phones since Adair entered, their excitement at a level high enough to power a small city. When he gets closer, they launch themselves forward, continuing to record. Before they can get within ten feet, his security smoothly intercepts them, redirecting the women toward the appetizer station with polite but unmistakable authority.

Adair notices me from across the room and, for a moment, intensity sparks in his eyes. Then Julia says something, and he turns his attention to her.

"They make quite the pair," Alex observes, his tone neutral.

As they proceed, I notice there's something almost protective in the way Julia positions herself, like she's both showcasing and guarding her prize. Adair greets people and introduces them to her, remaining in my line of sight but not approaching.

"He's not coming this way," Alex says. "And he's making sure you notice he's not."

"Is he?"

"You know, LT, I'm curious about something."

"What's that?"

"How committed Lord Byron is to this whole 'giving you space' routine." He steps closer, his voice dropping to that low, intimate tone he uses when he's about to cause trouble. "I wonder if a little test might be educational."

"What kind of test?"

"The kind where I put my hand on your waist, get near your lips, and see how long it takes him to abandon his noble restraint. Call it a social experiment."

"Alex..."

"Come on, it'll be fun. Besides, you said your radar's off in social situations. I'm offering to help recalibrate it by giving you something concrete to focus on."

"That's a terrible idea."

"The best ones usually are."

The warmth of his palm at my waist burns through the thin cotton of my dress as he draws so close the front of our bodies almost touch. His cologne—something with cedar and citrus—fills my senses, and I note the gold flecks in his hazel eyes as his lips descend toward me.

"Your breathing's shifted," he murmurs in my ear.

"Has it?"

His thumb traces a circle against my waist. "Interesting reaction for someone who's supposedly immune to my charm."

"This is for Adair's benefit, remember?" I manage, though I sound less steady than I wish.

"Is it? Because from where I'm standing, he's the last thing on your mind."

"Davia, Alex," Adair says from behind us. "Julia and I wanted to say hello."

Alex's lips quirk as he steps back. He removes his hand but remains close by my side.

"I'm Alex Gordon," he says to Julia.

"How do you know Davia?" she says.

"I'm her financial advisor. Among other things."

"You give such personalized service," she coos.

Adair's jaw tightens. "Davia, did you have any injuries after Wellington fell with you? I meant to call, but got caught up in a business ordeal, then had to rush to make it for this."

"Woke with a few bruises, that's all."

"Wellington is?" Alex asks.

"A Warmblood I own."

"Don't tell me you only buy horses named after famous Brits?"

A knot of men in suits enters, forestalling further conversation. At the center of the group is Bradford Kensington. Everyone pauses to take in the newcomer, and I notice Victor Hayes white-knuckling his wine glass before forcing away the tension.

What's that about?

In his mid-fifties, Bradford is of medium height with pale blond hair. He wears thick black-framed glasses, a light cardigan, and an assumed air of benign innocence.

He heads straight for us.

Adair and Alex straighten, and a slight crease appears on Julia's forehead as she takes in their changed demeanor.

Forcing myself to relax, I extend a hand. "Bradford, thank you for your generous donation to this wonderful cause." When his palm touches mine, I use my other hand to clamp his in a display of intimacy I don't feel. His amber eyes meet mine, assessing.

"When I found out you were involved with this charitable endeavor, I had to contribute," he says, his grip tightening. "Still playing savior to the masses, I see. How's Kyle Kavanagh?"

I wrench my hand free. "He told me if I ran into you, to give you his special regards."

A muscle in his jaw ticks. "How hospitable of him." He acknowledges Alex and Adair. "Gentlemen."

"Bought any stolen art recently?" Alex says. "Or poached another close friend's wife?"

"I've been busy. But I did hear you bought stock in my subsidiaries. I suppose even you recognize a profitable venture."

"I have in the past, but I moved the money. Found some alternatives with stricter ethics compliance and transparent leadership."

"Thought you'd be in Cannes or Monaco," Adair says. "There's much more excitement on the continent this time of year. But perhaps it would be boring for you without Brandt."

"You know I don't require my son's company to continue to have fun. Now, you haven't introduced me to this lovely lady, Adair."

Adair makes the introduction, and Julia studies him, which Bradford doesn't appear to notice. He shoves his hands into the pockets of his cardigan.

She's an observer. Will she buy his absent-minded professor act?

"Thank you for supporting the event and veterans," Julia says. "Did you or your family serve?"

"My dad was drafted into the Army for the Vietnam conflict, but his fluency in French got him reassigned to military intelligence. Vietnam was once French Indochina, so they needed people who could decipher captured documents or speak with contacts."

Julia gives a little gasp. "How admirable. Did you follow in his footsteps?"

"I chose to use my skills in the private sector. Building American economic power can be as patriotic as military service, but with conflicts played out in boardrooms rather than on the battlefield."

"How fortunate for the U.S. that your patriotism aligns with profit for your bank accounts," Adair says.

Bradford gives him a brittle look. "I—"

"Mr. Kensington!" Marilyn sweeps forward, followed by Vivienne and Elise. "We are simply thrilled to have you here tonight, and want to thank you for your incredibly generous donation."

"Yes, Mr. Kensington. Because of you, we were able to upgrade our show with the highest quality acts," Vivienne says. "It will be a glorious finale!"

He pushes his glasses further up his nose. "Do call me Bradford."

"What an honor." Elise's cheeks flush like she's in the presence of a rock star.

"I'd like you to meet our other donors," Marilyn says. "And get you something to drink."

"Of course. If you'll excuse me," Bradford says and follows the women, his contingent of suits positioning themselves behind.

Julia retakes Adair's arm. "I sense you don't like that man. Is he a business rival?"

"I don't want to ruin our evening by discussing him further." Adair flags a server. "Anyone want more wine? Let's have this nice young man retrieve it for us."

We all assent, Adair gives him a fifty for a tip, and he hurries away.

"That was unpleasant," Alex says. "Bradford coming here under the mantle of a generous donor when he's engaged in some kind of sick game makes me want to punch him."

"Game?" Julia questions.

The server returns with wine, and everyone takes a glass. "Like I said, let's enjoy our evening," Adair says.

"You're right." Alex slips his arm around my waist. "The night's young."

19

Kennedy's home is the meeting place for the weekend retreat to Serenity Springs. A luxury transport with tinted windows idles, and its driver stows mountains of luggage in a compartment.

"I think I should take my own car," I tell Kennedy after I park. "I'm co-chair of an upcoming charity event and—"

"Don't be silly! I understand Marilyn is working with you, and she doesn't have any problem attending. Besides, Brittany's documenting our departure for our followers. It's one of the last things we'll be able to post before we turn over our phones at the resort."

Crystalle says, "The trip will be a chance for us to bond even more as a group and process the loss of Samira."

"Her death was such a shocking tragedy," Brynlee says. "I know you were kindred spirits, Davia, since you both read that classic novel for our club's first meeting."

"I wish I could have known her better—" I begin.

"Is that all you brought?" Tiffaney points at the black duffel bag I carry. She and Crystalle stand beside multiple, oversized suitcases in pastels and signature patterns. "These are ours," she makes a circling motion to include Brynlee. "I mean, we have separate luggage for shoes, makeup, accessories..."

"I thought yours was already loaded," I say.

"That's only Kennedy and Brittany's," Francis says.

They packed like they're moving to Europe. Permanently.

The chauffeur finishes loading everything, wipes his brow, and is about to close the compartment when Marilyn pulls in half an hour after the agreed-upon departure time. She opens the rear of her luxury SUV and removes multiple pieces of luggage.

"Apologies for my tardiness," Marilyn says to us, not bothering to move her bags closer to the coach. "The club's head groundskeeper called about whether to reseed the east paddock before or after our event. Samira never gave him directions, rest her soul, so these decisions fall to me now."

"You have so much responsibility. I don't know how you handle it," Tiffaney says.

When the final bag is crammed in, the driver slams the bin shut with a definitive thud.

"Let's board!" Kennedy chirps. "Time for our pre-detox journey to begin."

The interior resembles a mobile nightclub with butter-soft leather seating arranged in conversational clusters, mood lighting, and speakers pumping out pop music.

I take a seat in the rear of the coach near an exit door.

Would getting overwhelmed by the company constitute an emergency?

"Davia!" Brittany waves a crystal flute at me. "You have to join our tradition. We always do a cleanse-prep toast before wellness weekends."

"It's like maximizing our toxins before we reset," Kennedy explains, popping a bottle with theatrical flair. Champagne sprays across the ceiling as everyone giggles with delight.

"I'm fine, thanks," I say, but Brittany shoves a filled glass into my hands.

"Don't be a buzzkill," she says. "The resort has a strict no-alcohol policy, so this is our last chance for days. Everyone! Raise a glass to the memory of Samira Westbrook."

"To Samira!" the women say, not melancholy in the least as they gulp the champagne.

The journey begins, and the music cranks louder. More bottles are opened, glasses are refilled, and Tiffaney begins to sing along to some song I don't recognize. The competing perfumes each woman wears—jasmine, vanilla, something floral—create a cloying fog in the enclosed space. I consider the champagne in the glass I hold, afraid to begin drinking for fear I might not stop.

Once we're out of Rancho and past nearby suburban areas, the transport climbs through remote mountain roads, each switchback taking us further from civilization. Cell towers disappear behind tree-covered ridges, and the road narrows to two lanes, with steep drop-offs on one side and towering granite cliffs on the other.

"Truth or dare!" Brynlee shouts over the loud music and conversation. "Davia, truth or dare?"

"I'll pass."

"That's not how it works," Marilyn says. "You have to pick."

Who knows what crazy ideas this crowd might have for dare? They'd probably make me chug a bottle of champagne while I dance in my underwear for Brittany and Kennedy's social media channel.

The women chant, "Truth or dare! Truth or dare!" and I say, "Fine, truth."

Tiffaney takes a long draw from her vape. "Spill—what's going on with you and Adair Monroe? He told everyone that the gorgeous brunette he brought to the donor party manages his equine interests and, since his stable is on the tour, he felt she should meet everyone. But we couldn't help noticing how he kept looking at you."

Everyone fixes on me, riveted with interest.

What do I say? We're drawn to each other like the proverbial moths to flames? He's kissed me a lot, but I have a man I love.

"Adair and I are good friends."

"B-o-ring," drawls Brynlee. "We all saw that magazine cover of you guys—"

The transport sways around a mountain curve, and Crystal lurches forward, dousing the others with champagne. This diversion ends further Adair commentary, as napkins are offered and drops are blotted. When everyone calms, Brittany yells, "Time for another group selfie!"

———

We reach Serenity Springs Wellness Resort, the main lodge emerging from the forest like a mirage of glass and stone. Floor-to-ceiling windows reflect the surrounding peaks, while clean lines of steel and timber blend into the wilderness.

"We're here!" Kennedy shouts into the transport's microphone, and everyone weaves to the windows to look.

"This place is majestic." Brynlee fumbles for her phone to take a photo.

Once the exclamations of appreciation die down, the driver does his best to stop everyone from face-planting as they exit. Uniformed staff appear from the lodge with carts and begin unloading the luggage with efficiency. While the others enter the lodge, I approach the driver. "Thank you for putting up with that." I give him a folded twenty.

His stoic expression never wavers as he pockets the bill, the look of a man who's hauled worse cargo than a busload of drunk socialites. "Comes with the territory, miss."

Inside, a serene woman in flowing linen gives us a soft smile. "Welcome to your wellness journey. I'm Lotus. We'll begin by releasing you from the burden of technology."

Staff members approach with silk-lined baskets, and most of the women place their mobile phones in them, but Kennedy films herself saying goodbye in a dramatic statement to her followers. When they reach Brittany, she clutches her hot pink phone to her chest. "Wait, I need to create more content. The lighting in here is incredible, and our followers expect updates."

"I understand, but—" Lotus begins.

"You don't!" Brittany screeches. "Kennedy and I have two million followers who depend on us for inspiration. This is part of our luxury brand."

"I'm sure you feel it's inconvenient, but it's mandatory," Lotus says in a tone you'd use on a toddler.

Brittany jerks back, almost taking out a meditation bowl display. "I'll post a few stories, then I'll give it up. I promise."

Lotus maintains her beatific countenance. "Sweet soul, your cosmic energy cannot flow properly with digital interference—"

"Cosmic energy can kiss my ass!" Brittany waves her phone above her head. "I am NOT giving this over."

"Britt, you're being *so* extra right now," Brynlee says.

"I'm being AUTHENTIC!" she shoots back, then trips over the cart holding her luggage and falls.

Two staff members hurry forward. One helps Brittany to her feet, while the other plucks the phone from her grip before she can react.

"No, wait—" Brittany reaches for it, but the phone has been placed in a basket and taken away.

Tiffaney takes a drag from her vape pen, but a staff member appears beside her.

"Sweet soul, we'll need that as well. Artificial stimulants block your natural energy flow."

I wait for another argument to begin, but Tiffaney is compliant.

Lotus claps once, a light sound that somehow commands attention. "Beautiful souls, let's channel this energy into something nourishing. Perhaps some cleansing herbal tea to help us all find our centers after the journey?"

More staff appear as if they materialized from the woodwork and guide the swaying women toward the dining room seating area, where plush cushions are arranged around low tables. Soaring timber beams and picture windows frame the darkening forest beyond. I notice each woman receives personal attention that seems caring, but is a choreographed effort to manage the chaos.

Francis gapes at everything as she's led to a seat. "This is like being at a fancy spa."

I release a prolonged exhale.

"That was exquisite pranayama mastery," Lotus says. "You must be an expert-level breath shaman. Here's some tea."

Thanking her, I take the proffered cup and make my way to where the others sit. A massive stone fireplace dominates an opposite wall, cold and dark in the summer warmth, and I pass a sleek beverage station with glass dispensers of water infused with cut cucumbers, lemons, and mint. The scent of fresh forest air wafts in through some open windows.

It's like camping in the woods with a 500% markup.

After thirty minutes of herbal tea and Lotus's gentle guidance about "releasing the day's energies," interrupted multiple times by inane questions from the intoxicated women, we're finally escorted to our accommodations. A soft-spoken staff member named River leads me down a hallway decorated with abstract paintings and pine branches preserved in resin.

River swipes the key card to Room 4 and pushes the door open. "Your sanctuary awaits." She urges me inside. "The bedding is organic linen, woven from heritage flax to promote calm, well-being, and vitality. It has a high vibrational frequency."

I wait for her to cite a peer-reviewed study. She doesn't.

"Sleep well," she whispers, and pads away.

A window frames a view of moonlit pines. The platform bed is positioned beneath a skylight, and a single armchair, upholstered in undyed wool, is placed beside a polished wood table. My black duffel looks pitiful in the room's understated elegance. A flowing cream-colored tunic and matching pants are arranged on the bed. Atop them sits a handwritten card in elaborate calligraphy:

Welcome, Sacred Being. These garments have been blessed with intention and will support your journey toward authentic self-discovery. Please wear only these during your stay, as synthetic fabrics disrupt the natural energy flow of our sanctuary.

—The Serenity Springs Team

I pick up the tunic. The fabric is soft, but it's essentially pajamas with pretensions. A lightweight cotton Japanese yukata jacket hangs in the closet, accompanied by a note stating that it's part of the mandatory dinner attire. A wicker gift basket tied with organic hemp ribbon sits on the bedside table. Inside are plush slippers, a water bottle engraved with inspirational quotes, a canvas tote bag bearing the resort's tree-and-mountain logo, a leather-bound journal, a pen, and a collection of organic skincare products.

The bathroom contains a thick terrycloth robe and, in a dresser drawer, fresh workout clothes are folded alongside a knit cap, gloves, and a flashlight.

Will we be required to burglarize each other's rooms to find our nirvana?

Wondering if the others will be excited or put out that they brought too many clothes, I go to the window and open it. I recall how many times my team trained in harsh conditions or withstood tear gas canisters, desensitizing us to the pungent chemicals. The only odor here is the scent of cleansing incense.

Before I left, Warden had called to say he was digging through intel to get the complete picture on a past threat he can't discuss due to its classified nature. When I told him what I'd be doing, he said, "While you're participating in chanting, sharing circles, or hugging strangers, be sure and analyze how you might adapt it for use in our hostile interrogations."

Ned had snatched the phone, shot me a prankster smile, and demanded to know all about this exclusive retreat. The other team members piled on.

"We hear you'll be wallowing in velvet," Hodge commented, his big frame taking over the screen.

K, his dark skin highlighted by the call's lighting, says, "Trying to flex, Bombshell?"

"No. And I think you used up your word count for the year," I told him.

"I checked your destination, and their biomarker diagnostic protocols are fascinating," Savant said. "They use peptide therapy combined with cryotherapy and red light therapy for cellular regeneration, but the real innovation is in their personalized IV infusion cocktails based on genetic methylation patterns."

"Good thing they're offering genetic optimization. I might need to evolve new patience genes to get through this weekend."

Kilburn hovered behind the others, arms folded, his pale blue eyes cold. "Forced intimacy with strangers. Nothing reinforces the need for solitude like being trapped with people you can't escape."

Hearing everyone's casual teasing, even Kilburn's, reminded me what real trust and bonds are like.

I draw the curtains and go to take a shower.

20

Soft bells summon us to the breakfast pavilion, where everyone in the resort wears the mandatory tunics, like we're members of a country club cult. The others arrive like survivors from a sinking ship stumbling onto a beach. Brittany and Crystalle wear their sunglasses indoors, and everyone dons a guise of pure misery.

"Good morning!" chirps a staff member as they pass, but their only responses are winces, snarls, or head clutches.

The breakfast spread features egg white frittatas with microgreens, steel-cut oats topped with goji berries, and fresh fruit. Pitchers of green liquid have labels promising "liver detox" and "cellular renewal."

Crystalle fills a glass. "Will this help my headache?"

"It's got activated charcoal and spirulina!" A staff member says. "Perfect for releasing toxins!"

Brittany sits next to me and begins to nibble the corner of a piece of toast. "I can't believe I have to look puffy in front of strangers."

"Right?" Kennedy says. "The *worst.*"

"It's not the worst." Tiffaney tosses her plate onto the table. "I'm crawling the walls without my e-juice. I doubt even their organic juice-juice will compensate."

I enjoy my full plate while the others pick at their portions like they're defusing bombs.

"Davia," Francis slides over. "There's a morning activity after this. Want to be partners? They're pairing people up."

"Partners for what?"

"A sharing exercise."

Francis appears to be less hungover than the rest, so I agree.

An hour later, we're arranged on meditation cushions on the floor of a tranquil room.

"Today we'll explore the gifts passed to us by our ancestors," the class instructor, Starlight, says. "Share with your partner what abundance you've received in your life."

"Want me to go first?" Francis offers.

I nod, grateful for the reprieve. She launches into a story about how she inherited her grandmother's fifty-two-piece China collection. "It was Lennox, like from the 1930s or something, and so outdated."

"Did you need that many dishes?"

"I wasn't sure what to do, so I gave the whole set to my preschool-age daughter for tea parties with her dolls. If she broke anything, it wouldn't matter."

"Sounds like a good idea."

"I thought so, until I found out Christie's auctioned the same set for nearly thirty thousand in 2002."

"Really?" I'm unsure what else to say about giving an heirloom collection to a child without first checking its value.

"Your turn."

I choose to go with something Francis might relate to. "My aunt left me a substantial inheritance."

"She did? How much?"

"Life-changing? But she added conditions if I want to keep the money, which is why I'm living in Rancho Suprema and serving on the Ladies' League board." I don't mention the date a millionaire every quarter or appear in the society pages requirements.

"I don't see how that could be a negative."

"I didn't appreciate her trying to control me by forcing me into a life I never wanted. But now I'm working on gratitude."

"What did you do before?"

"I worked as a personal assistant to a CEO and traveled a lot," I say, sharing my standard cover story.

"That is life-changing, then! I mean, what could be better than being rich?"

"I think it's a little more complicated than that."

"Complicated? Think of the opportunities. You can travel, enjoy spa days, indulge in delicious food, and buy expensive clothes, cars, and homes. And you've kissed Adair Monroe, which has to be the fantasy of most women. That's worth more than money!"

"I'll let him know he's priceless."

When the session concludes, there's a class combining Pilates with infrared light therapy, personalized cryotherapy sessions targeting cellular regeneration, and a meditation class featuring binaural beats calibrated to alpha brainwave frequencies. I recall my training in sensory deprivation, interrogation resistance, and underwater survival, and try not to laugh.

Our last class is archery. The range sits on a wooden platform overlooking a meadow, with targets arranged at varying distances. We've changed from our tunics into provided leather arm guards, fingerless gloves, and fitted athletic wear in the resort's signature cream and sage green colors. The equipment rack holds a set of wood bows.

"These arm guards are cute," Brynlee says, admiring the supple leather with brass buckles. "Very Katniss chic. I should consider something like this for my athleisure line."

Crystalle poses with her bow. "I feel like an Amazon warrior princess! This is so much better than those pajama tunics."

Our instructor, a woman named Astrid, demonstrates proper

form. "Remember, it's about finding your center." She draws the bowstring with grace, and her arrow hits the bullseye with a satisfying thunk. "The bow becomes an extension of your intention."

Brittany examines her long, dark blue manicured nails with concern. "Will this chip my gel polish? I had them done in Malibu so they'd look good on our content."

"The protective gloves will help," Astrid assures her.

Marilyn steps forward first, her posture rigid with determination. "I studied archery at a Swiss finishing school. Proper form is essential." She draws the string with theatrical precision, releases, and sends her arrow sailing past the closest target and into the meadow beyond.

"Don't worry, your aim will return with practice," Astrid encourages.

Crystalle screws up her face, aiming. The arrow drops three feet in front of her. "I was channeling my inner being to guide that shot."

"Your inner being is best friends with Marilyn's," Kennedy says.

Tiffaney examines her bow as if it might bite her. "Is this, like, ethically sourced wood? I'm very conscious about sustainability." Her first attempt sends the arrow sideways into a tree.

"I'm sure the tree appreciates your ethical consideration while it bleeds sap," Marilyn says.

Francis is next, and I wonder if she'll be able to pull the bowstring. She lands three arrows in the outer rings of the second target.

Brynlee exclaims, "Francis! You're like a secret assassin!"

"Beginner's luck," Francis blushes, but I notice her stance is textbook perfect.

My turn. I step to the line. The polished wood of the bow is lighter than the composite models I trained with. Draw, anchor, release. The arrow splits the bullseye of the most distant target. I nock another. Same result. And another. The group falls silent as I put six arrows into the center ring.

"I'm shook," Brittany says. "You're giving Robin Hood."

I set down the bow. "I grew up in South Dakota. Hunting was part of life."

Marilyn says, "How practical for you."

As we continue, without phones to perform for, the women's true natures emerge. Brittany asks Astrid for advice on her grip, her focus on the target instead of her nails. Tiffaney, Brynlee, and Crystalle stop making excuses and shoot, their competitive spirits sparking without the need for an audience. Even Marilyn, once her superiority complex deflates, asks a genuine question about her stance. Kennedy remains true to form, praising efforts with a condescending undertone. But for a few minutes, the performance drops. There's just the thwack of arrows hitting targets, and the murmurs of encouragement. They seem almost real.

An in-room personal massage and facial follow the classes, then dinner. The meal consists of a wild mushroom and lentil loaf, rainbow-colored vegetables, and chocolate chia pudding served with edible flowers. The women dig in, their appetites increased from the earlier activities.

"Everyone!" Kennedy stands at the end of our communal dining table. "I have the most wonderful surprise for tonight! We've been given a rare chance to attend a moonrise ceremony off-site to unlock our deepest, most authentic selves."

Authentic? What lies beneath the masks worn by these women? The archery session revealed glimpses, but how much was real versus performance?

Stop being cynical. Get through this, and you can go home tomorrow afternoon.

21

We gather in the lobby wearing our own clothes for the first time since arrival, the clicking of high heels signaling a transformation. Gone are the equalizing tunics, replaced by clothing proclaiming wealth and status. Kennedy sweeps in, resplendent in flowing white silk paired with statement jewelry that catches the light. Brittany opts for a designer denim skirt outfit and turquoise. The others follow suit with their own versions of elevated glamping couture. I wear black tactical pants, boots that can handle rough terrain, and a fitted black tee. The knitted hat from my room is stuffed in my pocket along with the flashlight.

Tiffaney takes in my outfit. "Are you planning to scale a mountain tonight?"

"You never know."

The same luxury transport that brought us idles outside, and our driver—the one I tipped yesterday—gives me a curt nod. I'm sure he's dreading another trek with this crew. At least they didn't bring luggage. The interior lighting is dimmed to a blue haze, creating what I'm sure someone thinks is a mystical atmosphere.

"I've restocked the champagne for the journey," Kennedy announces as we climb aboard, to cries of gratitude. Glasses are filled and refilled as we wind deeper and higher into the mountains. The women laugh louder with each mile, their hangovers forgotten.

Crystalle leans against Tiffaney. "I've never done a moon ceremony before. I wonder if we'll meet our spirit animals."

"It's sure to be life-changing," Kennedy declares, raising her glass in a salute.

The coach stops before a stone building shrouded by dense forest. Torches flicker along a path to heavy wooden doors.

We disembark, and Brynlee says, "Doesn't this look like a movie set?"

"I wish we had our phones," Crystalle whines.

"Yeah, Kennedy," Brittany scowls at her friend. "We should have gotten the resort to give back our phones. We need this for our channel. It's so theatrical!"

A figure emerges from the lodge. It's a man draped in a ceremonial robe of deep burgundy with intricate silver embroidery. A mask made of matching material with inlaid silver covers the upper half of his face, and wavy black hair falls to his shoulders.

"Welcome!" The word rumbles out, deepened by what sounds like electronic modulation. "I'm your guide for tonight's transformation. Please, leave all earthly possessions in your transport. The only thing you need to bring is your open hearts."

The women vibrate with excitement as they turn over purses and jewelry to the coach's driver.

"All possessions." He points to where the flashlight bulges in my pocket. I give it to him, but he lets me keep the knitted hat, perhaps a reward for my earlier tip.

The masked guide seizes one of the torches, sweeping it before him with dramatic flair. "Your journey to authentic selfhood begins now. This way."

The women fall silent as they follow, but some nudge each other and exchange excited looks. Nearing the building, I notice security cameras hidden amidst the decorative stonework. This place is well-monitored, like the resort. Whoever manages both is likely aware that they have to protect the golden geese as they ascend to a higher level of curated self-enlightenment.

I'm last in line, and the van pulling out of the parking area draws my eye. Was it to keep the women from fleeing the experience for some more booze, to make off with their possessions, or something else?

"Come on, Davia," Kennedy beckons.

The ornate wooden door groans open, revealing a cavernous stone chamber that swallows our group whole. The room stretches at least fifty feet across, its vaulted ceiling disappearing into shadows high above. No windows break the stone walls, which are set with iron sconces holding lit torches. Thick incense smoke hangs in the air like fog, coating the back of my throat and making the far reaches of the room difficult to discern.

"Oh my goddess," Crystalle says. "I feel a shift in the energy."

Tiffaney spins in an unsteady circle that almost sends her crashing into Brynlee. "It's giving ancient temple vibes, like we're in a movie."

Francis grabs my arm. "Davia, can you feel the spiritual power? It's making me dizzy."

That's the alcohol, Francis.

Kennedy claps with delight. "This is exactly what I imagined. I'm so grateful we got a reservation."

Marilyn gives a sage-like nod. "Highly authentic. This is how real ceremonies should be conducted."

As the women speak, I note every footstep or comment echoes off the stone. Despite walking in at ground level, something about the windowless chamber makes it feel subterranean, buried, like we've descended into the earth itself.

An altar laden with ceremonial objects stands before a circle of chairs. "Please sit," the masked figure invites, and everyone complies.

I take shallow breaths, trying not to gag on the thick air.

How long will this last?

The robed man takes position behind the altar, the silver in his attire winking from the torchlight as he surveys us. "Tonight, under the blessing of the full moon, we gather to shed the illusions that bind your higher consciousness. You have lived behind veils of societal expectation, trapped in cycles of material attachment that separate you from your essences."

Crystalle nods with enthusiasm, gripping the side of her chair.

"The ancient wisdom keepers understood that true transformation requires the dissolution of the ego-mind," the man continues. "Tonight, you will journey beyond the boundaries of your constructed identities, beyond fear, beyond the self that clings to comfort and control."

"This is so deep," Tiffaney stage-whispers to Brynlee.

The woo wizard raises his arms. "To facilitate this sacred passage, you will drink from the Cup of Awakening—a blessed tea infused with herbs that have guided seekers for millennia. This sacred brew will open the doorways of perception, allowing you to access dimensions of consciousness unavailable to the sleeping masses."

Pulling back one of his sleeves, he takes an ornate silver chalice carved with symbols off a brazier and fills silver cups on trays. When done pouring, he hefts the tray with solemnity and bows to each of us as we select a cup, his brown eyes intent. When finished, he returns to his position on the altar and raises his arms like a pastor doing an invocation.

"Drink deeply, sacred sisters. You might feel disoriented, but that's a normal effect to facilitate your journey into truth."

The women do as instructed, but I sip less than half of the bitter liquid. The unpleasant, astringent taste makes my nose wrinkle. When the figure turns, I tip the remaining contents onto the stone floor between my feet. I'm unwilling to take whatever consciousness-expanding journey this vile concoction promises.

What will happen now? Will I have to listen to everyone share their deepest secrets? Maybe how they buy discounted clothing at T.J. Maxx and pretend it's from Neiman Marcus?

"Now, we'll begin the transformation," the man intones, arms still raised. "Close your eyes and allow your consciousness to expand beyond the limitations of your physical form. Take a deep breath, in through your nose and out through your mouth." He demonstrates, exhaling with a lusty sound.

Here we go, I think, rolling my eyes behind closed lids. *More breathing exercises.*

Around me, the women follow his instructions with exaggerated exhales.

"Allow the ceremonial tea to guide you beyond the illusions of the ego-mind. Your breath is the bridge between your earthly self and your true form. Breathe and let go. Surrender."

Is this guy Eathr Bliss's brother?

Despite my skepticism, I notice it's difficult to open my eyes.

Has a day of mind-numbing activities finally caught up with me?

"Feel your inner being expand like ripples on a pond. You're safe to release control, safe to drift into the infinite wisdom that awaits you beyond the veil of ordinary reality."

His words seem to come from farther away now, though I know he hasn't moved. Around me, silver cups clink as they drop from limp hands onto the stone floor, and the women begin to slump.

I smack my cheek, fighting against an overwhelming urge to sleep.

Must be the hypnotic droning and this stifling air.

My chin drops to my chest. I force my head up, blinking rapidly, but my eyelids slam shut.

When I open them again, I lie on my side.

Groggy, I lift my head.

I'm in the forest.

In a cage.

22

My hands slide on cold, unyielding metal. I attempt to sit up. The scene tilts, a carousel. The metal bars of the cage go out of focus, double, then morph into skeletal bones. I squeeze my eyes shut. Open them. The bars are solid again.

Ghostly screams shred the air, and phantoms glide around me. The cage breathes, its bars expanding and contracting like the ribs of a living creature.

This isn't real. This isn't real.

Nausea hits like a punch. I heave up bile, then almost fall face-first into the mess.

Where am I? At Fort Bragg, doing escape training?

Sitting up is a battle. Each attempt sends the world spinning. My muscles won't obey. I try again. Fail. Rest. At last, I manage to prop myself against the cage wall, head pounding, fingers trembling against my skin. A metallic taste coats my mouth.

Was I drugged? When? Is this a chemical resistance exercise?

Kyle Kavanagh crouches before me, his blue eyes boring into mine. "Davia, you don't want to be the first person to die in a horror movie."

"Kyle?" This comes out as a strangled croak.

"Remember your training," he admonishes, then fades to nothing.

Training? My mind goes blank. Ideas near, then are swept away. A high, thin wail needles my ears, but all I can make out through the tight bars are the dark outlines of trees in moonlight. Are there people out there? Wild animals?

Observe. A cage. Locked?

Orient. Woods. Hostiles.

Decide. Decide what?

Crawling to the door is a marathon, each movement a negotiation with my rebellious muscles. I reach through the bars. A fresh wave of dizziness hits, and I pull back to dry heave, my body convulsing until I'm left hollow and shaking.

My operative teammates surround the enclosure.

Ned pulls at his scruffy beard. "We always knew you'd crack. Right, Warden? Why'd you let her on the team anyway?"

"'Cause she's hot," Warden says, and everyone laughs.

Kilburn places a finger against his temple and pretends to pull a trigger. "You're dead."

"You're wrong!" I shout, but the words come out garbled.

Are they wrong? I'm in a situation, and I don't know how I got here or what to do. I'm a failure. I'm a...

An M4A1 carbine is in my hands. I'm in a village consisting of mud-brick houses with corrugated metal roofs shaded by acacia trees. Overturned water jugs and cooking pots are scattered across the dusty, red earth. Women in indigo, crimson, and purple wrap dresses, men in simple cotton shirts and trousers, and children in school uniforms lie in bloody piles. Loose goats and chickens roam amongst the bodies.

The silence is broken only by the drone of flies. Cooking fires still smoke, and laundry hangs on lines, swaying in the hot wind. My team moves with soft footfalls, guns up and ready.

Blazing pain sears through my head. I fall.

Shot?

Lying on my side, I check my head, my body. No blood.

Where's my gun?

I struggle to stand and whack my head against something that slams me back to my knees. The vision shatters.

I'm not in Somalia. I'm in a cage.

Where am I?

Footsteps crunch on undergrowth, coming near.

"How much longer we gonna wait?" a man says.

"Boss said he's giving it another forty-five or so. These boujee bitches need time to wake up and be mobile enough to run before we release the college boys."

"Spoiled frats are getting antsy. Keep asking when they can start their hunt."

"Let 'em wait. The women are still drooling from the drugs." The men stop outside my cage, and I pretend to be asleep. "See? This one's still knocked out."

Women? Drugs? A hunt?

When they continue on, I force myself up again. I'm still unsteady and woozy, but adrenaline and a sense of urgency give me a tiny boost. A memory. I'm in a van with women going to a resort. Is that where I am? No, this is...somewhere else.

The cage forces me to remain hunched over, my shoulders pressed against the low ceiling. I shift position, working to find space to move, and brush my leg. A familiar weight. I pull up my right pant leg and find my .22 revolver in an ankle holster. How did whoever put me in here miss that? I slide the gun out and attempt to place my finger on the trigger.

I hit empty air.

Again. Fail.

Slow down. Assess... what? Assess the situation.

Guards. Time is...

Get it together.

What do I... what should I do?

Focus. I've got to focus.

Shaking, I place the revolver in my waistband.

Phase One: Get free.

What's phase two? Can't think.

Get out.

I thrust my arm through the door's bars again and touch the latch. There's no lock. Standard design. The weak point is the.... the word is gone. The thing that moves. Bringing myself to my knees for leverage, my bad leg spasms. I almost cry out, but bite my lip hard to stop the sound. I sag against the door.

Ignore the pain.

Open the door.

Kneeling, I try again. I pinch the lever with my thumb and fore-finger. They won't coordinate. I use my palm and slam it against the latch. It lifts, but not enough.

Don't quit.

Using all my strength, I hit it again. The apparatus scrapes, a deafening creak in the silence. I freeze. When a minute passes, I resume. The mechanism releases, and the door springs open.

Pulling myself out, I brace myself against the cage to stand.

Did that take five minutes or thirty-five? More?

Will those guards return?

The moonlight is too bright. Tactical...disadvantage. They'll see me first.

I've got to walk, I've got to...do what? What's my objective?

With caution, I place weight on my bad leg. It holds.

The trees are misty silhouettes in the darkness, and the ground undulates. I slap my face to clear my thoughts.

Count.

One-two-three-four...

The scene stabilizes.

The gun.

Patting my waistband, I find a knit cap shoved into a front pants pocket. I twist my blonde ponytail up and pull the cap on to increase camouflage. The movement sends another lancing stab through my head, the world rotates, and I drop to my knees.

Five-six-seven...

Taking out my weapon, I haul myself up.

Eight, nine...

Phase Two: Recon.

23

The ground is uneven, blanketed with pine cones and needles. My boot slides on a rock, launching me backward. I crash down, air bursting from my lungs. Stars blur and refocus above. Can I stand? I roll over, crawl to a tree, and lever myself up. Where's my gun? I pat my waistband. It's there.

Didn't I have it in my hand?

My cap. I put that on, then...what?

I bring my thumb toward each fingertip on my right hand. Miss. The gun will have to wait.

A chill mountain breeze braces me. I listen, straining, but the hoot of an owl is the only sound.

Operatives don't quit. We adapt.

Low crawl or walk? Crawling would be best in my state to mitigate the noise of my movement, but time will fly past. Rubbing my temple, I try to calculate how long it's been since I left the cage, but my thoughts remain blanketed by a haze.

I take a step. The ground twists, shadows move, and the forest tilts. Fixing my sight on a distant pine, I weave toward it like a drunk leaving a bar. When I reach my goal, I rest, then move on to a different rock, a shrub, or a tree.

How far have I come?

Keep moving.

A radio crackles.

Two men stand ten yards away, backs turned. A lantern on the ground illuminates their casual stance, their AR-15 rifles slung. I flatten against a tree.

"Frat boys are liquored up and ready," one says. "It'll be messy keeping them from breaking their necks in this terrain while ensuring they get some action."

"Heard the boss mention a billionaire—Monroe something— whose girl is here. Whoever smashes her first wins a prize."

My stomach heaves, and I break out in a cold sweat. I cover my mouth, working not to throw up. I've got to neutralize these men and gather intel. How? The .22 has seven shots, but my aim is compromised, and the sound will draw attention. Will my training be enough?

Pulling the knit cap off my head, I let it fall and step out. My stumbling footsteps alert them.

"Please," I say, the word slurred. "Please help me. I'm lost and..."

Surprise crosses their features. One comes toward me, frowning. "How did you get out?"

"Where...where am I?"

The other laughs. "We should get some before those brats. First come, first served."

One reaches for me. I grab his wrist and twist. His mouth flies open in silent shock as I kick him into the second man. The guards double, their edges indistinct, then snap back to two.

"What the hell?" the second yells as they untangle from each other.

"The dope's made her unpredictable," the first says with a grin. "You know what they say about crazy women making the best—"

Drawing my .22, I blink to clear my vision, aim for center mass, and pull the trigger.

He clutches his chest and drops.

The second stares at him, stunned. A loud horn blares. His radio sparks to life, a man saying, "The hunt's begun! Get ready."

By the time the remaining guard's brain kicks in and he moves to unsling his rifle, I'm on him. I jam my gun into his stomach, my grip faltering.

"Don't move."

He doesn't comply, dragging the rifle over his head.

I lower my weapon to the outer edge of his thigh and fire. He cries in agony, falling onto his side. His abrupt movement disrupts my tenuous balance, and I topple.

He curls into a protective ball, clutching his leg while I struggle to my feet. "You-you shot me!"

"Tell me." I pause. "Tell me. What's happening."

The man moans, but doesn't answer.

I step on his injury, and he cries out.

"How many more guards?"

"One other at the...god, I'm going to die. I'm..."

Bracing my gun with both hands, I aim at his face. "How many?" My words are now cold and clear.

The terror in his eyes is real. Or is it? "One more at command."

"How many other people?"

Tears spill down his face. "Eight college boys and our boss. Going to chase some women for sport."

"These women. How many?"

"Seven, eight?"

"Who are they?"

"Dunno. Boss likes them pretty for the," he gasps. "Premium clients."

"Are they in cages?"

"Not now. They open when the games begin."

"Games?" I hiss.

"The women get released and try to escape." He moans again, rocking. "They can't move fast due to being drugged. Easy prey."

"How many times have there been 'games'?"

Taking in my flat stare, he stammers, "Three? Four? I don't know."

Pushing aside my fury, I fumble for a pair of handcuffs that dangle at his waist. "Put these on."

"I'll bleed to death!"

"You'll live, unlike your friend."

Once he's secured, he uses his restrained and bloody hands to grip his leg injury again. The trees swerve and sway. I close my eyes and manage to put my .22 in my waistband. When I can refocus, I take his radio and retrieve his rifle. The dead guard lies on his back, his weapon beneath him. The strength to move him is beyond me, so I stomp on his radio with my boot.

"Which way is the command center?"

The man uses his chin to indicate uphill and to my right.

"How do I get in?"

His jaw sets, but this small show of defiance disappears when I do a quick check to see if the rifle's loaded.

"One entrance, one guard monitoring camera feed from," he coughs. "Body cams on the participants. And maybe the boss. Sometimes he likes to get out and watch."

"Can't wait to meet him."

As I turn to go, he stammers, "Who—who are you?"

I bare my teeth in a smile that doesn't reach my eyes. "I'm Adair Monroe's girl."

24

Phase Three: Subdue or eradicate remaining threats.

The drug's effects have eased from a tidal wave to a haze, but exhaustion weighs my limbs like lead. I plod toward my goal of finding the command center, numb despite the urgency. Sooner than I want, I stop and lean against a tree while my leg continues to ache.

Can I do this?

I recheck my grip on the automatic rifle and my .22 to bolster my confidence, grateful my coordination is returning. The radio clipped to my pants has been quiet, giving me some comfort that the guards haven't been discovered.

Memories filter in, but they're never complete. I can't connect how I got here or what happened to any concrete images. What the guard said leads me to guess that the other women are either from my group or are similar to them.

A terror-stricken scream jolts me.

Someone stumbles downhill, a woman. Trees separate us, and I can't tell who she is. She weaves, not moving fast. Two men in their early twenties follow her, laughing. One calls out, "Don't waste your energy, sweetheart. You're going to need it for us!"

"We'll make you scream some more soon!" roars the other, his voice cracking with a half-laugh.

Operative instincts override my stupor. I raise my rifle and step into their path, planting my feet on the heaving ground. "Stop. Hands where I can see them."

Confusion spreads as they slow to a standstill.

"Why?" a blond challenges. "Guards aren't supposed to interfere."

The other's fingers scrape his wild, dark curls. "Yeah, like, she's getting away! We paid mega bucks for this."

They wear tactical vests, boutique camouflage, and boots that have never seen real combat. I slam my rifle butt into the red lights of their body cams, shattering them, then flip it around.

"Do you have cuffs or restraints?"

"Is this part of the game?" The blond sways a little, alcohol fumes drifting toward me. "I mean, this is like Call of Duty, right?

"I bet it's an upgrade," the other says. "To make things more realistic."

"Answer my question."

"Here." The dark-haired one removes two black plastic zip ties from the front pocket of his vest.

"Tie up your friend."

"Is *he* going to be prey now? That's fire."

"I won't..." the blond begins. I press the barrel to his temple, a move I would never do at capacity. A gamble.

"*Hahaha*, Carl." The other nearly chokes laughing. "Think any of our group's on the DL about guys?"

"C'mon, Derek. Don't do this," Carl says. "We need to catch some girls."

But Derek binds him, grinning. "Now, you'll be a target."

I slam the stock into the back of Derek's head, and he crumples. I take the other tie and restrain him while his friend watches with eyes like saucers.

"Turn around," I tell Carl, and he complies.

He falls with a grunt, his head making a solid *thunk* against a boulder.

Shifting my attention from their prone forms, I check the area, but their intended victim is nowhere to be seen.

How many more hunters? What did that guard say? Can't remember. Focus on the objective.

Reorienting, I continue up the slope. The trees thin, and a rock-strewn clearing appears. A woman is on the ground, a man astride her, fumbling at the front of his pants.

"Stop, please stop!" she begs. "Please."

He strikes her in the face.

It's Francis.

The man reaches to his side and pulls a hunting knife from a sheath. "Shut up or I'll cut your face open. Or your neck."

I raise the rifle. "Drop it."

The knife glints as it falls.

"Stand up," I order, closing the distance between us, searching for the light of his body cam. It's centered on his tactical vest like the others, and I smash it with the buttstock with so much force that it knocks him backwards.

"Hey!" he cries. "That was a little too real for me."

I keep my focus on him, not Francis, who tries to straighten her torn clothes. "Do you have zip ties or cuffs?" I say to the man.

"Two sets of handcuffs, but..."

"Take them out."

"Why? Was I supposed to tie her up first or something? I thought we got to do the hunt however we wanted."

"Take them out, and drop them."

He complies, but my actions sap my energy, and my rifle droops. "Francis. You need to. Cuff him."

She's on her knees, wiping tears from her face.

"Francis!"

Her swollen eyes are glassy. I repeat her name, louder. At last, recognition dawns. "D-Davia?"

"Bind his hands and feet."

"Aw, come on. I'm not supposed to be a prisoner!" the man says, but Francis picks up the cuffs. Her fingers don't close, and she drops them.

"What is...what is wrong with me?" she slurs, then vomits.

When she's done, I say, "Try again."

It takes time, but she secures him.

"How many more of you are there?" I ask the man.

"You're a guard, you know that."

How many are left? Can't...think. Should I try to take them down?

"Davia, how did we get here? I can't, I can't..." Francis breaks into tears.

"I don't want to leave you, but I've got to locate the command center."

"What if there are other men?"

"Pick up his knife and hide."

"But, but, what if someone finds me?"

I stride to the bound prisoner and slam my rifle butt into his head. "You deal with them, okay?"

Without waiting for a response, I limp into the trees.

25

Thinning underbrush offers the lie of easier going. My foot catches on a hidden branch, and I go down hard. Getting up is a battle I almost lose. A shout rings out from my right —a clear chance to intercept. My leg buckles, and the opportunity is gone. If I weren't running on fumes, could I save more women fleeing through the forest?

The scent of wheat and engine oil cuts through the pine. My dad stands beside me in his dirty coveralls. "Davia, do what you can, where you can, wherever you are."

His figure dissolves.

A high-pitched scream carves the night, then chokes off. The sound is close, so I divert from my intended destination. I twist through a dense stand of saplings, ford a shallow stream, and climb its muddy embankment. Coming into a clearing, I pull up short.

Brittany lies discarded on the ground, an arm bent beneath her at an unnatural angle. Moonlight glints on her waxy skin and the white of her unmoving eyes. Her denim blouse is torn open, her skirt yanked to her ankles, her long platinum blonde hair drenched with blood.

A barrel-chested man pushes himself up, zipping his pants.

"Your turn, Brad," he says to a man of similar size who waits nearby.

"Jeez, Nathan. Did you have to bash her so hard with that rock?"

"Bitch tried to scratch my face with those talons! Our football photos are on Monday."

"Think she's the Monroe girl?" Brad's hand fumbles with his fly. "If so, we'll split the cash."

"Actually," I sling my rifle and draw my pistol. "She's not."

"Oh?" Brad's lips peel back from his teeth as he drops to his knees. "Guess we'll have to look for her. That'll be our next prize, right, Nathan?"

Nathan nudges Brittany's limp body with his boot. "If she's as fun as this one…"

Noise no longer matters. I pull the trigger. Nathan's shoulder explodes in a spray of red brighter than the light on his body cam.

"What the…" Brad flinches back.

Trigger discipline. One shot, one hit. Another shoulder explodes. Brad screams a high, animal sound.

"I made sure not to aim for your faces, but I'm certain your football careers are over."

I crouch beside Brittany. The thick smell of blood mixes with the fresh night air, and I check if she's breathing.

She's not.

The radio at my belt lights. "Base to patrol unit two. Come in. Base to patrol unit two. Come in."

Two units? Did that guy I shot lie to me about the number of guards?

Blood from Brittany's head wound soaks the earth in a wide pool. Pressing my fingers on her neck, there's no pulse. Will CPR and my field medic training help?

Seconds tick.

There's no change.

Her pupils are fixed and unresponsive.

Decide.

I run the cold, clinical checklist from my medic training.

Crushed skull. Major blood loss. No pulse. No respiration.

A clean, sharp clarity burns away the haze in my head. Rising, I begin to retrace my steps.

"You're...leaving?" Nathan gasps.

"You can't do that! We'll die," Brad says, voice faint. "We need an ambulance."

"Do you think I care?" I raise my revolver again. "If you like, I can guarantee you won't make it."

Their pleas become whimpers, and they curl in on themselves.

"I suggest you don't move," I say, and leave.

Backtracking, I recross the stream, then sag against a tree. I stash the .22 and bring the AR-15 to bear.

Can't save them all. Keep moving.

The terrain grows steeper, each step a trial for my deadweight leg. Undergrowth, fallen logs, and loose rock slow me further. The trees become so thick that I lose my bearings. The frequency of my breaks increases, each pause a battle against the urge to close my eyes for a minute. Only a minute.

A murmured conversation reaches me.

"Wonder why our other patrol unit's not answering," says a man. "Perimeter security's stable, same with the lodge."

"Maybe they decided to join in. It's one of the perks of our jobs, so it's happened before," says another.

"It's happened a *lot*. Why let these spoiled brats have all the fun?"

The two laugh, a harsh sound that carries.

The radio at my belt comes alive. "Base to patrol unit two. Come in. Over."

"Did you hear that?" one of the unknown men says.

"Came from over there."

They move without stealth, crunching across dry twigs.

"Hey, Lucas! Jack!" one calls. "Where are you?"

Recognizing I don't have the stamina for a fight, I take the radio from my belt, place it on the ground, and bleed into the under-growth. A broad-shouldered man emerges from the gloom, a leaner one behind him. Both carry assault rifles.

"Think they dropped it in the chase?" the big one says, bending to retrieve the device.

"Could be. But their cameras have been off for a while, and some of the participants' feeds have also gone dark."

"The organizers keep cutting costs. Probably crap equipment."

"Base to patrol unit one. Base to patrol unit one."

"This is patrol unit one," the big man says into his radio.

"We've got a problem."

'The men stiffen. "What problem?"

"Two hunters are down. Repeat. Two hunters are down. Maybe more. Over."

Cautious now, the men peer into the woods around them. The dispatcher barks, "Move to quadrant six. Now." They rush away.

After a beat, I continue uphill and find a path bounded by a low brick wall. Every step on the gravel is a pistol shot that can't be silenced. A long stone lodge resolves out of the darkness. I shuffle along the building's wall, searching for a door. One flies open ahead of me. A man with a pistol storms out, barrel sweeping toward me, but my rifle is already at my shoulder.

Our shots are almost one. His round tears into the wall by my head. Mine punches through his sternum, and he goes down.

I step over his body, kick his gun under a bush, and flatten myself against the building near the open door. Edging forward, I peek inside.

Multiple screens show different views of the surrounding forest.

Two people are on their feet, staring at the door.

Kennedy and Eathr.

26

Champagne flutes dangle at their sides, liquid spilling to the concrete floor. Draped on a chair behind Eathr is a silver and maroon robe and a black wig. He wears a T-shirt and jeans, the most regular clothes I've ever seen him in, and he scrubs at a smudge of Kennedy's lipstick that clings to his mouth.

"Were you two so engrossed in drinking and kissing, you didn't check the feed or listen to what your security said?"

Kennedy takes a stumbling step back, almost colliding with Eathr. "Davia. How did you—"

"Brittany's dead."

Her face blanches as white as her pricy silk outfit. "You're lying."

Fury flashes, helping keep me upright. "Were you expecting her to 'only' get raped?"

Kennedy's shock dissolves so fast, I question her initial reaction. "So what? She's out partying with a different guy every weekend."

Behind Eathr, the screens show jerky footage from body cameras. Shaky running shots of dense forest, branches whipping past, a flash of Marilyn's fearful face as she disappears behind a tree.

The comm system beeps, a tinny, insistent tone. "Patrol unit two to base. We have two participants with gunshot wounds. They might not make it. Call an ambulance."

Eathr's brows jerk upward over brown eyes. "Did you shoot someone?"

"Did you lose your blue contacts? Call this off."

"I can't. The hunt runs until the horn sounds. Which is..." he checks his watch, "three hours from now."

"Patrol unit two to base. Calling to confirm an ambulance is en route. Over."

As their request ends, Kennedy inches toward a rusted wrench lying on a bench.

"I wouldn't," I tell her. "And Eathr, if that's even your name, there has to be a signal in case your event gets compromised."

"Sorry." He pushes his long, blond hair off his face. "Rules are rules."

Emergency protocols. Every operation has them. Even this sick game would need...wait. The horn. It won't only be automatic. Why is my brain working so slowly?

"Where's the button to sound the horn?" I demand.

One side of Eathr's mouth pulls up. "You think—"

Bang.

The shot is deafening in the enclosed space. Kennedy covers her ears and cowers. The acrid smell of gunpowder fills the air as Eathr clutches his upper arm, blood welling through his fingers.

"Rethink your answer." My leg quivers, and I shift my weight. "Your turn, Kennedy." I point the muzzle at her.

"Don't shoot me!" she begs. "It-it's over there." She points to a blinking green light past Eathr as he bends over in pain.

"If you're lying, you're dead. Got me?"

She nods with vigor. "I'm n-not."

"Go push it."

"Kennedy, no!" Eathr tries to stop her despite his injury, grabbing her arm and staining her white outfit with blood. "We can't or we're done for."

"God, Eathr. Has all the time you spent breathing incense rotted your brain? She'll kill us."

"You're the one who told me she should get invited into your book club as potential prey. And she even *read the book*! But you wrote it off as people pleasing, trying to curry favor with you like the others."

"Who's to blame isn't the point right now," I snarl. "Hit. The. Button."

Kennedy rips her arm loose, stumbles over, and slams her palm against the flashing mechanism.

An earsplitting horn sounds.

"You know we'll pay for that!" Eathr shouts. "You know they'll—"

"Shut up," I order. "Where's the meeting point for the hunters?"

"Here," Kennedy says.

"Be specific."

"In the main room of the lodge," she clarifies. "There's a lavish after-hunt meal prepared, but they won't be happy if they didn't get to...to..."

"Kennedy, call 911. Tell them there's been a murder and sexual assaults at this location with multiple perpetrators, security, and victims. Give them the exact address and details about the men, the hunt, all of it. If you try to give false information, I'll put a bullet in your head before you finish the sentence. Are we clear?"

"Don't do it!" Eathr says. "Don't, Kennedy or—"

"Or what? I'd rather take my chances later than die here in this decrepit place filled with spider webs and rat poop." Kennedy crosses to a dusty telephone on the wall and stabs in the number.

27

Kennedy gives the operator the information, then covers the phone to say she's been told to remain on the line. Eathr sinks into a chair, clutching his arm, his shoulders hunched. Unable to remain standing, I drag a second chair in front of him and collapse into it.

Think. Their blink rate went through the roof when I got here. Stress. By my presence or more?

"Who are you afraid of?" I say to Eathr.

He straightens. "Not telling. You'll never see them coming."

"Kind of like you tonight."

Behind him, the monitor scenes change. Body cams show the lodge interior, now bright with lights. Tables laden with food and bottles of alcohol are approached as the hunters straggle in. There are still feeds from the woods, but it's of the two guards crouching over the injured hunters.

"The participants will expect me to give them a congratulatory speech," Eathr says. "It's a tradition."

"Are they repeat customers?"

He doesn't answer.

"Tell me about the women. There have been other hunts—"

"How do you know that?"

"Amazing what a bullet wound will do to loosen tongues."

"Some might talk, but this," he sneers at his bleeding arm. "This won't make me tell you anything." He stretches out his legs, a pantomime of ease that the tightness around his eyes betrays.

I winged him on purpose. Was that a mistake?

"How do you keep the victims silent?" I press. "Buy them off? Blackmail?"

Eathr says nothing.

Kennedy hangs up the phone and bites her lower lip.

"They can't have let you get off the line," I say. "Not for something this serious."

"I gave them the information they needed. You heard me! My nerves are shot."

I stand again, gripping the chair with white knuckles so I don't topple from fatigue. "How do you keep the victims from reporting what happened?"

"We—" she shoots a nervous glance at Eathr, who leaps to his feet.

"Kennedy." The word is as hard as the crack of a whip.

"We give them more of the tea, but diluted." Kennedy talks fast. "It causes, uh, memory gaps. They might know something happened afterwards, but they think it's due to getting drunk."

My head pounds, and the room tilts, but I keep my face impassive.

"What's in the tea?"

Eathr and Kennedy don't answer, their features rigid. I throw Kennedy two zip ties I retrieved from one of the hunters. "Tie him."

Kennedy picks up the restraints, and Eathr backs away. "No way this is happening."

"It's been a long night and I'm not at my usual standard." I point the gun barrel at his chest. "So this time my shot will be for a larger target area."

He freezes.

"Have him sit and bind his ankles, too," I say to Kennedy.

When she finishes, I command her to sit in another chair. She does, but her eyes glint with fury before she drops her head, her black bob obscuring her face.

Will I have to fight her? Do I have the strength?

Slinging the rifle, I stand before her with the zip ties, but she doesn't look at me. As I bend to secure her wrists, Kennedy launches upward, slamming her shoulder into my chest.

The impact sends me backwards, and my legs almost give out. Kennedy lunges for where the .22 sits in my waistband.

"You're not ruining my life!" She scrabbles for the gun.

I deflect her arm, but she grabs a chunk of my hair and tries to snatch it from my head. Pain shoots across my scalp. She rakes at my face, her nails aimed for my eyes.

"You're a nobody!" She kicks at my legs. "You don't have any followers!"

"And you don't have any training."

Locking onto one of her wrists, I manipulate the joint past its range of motion.

"Let go!" she cries, but I increase the pressure until she drops to her knees.

I bend and retrieve the zip ties. Kennedy tries to twist away, but the pain compliance hold keeps her in place as I cinch her wrists behind her. I crank them so tight, they cut into her flesh.

"You have no idea who you're up against," she gasps after I shove her into the chair. "You'll die!"

"Fill me in." I bind her ankles.

"Don't say a damn word, Kennedy!" Eathr yells.

She responds with a sardonic laugh. "She won. We're dead. DEAD."

"If that's true, protective custody might be in your future." I glance at the screens, checking positions. The four remaining hunters are huddled together, eating. The other guards remain as before.

The duo falls silent, communicating in a furious language of tight features and hateful glares.

"I assume the transport driver's in on this?" I comment while ensuring Eathr's restraints are tight. "Guess I shouldn't have tipped him."

They turn their heads away, neck and jaw muscles clenched.

If I don't keep moving, I might collapse.

A laptop glows on a desk, its screen the same mosaic of the horror outside as the other monitors. A USB drive is plugged into it. I bend closer, my vision swimming. The text on the screen below a folder blurs into gray lines, then snaps into focus: Operations Archive.

Right-clicking, I select "Copy to" the USB. A progress bar appears, but is a slow crawl. 10%. 20%. My hands tremble as I wait. Kennedy fidgets in her chair. Conversation from the lodge grows louder, and the hunters clink glasses and dive into the meal.

The bar hits 50%. 75%.

Come on.

89%. Kennedy mutters something to Eathr.

95%.

Complete.

I remove the drive, the metal warm in my palm, and shove it into my pocket. Kennedy and Eathr watch me with the hollow stares of the condemned.

"Why is this all being recorded? Do you rewatch it on dull Saturday nights?"

Eathr straightens in his chair, trying for his usual arrogance, but sweat beads on his brow. "Like Kennedy says, you have no idea what you've done."

"I intend to find out."

The faint wail of sirens carries a distant promise of relief.

Plenty of time for things to go wrong.

———

Can't have the first deputies walk into this blind. Those drunk hunters in the lodge might become belligerent or run. Kennedy and Eathr might make up some story about me being the real threat.

Verifying the predator duo can't get loose, I step outside, move along the building's length, and place the rifle on the ground behind a bush where it's not easily seen. With effort, I return the .22 to my waistband and drop my shirt to cover it.

The red and blue flashes of multiple sheriff's cruisers light up the trees as responding deputies turn onto the road leading to the lodge. Following behind are ambulances. The four remaining hunters come outside, but don't run, hovering by the door.

Two deputies approach, guns drawn, and I raise my hands.

"I'm Davia Glenn," I say. "I made one of the ringleaders call 911."

"Do you have a weapon?"

"My waistband."

While she pats me down and secures it, I give her details, stumbling over my words. She keys her radio, calling for more units and EMTs.

The adrenaline fade is a physical blow. A tremor starts in my core, and my legs dissolve. I hit the gravel on my knees.

The world dims, then goes black.

Consciousness returns in fragments. Someone's speaking. "What are her injuries?"

A paramedic replies. "Drugged. Cuts, scratches. Can't say more until she's awake."

I push up on an elbow, saying, "Rodriguez."

"Miss Glenn," Detective Robbie Rodriguez breaks off to come closer. "How do you feel?"

"Alive. Did you...did you find the others?"

He pushes a strand of black, wavy hair from his forehead. "Five women are alive, one deceased. Can you tell me what happened?"

"I have memory gaps."

"Do the best you can."

I give him edited highlights. The cage. The hunt. The command and guards.

He listens, and doesn't grill me. "We found some underground tunnels beneath the main building. There were flatbed carts, and we think they loaded unconscious victims onto them. A mechanical lift system raised cages containing the victims to the forest level. Pretty sophisticated."

"I'll second that." Detective Montoya comes up beside Rodriguez and says to me. "You good?"

"Alive," I repeat. "Did you arrest Kennedy Connors and Eathr Bliss? The others?"

He nods. "Didn't buy their protestations of innocence, especially after reviewing the footage."

A paramedic interrupts. "We need to get everyone to the hospital now."

I begin to protest, but Montoya says, "For once, let others handle things, okay? I texted Sherilyn to meet you."

28

The antiseptic smell hits me before I'm fully awake. There's an IV in my arm, I wear a scratchy gown, and monitors beep. Another hospital, like the many I've been at before.

"Davia?" Sherilyn rises from a plastic chair beside my bed, brows knit. "How are you feeling?"

"How long have I been here?"

"A few hours. They ran blood work, then pumped fluids into you to clear whatever drug cocktail was used. They want to keep you for observation."

"The others?"

Sherilyn's expression darkens. "When I first got here, everyone was in the ER. Francis is doing the best. The other four..." She pauses. "Crystalle wouldn't stop crying. Tiffaney kept asking for someone to call her mom, but couldn't remember her phone number. Brynlee got hysterical if anyone touched her."

"Marilyn?"

"Conscious but unresponsive."

A flash of Brittany, partly clothed, lying in blood.

"At least they're alive."

"Did someone die?"

"Brittany Guinn, betrayed by her bestie, Kennedy." I pick at the IV tape. "I need to get out of here."

"The hell you do. Ric warned me you'd be like this and—"

"I'll rest better at home. Get me a doctor. I'm releasing myself."

"Davia—"

"I mean it. Find my clothes, will you?"

Getting dressed is a slow process. I pull on the stiff, filthy pants and shirt. When I shove my feet into my boots, the dampness from the creek I forded still clings to the leather and soaks into my socks. It's a cold, unpleasant reminder I don't need. My body aches, my leg can barely hold my weight, and all I want to do is sleep. By the time Sherilyn finds someone, I endure a lecture, and the disapproving doctor lets me leave, I almost regret not staying. Almost.

"You can hardly walk, and those clothes are filthy. I should have brought you some clean ones, but I wanted to get here fast," Sherilyn says as I hop into the wheelchair she holds. "And you look worse than after your last shoot-out or whatever it was. But at least there's not blood everywhere. The memory of that still freaks me out."

"I'm fine."

She scoffs. "You don't know what that word means."

We wheel down a long hall, me locking down the tumultuous emotions that fester in one of my many trauma memory vaults.

"Davia?" A call comes from a room we pass.

Francis Downs stands inside, holding an IV pole. She's in a hospital gown and looks like a lost child.

"Francis." I get out of the chair, holding the doorframe to support myself. "How are you?"

It's a stupid question. I know how she's doing.

"I-I don't know." She wraps her arms around her tiny frame and shivers, appearing decades older than she had at breakfast at the resort that morning. "I remember being at Serenity Springs, then everything gets fuzzy, like a nightmare I can't recall. But the fear...the fear remains. I was in some kind of locked container. It opened, but for a long time, I couldn't move. I was so woozy and uncoordinated, but I finally managed to crawl out. Once I was able to stand and walk, a man chased me. He caught me and..." She touches her face, where a bruise is visible.

"Do you remember me finding you?"

"Yes." Her word is a whisper.

"Did something more happen after I left?"

"No. I hid in a hole between some rocks. I pulled branches over me. But every twig snap, every sound, I was sure another man was coming for me. The time it took until a sheriff got there was torture." She breaks down, great, heaving sobs wracking her entire body.

Sherilyn retrieves some tissues, gives them to her, and pats her gently until she quiets.

"What do we do?" Sherilyn whispers when she rejoins me.

"Francis, the people who did this got caught," I say. "It's over."

"But why?" Her eyes plead for an answer I don't have. "Why would anyone...?"

"I don't know," I say, and it's the truest thing I've said all night. "Some people are monsters."

"Do you have anyone we can call?" Sherilyn says.

"My husband's on his way, but..." Alarm crosses her features, and she takes some shaky steps toward me. "Davia, you can't go yet. You can't."

I sit in the wheelchair, strength waning. "The doctor released me."

Francis's pale face turns ashen. "You're really leaving?"

A man accompanied by a nurse hurries toward us. When he sees Francis, he rushes to her and gathers her into his arms.

I tilt my head toward the exit and tell Sherilyn, "Time to go."

———

Once I'm home, showered, and in bed, Sherilyn comes in carrying a tray of scrambled eggs, toast, and a mug of chamomile tea.

"Thank goodness I purchased these trays after the last time you got hurt. I mean, I somehow knew you'd need them. And they've got this dainty flower design that, I hope, will make you appreciate delicate décor. Want me to help you drink some of this tea?"

A memory. Silver cups dropping from limp hands.

"You didn't put drugs in it, did you?" I joke to cover my sudden unease as she places the tray on my lap.

"I didn't, but you're not going to be happy with me. I called Adair."

"What? Sherilyn—"

"This makes me feel sick to leave you, but I'm locked into Rancho Suprema Cultural Center's grand opening. It's a massive public project with penalty clauses that would bankrupt me if I don't oversee the final installation personally. Believe me, I argued with my lawyer about not going, but she said there's no way out."

"It's okay. José is here and he can—"

"He's not. Did you forget he flew to Mexico City for a vacation? His cousin's filling in. And your housekeeper, Ana, is in Los Angeles. I knew you'd be angry, but I am not going to leave you here alone."

"Please call Adair and—"

The doorbell rings.

"That's probably him." Sherilyn rushes out of the bedroom while I swear. Should I hide beneath the comforter?

There's a distant conversation that I can't hear, then Adair appears in the doorway. When our eyes meet, visible relief relaxes his features. He nears my bed, saying, "Don't be mad at Sherilyn. She's in the kitchen putting away some food Alain made for you. My bodyguards are outside checking the perimeter."

"You don't need to—"

"I'm not leaving." He maneuvers an armchair over. "Do you want me to help you eat? I can pretend the spoon's an airplane and fly it into your mouth."

"Adair."

Sherilyn comes in. "Everything that needed to be refrigerated is. Do you want me to pick up anything while I'm out?"

"Go," Adair tells her. "I can take care of any needs from here out."

"Text me updates."

She leaves without fussing, perhaps recognizing she's pushed me to an edge. I force myself to eat half the eggs and a few bites of toast before I give up. Adair takes the tray and leaves the room. When he returns, I say, "Do you know how to do dishes?"

"I dressed down in case I might come in contact with manual labor." He wears a faded T-shirt and jeans. "Sherilyn gave me the edited version of what happened, so all you need to think about is sleep."

When I close my eyes, my mind doesn't shut off. Thoughts spiral. Women hunted for sport, college boys dressed like pretend commandos, Kennedy and Eathr's fear of an unknown person or persons. Who?

"You're thinking too loud," Adair says.

I open one eye. "Am I disturbing you?"

"Your tendency to overanalyze is showing in your pensive expression." His tone is tender, and he smooths the comforter over me. "Please rest."

There's something about having him here, and it's not about protection. I've slept alone in worse places than my own bedroom. But his presence fills me with quiet companionship.

As I drift off, Adair covers my hand with his.

Warmth spreads through my chest, a feeling of calm, and I'm able to release my thoughts and sleep.

<h1 style="text-align:center">29</h1>

When I wake, the sun wanes. Getting up to use the bathroom, my body protests with a chorus of complaints. A sudden, hot twinge in my side makes me stumble. Cuts on my arms sting, my muscles ache like I've been in a car crash, and there's a persistent fog in my head that sleep hasn't cleared. My injured leg throbs like background music I can't tune out, reminding me that adrenaline did the heavy lifting during the hunt.

I note an empty chair pulled close beside the bed, and a pang of disappointment catches me off guard. Why would I expect Adair to still be here?

A tray with a filled water glass is on the dresser, along with my phone on a charger. I power it on, returning from the bathroom to find a number of voicemails and texts I'm not ready to deal with. I'm functional, but not fully capable.

Warden told us you're getting soft.

My team wasn't in that forest; it was a hallucination. Then why do I hesitate to text or call Warden? Because I'm sure he'll be furious, questioning both how this happened and my actions.

Setting the phone down, I drain the glass, aware I need to hydrate and flush any lingering toxins from the drug cocktail. Still in the yoga pants and tank Sherilyn gave me after a shower, I decide that changing clothes is beyond me.

"Davia, you're awake," Adair says from the door. He's in different clothes, khakis paired with a short-sleeved blue linen shirt. He goes directly to the tray. "I'll get you a refill."

"You weren't here all night, I hope? I'm a little unclear on time."

"You slept for almost eighteen hours. Jason had some clothes delivered for me. He also coordinated the retrieval of your belongings from Serenity Springs. Be right back."

Gratitude fills me, and something more. Adair isn't hovering or treating me like I'm fragile. He's made no romantic gestures or declarations, keeping his focus on the practical, and his distance allows me to relax. I smile at him when he returns.

"Get in bed," he orders, and I do. The tray he sets on my lap holds a carafe of water with a newly-filled glass, a cup of chicken soup, and a plate of bite-sized quiche. "I tried to figure out what might be best, but Alain went completely mad and sent coq au vin, ratatouille, some kind of fish in white sauce, three different soups, and enough pastries to stock a bakery."

I try a spoonful of the soup, the warmth spreading through me, and sigh at the broth's elegant taste. "This is perfect."

"Want me to help you eat? I can pretend I'm a train and make choo-choo noises while I feed you quiche."

"Where did you learn how to get fussy kids to eat?"

"The orphanage in Africa that I fund. And is that a yes?"

"It's tempting. I'll have to tell everyone the world's hottest bachelor knows his way around uncooperative kids."

"Please don't. The tabloids will say it's because I have loads of illegitimate children."

"I forget how public your life can be. Don't worry, your secret's safe."

When I finish, he picks up the tray and puts the water carafe on the dresser.

"Want me to leave while you return calls?" he nods at my phone.

"I'm not up for it."

"You should go to sleep."

"And you should go home. Your business—"

"Has been conducted from your office. Jason gives me so many updates, I could be anywhere." His cellphone rings. "Speaking of. Excuse me."

Taking the tray, he exits. I allow contentment to fill me, recalling Detective Montoya's advice about letting others handle things. When Adair returns, his demeanor is more serious.

"Is everything okay?"

"Jason's been keeping tabs on the investigation into what happened to you and the other victims, and—"

"I'm not a victim," I snap.

Adair perches on my bed. "Really? You were drugged and put in a cage to be hunted. Tell me how you define that."

"A challenge."

He opens his mouth, then reconsiders. "I understand you prefer to be viewed as invincible, but sometimes...anyway, Jason's sources at the sheriff's department said a review of the recording made investigators believe this is a blackmail operation. There was a file with videos from other hunts showing women "confessing" to things like racist attitudes or criminal activity. They were still drugged, and I'm not sure any of it was true or if they were manipulated to keep them quiet. The male participants were all from wealthy and influential families, which is another blackmail opportunity."

I run through the facts like I'm in a briefing. "Did he find any specific names or clues about the organizers?"

"Not yet. But you know Jason. He'll keep at it with his Moneypenny, Jenny."

Recalling Jenny, a woman in her late thirties whom I met the prior month, I say, "She's quite matter-of-fact and sensible. A perfect match for him."

"The office has a betting pool on when they'll get together."

"If they do begin a relationship, will that lighten him up?"

"Doubtful. He's been tight as a tick since he was a teenager."

"I don't expect you to know, but have you heard anything about the other women?"

"No. Jason zeroed in on the operation, and Sherilyn didn't give me any updates."

The memory of Francis at the hospital makes me shudder. If she were the strongest...

"Davia, I'm sure you think you're ready to help Jason find answers, but you need to sleep some more."

"You're right, but I'll be okay without you rearranging your life to stay here. Go home."

"But—"

"I'm going to sleep, and if I'm hungry, it sounds like there's plenty to choose from." I sit forward, place my hand over his, and kiss his cheek. "And thank you, Adair."

30

The next morning, I enjoy one of Alain's pastries on the patio. It's pain au chocolat, a flaky, buttery croissant wrapped around sweet, slightly bitter chocolate. Hot tea is the perfect accompaniment, and the sun warms my bare feet.

My phone shows a video call from Warden. I lick the pastry flakes and chocolate clinging to my fingertips and answer.

"How'd your weekend retreat go?" he says.

His features are relaxed, and I stall. "It's Tuesday. Did you give me a day to recover?"

"That arduous, eh? Let me guess—forced meditation, overpriced smoothies, and group therapy sessions about releasing your inner goddess?" His teases fades. "What happened?"

"Mm...a lot?"

"Since I won't buy a five-star wellness retreat was too difficult for you, you need to tell me everything."

As I do, I wait for him to interrupt, to question, to react, but he only listens. When I finish my account, his expression is grim.

"Thank god your training saved you. Given the circumstances

and your impaired state, your tactical decisions were sound and effective."

I blink. "That's it? No lecture?"

"Would it change anything? I love you, Davia. I'm relieved you're alive." His eyes are soft, full of concern. "And you're saying the sham shaman I met and the head of your book club was behind it all? That's hard to believe."

"They were the on-the-ground guy and the recruiter, not the true boss. Eathr was more afraid of whoever was at the top than me with a gun."

"Any clue who's running the operation?"

"I took a thumb drive from a computer on site. I haven't looked at the files yet."

Warden scowls. "If you haven't, that means you're a wreck."

Not meeting his eyes, I say, "I slept a long time due to the drugs, have some scratches and cuts, got dehydrated..."

He rolls his index finger to speed me along. "And?"

"My leg is jacked again. It was improving, but then I took a spill from a horse, and..."

"You fell off Ace?"

"No. It happened at Adair's." I give him the details.

"Are you sure it was an accident?"

"You sound like Jason. Yes, I'm sure. The pain got better, then this happened. The cage was cramped, the terrain rugged, my footing unstable—"

"I shouldn't have left."

"And that would've helped how exactly?"

"I'd be there to hold you, to look at the drive, to help figure out who's behind all of this. What about the other women?"

"No updates since the hospital, but I doubt they're doing well. Tell me you've been productive at least."

"It's been slow. You know how this goes: piece together incomplete statements and lies from sources, find paths that lead to dead ends, and try not to speculate." His cheeks puff out, then he exhales. "I have my suspicions, but I need more."

Three years of training and running missions beside Warden has taught me to read his body language, his nuances, and all the concerns he tries to mask. "I can tell whatever your working on is serious."

"You know we can't discuss it."

"Will you be able to come back?"

"If the threads I'm following lead to something conclusive, maybe." He hesitates. "I've been cleared to return to work, passed the fitness."

"That was fast."

"The break gave me time to heal."

"I'm glad, it's just..."

"I know."

Silence follows.

"I should let you go check the drive," Warden says at last.

"Yeah."

"Call me if you find anything."

———

The thumb drive contains data from eight previous "hunts" over a two-year period, including graphic footage. The hunters' reactions after successful rapes or murders are uniform. They whoop, high-five, and celebrate like they're at a bar cheering on their favorite sports team. A file labeled "Insurance" shows drugged women making slurred "confessions."

Everything's coded. There are no names, only labels like "Client 22" or "M. Facility Rental." The considerable money involved is startling. Despite cutting corners with security, this appears to be a professional criminal organization with serious backing.

I copy the files and text Montoya.

Call me.

Returning to the kitchen, I turn on the burner beneath my teapot, thinking about the information while the water boils. The kettle whistles right as Montoya's name flashes on my phone screen.

"What's up?" he greets, sounding rushed.

I turn off the burner. "Are you at another scene?"

"No. Are you better?"

"Yes. I went to wash my clothes and discovered a thumb drive in the pocket of my cargo pants." I give him the broad strokes of what it contained.

"And I take it you have no memory of how you obtained it."

"I don't."

He sighs. "We have the laptop, but you need to get it to Rodriguez. Are you up to driving?"

"I'll find a way."

We disconnect, and I say, "Darn it. My car's still at Kennedy's." After I dress, I retrieve the Rover keys and go to the garage to find the Maserati is parked inside. Adair and Jason thought of everything. Should I text Adair and thank him? No, get the thumb drive delivered first.

When I check in at the San Diego Sheriff's HQ, I hope to leave the envelope containing the drive, but the deputy on duty says, "Detective Rodriguez said to tell you to wait."

Rodriguez is out of the elevator before I finish clipping on the visitor badge. "Let's go upstairs."

When we're in an interview room, he says, "Ric, I mean Detective Montoya told me you 'forgot' you had the drive. Neither of us believes you."

"My memories from that time are muddled. Some are clear, some are like looking through frosted glass."

"You gave me a detailed account of what occurred when you confronted Eathr Bliss and Kennedy Conners at their command center. The drive had to be from there."

I shrug. Giving up, he says, "We looked through the laptop, and the drive is likely duplicative, but the information is—"

"Did anyone talk?"

"Bliss said nothing, demanded a lawyer. Same with Connors."

"How about the participants?"

"They made some incriminating statements on scene, but have high-priced lawyers now. They're all from wealthy families. Even the security guards won't talk."

"Did they get released?"

"Fortunately, no. For now, anyway. There's a bail review coming up."

"Have you spoken to the other women?"

Rodriguez's brown eyes shutter. "They're all traumatized, some more than others. Francis Downs was the only one who escaped without being sexually assaulted. Tiffaney Blaze moved in with her parents, Brynlee Starr upgraded her security system, and won't leave the house. Marilyn Voss remains hospitalized. She got the worst of it."

"Brittany Guinn got the worst of it."

Another detective I don't recognize knocks on the door and summons Rodriguez into the hall. When he returns, his expression is grim. "Connors is dead. Bliss is in critical condition."

"What?"

"Found in their jail cells. Not sure what happened yet, but deputies think they both tried to die by suicide and only Connors succeeded."

"That's..." I shake my head. "Do you really believe that?"

"I need to go." He escorts me to the elevator. As the doors begin to slide shut, he says, "If you remember anything else, contact me. And be careful, okay?"

31

efore I pull out of the parking spot, I send a text to Adair.

Thanks for delivering the Maserati.

He calls. "Davia, I was about to text you. Is it okay if I pick you up? Jason needs to see you."

"I'm out." I don't tell him where, needing time to think about the news of Kennedy's death and Eathr's alleged suicide attempt. "Be there soon."

When I park in the portico before his sprawling mansion, Adair comes out, opens my door, and offers his hand.

I let him be a gentleman, placing my fingers on his. "Thanks for the courtesy, but you know I'm fine."

"Even if you were in intensive care with a life expectancy of moments, you'd say that." He searches my face. "I've said this before, but I don't want to lose you."

"I'm a survivor."

"Yes, but please stop testing your luck."

"Did Jason figure out who's behind the hunts?"

"I'll let him tell you. Let's go in."

When we take the stairs to his front door, a twinge of pain causes me to stop for a second. Thankful Adair is ahead of me, I grit my teeth through the remaining steps.

Inside, he says, "I should carry you."

"I'm good."

"Liar. The color left your face, and you stiff-legged it."

"You noticed?"

"You told me to up my observation skills, so don't get sulky when I do."

Walking much slower than his usual pace, we cross his foyer, go down a wide hall decorated with oil paintings and statues in alcoves, and take an elevator to the floor containing Jason's office.

Inside, people are busy at different workstations. Jason wears his standard suit and tie, staring at a television screen, fingers cupping his chin. The sound is off, but a "Breaking News" banner scrolls across the bottom and states one inmate was found dead by suicide in a county jail, and another is in critical condition.

"I turned over the thumb drive to Detective Robbie Rodriguez when the news broke," I say. "Kennedy's dead, and Eathr's on his way to a hospital."

Jason considers. "The Sheriff's taken a lot of heat for jail deaths, something like ten or twelve a year. There's always a new story about lawsuits being filed over neglecting prisoners, not rendering timely aid, and suicides, etcetera. But two in one day, and in different facilities?"

"When I confronted them that night, Eathr's main fear was of whoever ran the operation, and Kennedy was willing to do anything to stay alive. Neither seemed suicidal."

"Let's talk over there." Adair indicates Jason's in-office sitting area. It's furnished with a comfortable couch and chairs, with water in a pitcher and glasses on a coffee table. Adair fills a glass and gives it to me.

Jason comes over, saying, "I chose Eathr Bliss as the starting point for our investigation. His real name is Joshua Thompson."

"I knew that had to be a made-up moniker," I say.

"He went from guided meditation videos filmed on his phone in a cheap apartment to a professional brand with high-end production in a short period. He's been rebranded twice in two years. Latest company uses a Delaware shell structure with professional place-holder officers who've never met him."

"Did you check his website?" Adair says.

"Yes. He offers high-end, expensive seminars and private coach-ing. Classic case of serious money packaging a nobody into an influencer."

"The hunts have occurred for a few years." I fill them in on the thumb drive. "I'll get you a copy of the contents."

"Jennifer, will you bring me my tablet, please?" Jason says to a blonde woman in a starched blouse and skirt. She approaches and hands him the device. "You recall Jenny Madison?"

We nod at each other, and she returns to her desk, while Jason makes some notes. "Eathr's been around about two years," he says. "Probably grooming college-age men from prominent families."

"For what purpose?" Adair says. "Blackmail? Control?"

"Not sure yet," Jason says. "But I still need to do a trace on any known participants and who their parents are, which companies they might be affiliated with. See if we can find a connection that way."

"We checked on who rented the location where this happened," Adair says. "The name led to another shell company with profes-sional placeholders as directors. We'll need to trace money flows, not incorporation docs."

"Can you tie its listed directors to anyone?" I say.

"Dead end. They all work for the same corporate services compa-ny," Jason says.

I take a drink of water. "Anything else?"

"Only what you already know," Adair says. "Kennedy's legitimate follower base made her perfect for recruiting."

"She's definitely someone who women aspire to imitate." I think about how the attendees at the book club acted, fawning over her. "I'm confident she wouldn't try to kill herself."

"And now she's been silenced," Adair says.

"If this was a hit on Kennedy and Eathr, it takes a big bankroll to pull off," Jason says. "Perhaps the sheriffs will figure out what happened after reviewing their security footage."

"Davia, you look knackered," Adair says. "Let's quit for now."

I thank Jason for his research, promise to send him the drive files, and follow Adair to the elevator.

"I know we don't have answers yet, but you know Jason. He'll keep pushing," he says.

"How's the betting pool going about Jason and Jenny?"

"Most have bet they'll be a couple by the end of summer, but I think sooner. Did you see that brief brush of hands when she gave him the tablet?"

"Ooh, you are noticing more details."

"If I'm going to continue to hang around you, even with body-guards, sharp eyes are the best way to avoid Davia dangers."

32

When I'm almost home, Alex calls. "Hey, LT. I spoke with Elise about the horse event, and she told me Vivienne has taken over all the decision-making. Since I know Marilyn hasn't been arrested for Samira's death yet, and she clings to that riding club like a reality star desperate for relevancy, I concluded something happened."

"You're not wrong."

"Want to tell me? I had lunch delivered to my office, and there's enough for two. And before you refuse, I have some info from digging around in the file from Samira's computer that we should discuss."

Am I too tired? It's lunch, not a high-stakes operation.

"Be there in ten."

Gordon Financial is located in an office building in downtown Rancho Suprema. The elevator opens directly into a reception area on the second floor. The space balances modern efficiency and understated luxury. Polished concrete floors, clean lines, and chic furniture whisper expensive rather than shout it.

A young man in his mid-twenties sits behind a desk, his dark hair styled and his navy suit tailored to fit him. He glances up from his computer screen with a smile that says he's comfortable scheduling meetings with billionaires.

"Miss Glenn? Mr. Gordon is expecting you. This way."

He leads me past a series of offices where men and women are focused on their screens to a sizable corner suite. The door is open, and Alex is at his desk in a gray tailored suit, tie loosened, reviewing documents on dual monitors. When he sees me, he stands.

"Thank you, Camden," Alex tells the receptionist. "Is the food set up in the conference room?"

"Yes, Mr. Gordon."

"Make sure we're not disturbed."

After he leaves, Alex says, "You look dreadful."

"Thanks?"

"Are you up for this?"

"Yes."

Alex gestures toward an open door. "After you."

The adjacent conference room has a glass wall. He presses a button, and the glass frosts to opaque for privacy. The conference table is a single slab of dark wood, surrounded by leather chairs with a kitchen area along one wall.

"I can tell you had more than a bad weekend. While we eat, perhaps you'll catch me up." He gives me a plate. "You have a choice of brioche grilled cheese or ranch beef dip sandwiches and salad."

We make our selections, sit, and I provide a brief account of what happened at the hunt. He doesn't interrupt and, when I finish, he says, "Those women will never realize that without you, they might not have made their next Botox appointments."

"You really are a cynic, aren't you?"

"I'd rather state the truth than skirt around it, like you." Alex picks up his grilled cheese. "The part I'm struggling with is Kennedy being a mastermind. I always assumed she and Brittany shared a brain cell on alternate weekends."

"I thought the same. Did you ever encounter Eathr Bliss?"

"Fortunately, no. Heard about him, though. He lured some of my clients into his warrior weekends, and several paid for private sessions. From what they said, he's good at reading people and identifying their pain points in life. I put it down to being a clever con artist, but now it seems more sinister."

I tell him about the Eathr and Warden exchange, and Alex begins laughing so hard he nearly chokes. After he regains control, he says, "I would've paid half my fortune to see that. It's shocking that Eathr came out of it alive. He must have angered someone much less restrained than Warden to nearly die in jail."

"That problem is finding out who. For now, let's focus on what you found in the riding club records."

"Why don't we finish eating first? The info's on a tablet on my desk."

"Your office is nice. With your personality, I expected something less sedate."

"You should see my New York branch. It's all dark wood paneling and leather-bound books, an old-money aesthetic to make the clients feel like their great-great-grandfathers would approve. This place is less formal for the cool Californians."

"You kept your office back east?"

"The one in Manhattan. Half my clients think anything west of the Hudson is a foreign country."

"How did you get into finance?"

"Business degree from Columbia. Then I took a job at a major firm to learn the ropes. Hated the rivalry, so I went out on my own. Struggled for a while. The turning point came in 2020 when I spotted the pandemic early. Sold my clients' stocks before the crash, made aggressive bets against the market, and then bought world-class companies at bargain prices when everyone was panicking."

"And that made you a lot of money?"

His eyes hold mine. "Are you asking because you might want to merge our assets? I can guarantee some exceptional returns."

The double meaning hangs between us, and a laugh escapes me at his utter shamelessness.

"No wonder most women can't resist you."

"But you're not most women, are you? Not many find dangerous situations normal."

"Speaking of dangerous, where were your gun and fighting skills honed?"

"Private club in the Hamptons. The rich pay fifty grand a year to play soldier on weekends. Turns out hedge fund managers enjoy shooting things after a bad quarter."

When we finish our lunch, Alex says, "Leave everything. I pay Camden way too much to clean up after me."

We return to his office, and he indicates a couch. "Have a seat. Let me grab my tablet to show you the data."

When he sits beside me, I say, "Please use terms I'll understand."

"Afraid of a little math, LT?" His expression is pure mischief, the kind that probably got him out of—or more likely, into—trouble his entire life.

"How about you cut to the findings?"

"Here I thought you enjoyed my company. Okay. Someone's been paying a vendor who doesn't exist. The amounts are small enough to fly under the radar, but they add up. I compared the actual invoices to the bank records to verify."

"Do you think it was Samira?"

"Unclear. She'd only been manager a short time, but the file contained data going back five years. Marilyn, Elise, Vivienne, or anyone else with access is a suspect."

"Elise and Vivienne? I thought Samira hired them for this event only?"

"They're the go-to business to aid past riding club shindigs. They provide organizations with additional support, take over the accounting, and line up contracts with vendors."

"So, they might also have had access across multiple years?"

"It's a good bet. There are also payments to Meridian, like the note Samira made. I can't trace what for."

"Was it a lot of money?"

"To me, no. About fifty grand."

"Your perception is seriously skewed."

"I'll admit it. The fewer zeroes, the less interested I am."

I consider the info. "Meridian invested in Crown Point, Victor Hayes is having money problems, and now there's a payment from the riding club to Meridian. My headache is resurfacing."

"In the future, I'll remember to avoid complex finance discussions when we're together. Are you still having issues from the weekend?"

"I'm tired."

"For now, I'll let you pretend you're a battle-hardened warrior laid low by a discrepancy." He stands. "You need to rest. Come on, I'll walk you out."

33

Two days later, I'm at the Rancho Riding Club for the rehearsal. A massive, red and gold striped tent surrounds the main arena, resembling a circus, its steel framework supporting arches high overhead. The tent's entrance features dramatic red velvet drapes held open with golden ropes, creating a grand threshold. Inside the big top, sound technicians test microphones, lighting crews adjust spots and floods, and crews string thousands of tiny white bulbs above temporary bleachers.

Vivienne strides through it all, headset on and holding a clipboard. She barks orders while dodging a prancing horse being led past her. "Davia, there you are," she greets. "I'll introduce you to Talia, the equine performance coordinator. She'll walk you through everything."

I follow her past handlers, who are leading two matched gray Andalusians with pewter coats polished to a high sheen, to where a striking brunette with intricate arm tattoos stands beside a white stallion tied to a post. Vivienne introduces us, then says, "I need to go. We're setting up another tent for the concert and arranging seating in the main courtyard for the barbecue. Elise is helping me, but it's been a lot to manage since Samira died and Marilyn's out of commission."

"I'll show you where your costume and changing area will be," Talia says. The way she holds her spine, shoulders pulled back and down, is pure Adair. I see his years of ballet training in her posture. "What's your riding skill level?"

"Advanced, but western."

She lets out a soft 'tch' from the corner of her mouth.

"What's your background?" I say to divert a censorious lecture.

"All of the performers who have been hired for this event began riding as children in dressage and show jumping, in Europe for the most part," she explains as we exit the tent. "Many trained at École Nationale de Cirque in Montreal or circus academies in France and Russia. They're skilled in acrobatics, dance, and aerial arts, as well as horse choreography."

Maybe I could do an Annie Oakley routine. Shoot a cigar out of a donor's mouth while galloping past?

We enter a white auxiliary tent that holds rows of clothing. "Your costume will be on this rack with your name on it, so come here and get dressed after the barbecue."

Before I can ask questions about my outfit, Chase enters, and Talia's lips part. He kisses both of her cheeks. "I came to find you to see which horse I'll ride."

His muscular, tan arms have a pale band on his left wrist where he wore the Longines watch, and my mind returns to Samira's murder.

"Do you know Davia Glenn?" Talia says.

"Nice to see you again." His gaze licks over me. "Where's your lunch date?"

"He resides in Virginia."

"Long-distance relationships never work, you know. If you need someone local..."

"Let me introduce you to your horses," Talia interrupts and walks out.

"Looks like you blew your chances with her," I say to Chase as we follow.

"Talia? That was a lifetime ago. I have a much shorter attention span these days."

"If Samira were still alive, I'd tell her how smart she was to dump you."

His swagger, all rolling shoulders and easy grace, hitches for a single step, then he says, "You didn't know her like I did. She came with her own set of issues."

"They'd have to be pretty substantial to catch up with yours."

Talia pauses beside a jet-black horse with a flowing mane braided with gold ribbons. Grooms buzz around stately horses tied nearby while others push carts loaded with elaborate tack. Saddles are adorned with crystals, bridles with silver conchos, and there are colorful plumes that will transform the horses into fantasy creatures.

"Davia, this is Antonio," Talia says, introducing me to a man with black hair and a swarthy complexion. "He's in charge of preparing Luciano. The rehearsal's in thirty minutes. Antonio will assist with your warm-up, then bring you to where I'll help you with your routine. See you soon."

She walks away, Chase running after her, saying, "Wait up!"

"I need a few moments to finish saddling him," Antonio tells me.

"Of course."

There's a nearby bench beneath a shade tree, and I take a seat. Julia comes out of the main barn's wide opening.

"Davia?" She joins me. "How are you? Adair's been so worried."

Is she referencing my fall from Wellington or more recent events? Would Adair have told her about the hunt?

I stand. "I'm fine. Are you going to ride in this?"

"No. I came with Adair and the twins. They're too young for the evening performance, but pleaded with us to see the horses. Adair called someone to get permission for them to do a walk-through."

"Where are they?"

"Waiting at the car. I told them I'd make sure it's not too crazy."

"That's smart of you."

"Vivienne gave me the all-clear, and I texted Adair where to meet me. He should be here in a moment."

"Ms. Glenn?" Antonio calls. "Your horse is ready."

"Excuse me." I take a step, and a sharp pain shoots down my leg. Wincing, I stop.

"Are you okay?" Julia says.

"Old injury. It flares up from time to time."

"It probably didn't help when you took that spill from Wellington." Her brows pinch together, watching as I rub my leg.

Adair exits the barn with Evie and Emily holding his hands. The girls try to pull away when they see me, but Adair bends to tell them something, and they stop. He looks back at his lone bodyguard, says something to him, and he stays a distance away.

When they reach us, the twins shout my name and throw their arms around my legs. I flinch from a flash of pain, but hug them.

"Girls," Adair says, "why don't you go with Julia? She'll take you to see that big red tent. And what did you promise?"

"To always hold hands with one of you," they intone, then squirm with excitement as a horse in full equipment and plumes is led past.

"Feel better," Julia says to me before taking the girls and heading away. She looks back, her smile fading as her gaze flits between us.

Adair says, "Is it your leg?"

I nod.

"I have this specialist you should see—"

"Miss Glenn?" Antonio calls. He holds Luciano's reins, and the big animal weaves around him, restless. "We're running out of warm-up time."

"Have you turned him out, let him work off that energy?" Adair asks.

"*Sì, Signore.* He's, how you say, a spirit."

"Spirited, *vivace*," Adair says, switching to Italian for a rapid-fire conversation with Antonio. He ends it by telling me, "I'll warm him up. And don't you dare protest."

"*La ringrazio molto*," I say, my thanks heartfelt.

Adair pulls me against him. "Go sit down. If you're not better when I return, you won't be riding. Do you understand?"

"Yes."

"See you soon." He goes with Antonio toward a practice arena, his bodyguard following.

Settling back on the wooden seat, I massage my leg. Did the hunt exacerbate my injury? Will this be the end of my time as an operative? No, stop those thoughts. I'll recover. I have to.

People leading horses and others pass by, all intent on their tasks. As the day progresses, the temperature continues to rise. The air is filled with the aroma of hay and horse sweat, yet Adair's cologne lingers from when he pressed me to him.

Don't think about Adair. That road is riddled with problems.

Elise rushes by, then skids to a halt. "Davia. Are you here for the practice?"

"Yes, I'll meet Talia soon. What have you been doing?"

She flops onto the bench beside me with a weary sigh. "Running non-stop since dawn. Coordinating hay bale placement for aesthetics, mapping food stations... I'll have a new constellation of freckles by sundown, sunscreen or not. What about you?"

"I have a leg injury that's bothering me. Adair's warming up the horse I'm using in the performance."

"I thought you said you weren't dating him. Are you now?"

"He's a friend."

She looks skeptical, but doesn't press. "Do you want some water? I have bottles in a mini-fridge in the barn."

"Thank you, but I'm good."

"I'd best get going." She pushes herself to her feet, the fatigue evident in her slow movement. "Vivienne will scold me if a single thing is out of place."

"I thought your sole duty was the accounting with Alex."

"With Samira's death, and Marilyn in the hospital, our duties expanded into all of this."

"You should have reached out to me."

"We tried a few times. Your phone went straight to voicemail. We figured you were occupied."

"I was at Serenity Springs. They made us turn over our phones." Hers was likely one of the many calls I lacked the energy to return. "I'm sorry so much of this fell on your shoulders."

"I'm scheduling a coma for the week after this wraps."

I laugh. "Let me know how I can help going forward."

"Help?" a man says from behind me. "I'm sure my donation will keep them from bothering you."

"Mr. Kensington!" Elise exclaims. "It's so good to see you here."

"I told you to call me Bradford, remember?"

I rise, my face impassive. Bradford pushes his thick-framed glasses up his nose and gives me a smile that doesn't thaw his steely regard.

"I'll get you some water!" Elise bustles away, passing Bradford's bodyguards, whose suits contrast with the riding and casual attire around them. They take up positions a discreet distance from Bradford, their postures relaxed but their eyes constantly scanning the area.

"Checking to see if your money's being well spent?" I say.

"You having to be polite to me is worth the cost."

"But I don't."

Bradford doesn't wear his usual cardigan, and he reaches for pockets that aren't there. "Heard a rumor you and your book club members had some trouble during your resort outing."

"Oh? You mean when some of us didn't elevate our consciousness to the correct level?"

He tilts his head. "I heard something much more, um, physical occurred."

"Did you?"

"I like to keep tabs on your life."

Adair rides up on a subdued Luciano, dismounts next to me, and Antonio takes the reins to lead the horse to a water trough. Adair's bodyguard takes in Bradford's men and tenses.

"Bradford. It's surprising to find you here," Adair says.

"Surprising? I'm a donor, like you."

"It astonishes me that your business doesn't take you else-where." Adair emphasizes the last word.

"But being in Rancho is so...entertaining."

"Mr. Kensington," Julia greets as she approaches with the girls, who bubble with excitement from their adventure. "How nice to see you again."

"Julia Darrow, right? And hello, young ladies." He pats the girls' heads. "I met you last month, but I don't expect you to recall."

Julia holds onto the twins and gives Bradford a friendly smile. "I didn't expect to see you again so soon. Thought you'd be busy running your empire."

"It runs itself for the most part. I've invested wisely in the next generation."

Elise returns, carrying two water bottles. "Here you go, Mr. Kensin—Bradford, Mr. Monroe."

"The girls probably need those more than I do." Bradford indicates the twins.

"That's so kind." Elise gives the water to Evie and Emily, who thank her politely.

"Why don't you let me preview the concert set-up?" Bradford says to Elise.

"It will be my pleasure."

Bradford looks thoughtful as Elise continues to provide a stream of information about the event. Kensington's bodyguards fall into step, a two-man formation that parts the crowd without a word or a touch.

The moment they're out of earshot, Adair says, "Davia, do you think you can ride?"

"What's wrong?" Evie says.

"Are you hurt, Davia?" Emily stares up at me with a worried expression.

"My leg had a cramp, that's all. I'm sure I'll be fine."

"You're Davia's knight," Emily says to Adair, fists planted on her hips. "You're supposed to always protect and care for her."

"Don't worry. I promised her we'd all live happily ever after. Maybe even adopt a dragon." Adair grabs their stomachs and roars, and the girls giggle.

"Davia, do you want me to find some ice for your leg?" Julia says, but Adair interrupts.

"Did the girls get to see everything?" he asks.

"What the coordinator said they could, yes."

"Then would you mind driving them to Stacey Templeton's? I'll stay and help Davia."

"Of course," Julia says with forced brightness, but her expression is strained.

The twins hug both me and Adair, then go with her.

"You know she has a crush on you, right?" I say to him.

"She's an employee and I've been plain about my boundaries."

"Boundaries can't keep out feelings."

"I have no control over that," he says, his attention already on the horse. "Can you ride?"

"I think so."

We follow Antonio and a quiet Luciano to a mounting block near the main red tent. Jeremy leads a big chestnut gelding toward it, expression downcast.

"Please go first," he says when he notices us. "And, Ms. Glenn? Are you okay? Marilyn said you were with her at, uh, the resort."

"Yes," I say. "Have you seen her?"

"I went to the hospital every day. She got released yesterday and is home, but..." He shakes his head.

"When you see her next, please send my regards and tell her I hope she'll be better soon," I say, knowing these are platitudes and they solve nothing.

"I will." He motions to the mounting block. "Go ahead."

I step into the saddle, and a spike of heat shoots down my leg. I suck in a breath, gather the reins, and point him toward the tent's opening.

34

Montoya texts me a day before the charity event: *Call me.*

"What's up?" I say when he answers.

"A few things. First, Eathr Bliss escaped from the hospital."

"How?"

"He was taken to a different floor for a medical procedure. A deputy was present. He unhandcuffed him and waited outside the exam room, but a brawl erupted between two families, forcing his intervention. When he subdued them, he secured the corridor, returned, and checked. Eathr was gone."

"Did someone kidnap him?"

"We're still looking into it. We're getting a warrant to obtain footage, if it exists."

"Doubt he'll come after me. Even if he does, he's not much of a threat."

"You cost him everything, so be careful."

"Anything else?"

"Need to check your statement about what Victor Hayes told you when you went to Crown Point."

"Which part?"

"Tell me exactly what he said again."

"Is this a memory test?"

"Just tell me."

I go through what I remember, saying he called Samira the morning of her death at around six-thirty a.m. and told me about her relationship with Chase.

"How did he seem that morning?"

"His primary concern was getting additional insurance for the tour in case he got sued, and he was happy Samira split from Chase. Why?"

"When we reviewed the footage from the riding club, we found him on camera, walking past one of the barns around six a.m. on the day she was murdered."

"He definitely told me he called."

"You sure? Is your memory up to speed?"

"Yes. Samira wrote his initials and something about Crown Point financials on her notepad, right?"

"And a note: Check Meridian connection," Montoya says.

"Like I told you, Meridian invested in Crown Point, and I heard Victor has had some financial issues. Maybe she wanted to be sure about his donation for the event."

"He told me the same story, that their investment helped him upgrade and keep his premier west coast facility title. But he also said he only called Ms. Westbrook that day. He's lying about something, but I can't pin down what. Yet."

"What about Marilyn Voss, Jeremy Maxwell-Price, and Chase Matthews?" I list.

"Robbie, I mean Detective Rodriguez, spoke to Marilyn yesterday. She's doing a little better, and he mainly went over details about what happened to her during the hunt. But he told me she said she was so caught up in trying to get her riding club job back that she lost perspective, and regrets being so petty to Samira."

"What about her keys?"

"She said she really did lend them to Samira that day."

"Do you believe her?"

"Marilyn described Samira as being upset that morning, distracted about something. I don't think she's lying, well about that part anyway. What happened to Marilyn has also made Jeremy much more forthcoming. Said he was stressed that he might lose sponsors if he didn't win more, and he pushed hard to get more arena time. When I say "pushed," I think he means that literally. He said he feels like a complete ass for focusing on his own riding career and taking it out on Samira."

I tell Montoya about my more recent encounter with Jeremy. "Not that I believe his attitude change will last, but what happened to both Samira and Marilyn might have caused him to do some self-examination. Which leaves Chase."

"He claims he didn't get there until right after the Ranch Patrol secured the scene. Said he and Samira fought outside her office the evening before her death. That's when his watch probably fell off. There weren't any witnesses that we could find, but we did ask for anyone with riding club footage from their phones to submit it for the day of her murder."

"And?"

"I need to check with the tech looking at it, but no one's called me. I've been pretty busy, as you know."

"Are there any other suspects?"

"Alex Gordon informed me about the accounting discrepancies," Montoya says. "Said someone's siphoning off money from the riding club."

"I met with him about that yesterday."

"Which adds an unknown embezzler to the suspect list."

"Do you think Kennedy's death was a suicide? And before you wonder how I know, I was at the station to give Detective Rodriguez the thumb drive when he got notified."

"You know I can't discuss that."

"Any leads on who might have been running the hunts?" I don't tell him I sent the drive files to Jason McCall and his team.

"More information, I can't discuss."

"Are you coming to Hoofbeats for Heroes with Sherilyn?"

He sighs. "She sprung for tickets because she says it's essential for her business to be visible in the community."

"See you then."

———

The night before the event, I go to Stacey Templeton's for an early dinner, and a special treat she says will be a complete surprise. I think back to the first time I met her, when she introduced me to her previous turkey companion, Triple T4. What could top that?

Before I can ring the bell, the front door of Stacey's mansion opens.

"Davia!" Evie and Emily rush toward me in pink and purple tutus with sparkling tiaras perched on their blonde curls.

"We're putting on a show, " Emily declares.

"With Triple T5!" Evie adds.

Stacey appears next, wearing a flowing cape made of peacock feathers and a spectacular crown that catches the light with the cold, hard fire of diamonds. "Welcome to the Inaugural Templeton Turkey Spectacular. We're dedicating tonight's show to the memory of the brave Triple T4, rest his soul."

Behind her, Adair emerges looking sheepish. He has a purple satin sash draped across his chest and a tiara balanced on his head. When he nears, he whispers, "Don't say a word."

"I wouldn't dream of it."

"Wait!" Evie rushes inside and returns carrying a pink feather boa. "Put this on, Davia!"

I loop it around my neck, not asking where my tiara is for fear I'll be forced to wear one.

"This way!" They skip along the house with Stacey close behind.

"They got this idea from going to the riding club and seeing the glamorous costumes and horses," Adair says.

"I think your ensemble makes you look dashing," I say.

"Does it now?" With a cheeky grin, he puts a hand on his hip, and imitates a runway model as he sashays toward a side gate.

In the backyard, wrought iron chairs form a semicircle around a "stage" marked by rope lights strung between trees, and poles hold billowing white bed sheets for walls to give it a tent-like effect. A desk lamp has been repurposed into a turkey-sized spotlight, and glitter is scattered across the lawn for added glamour.

Triple T5 struts to the area's center, a cape that matches Stacey's covering his white feathers. He wears a tiny crown secured with elastic under his red wattles.

"Ladies and gentlemen!" Evie calls through a toy megaphone. "Welcome to the most amazing turkey show ever! The star of tonight's show is Tiberius Torston Templeton the fifth!"

The girls make a grand, sweeping gesture toward the turkey, who wanders away from them and across the manicured lawn. Evie runs to guide the bewildered turkey back.

"First, he'll demonstrate his jumping skills," Emily says.

Evie faces him toward a row of pool noodles balanced horizontally on two-foot-high pots. Instead of doing as ordered, the turkey strikes a series of poses, puffing out his chest and fanning his tail feathers

"You have to jump!" The twins cry, then demonstrate what they want, leaping over the barrier and back. T5 ignores them to preen a feather on his chest.

Emily's face falls for a second before she brightens. "He's going to fly next!"

"Fly?" I whisper to Adair.

"They're convinced he'll take flight if asked. I've been designated as his flight instructor, despite his wings being clipped."

Adair runs to stand with the twins, striking an identical pose of hopeful expectation. "He failed every single one of his lessons," he confides to the audience in a stage whisper, "but we believe in the power of the spotlight, right, girls?" `

"Come on, T5. FLY!" the twins shout, pointing skyward.

The turkey bobs his head, walks a distance away, then runs toward them, flapping his wings. It sounds like a deck of cards being shuffled, and he lifts maybe an inch off the ground.

Evie and Emily jump up and down in their excitement. "He's flying! He's flying!"

"Give him a treat," Stacey says, and the twins take grapes, pieces of lettuce, and some grain out of a nearby bowl. They let it spill onto the ground before T5, who pecks at their offering with enthusiasm.

When he finishes eating, Stacey says, "Now for T5's signature move." She unfurls a scroll with words written in elaborate calligraphy, clears her throat, and announces, "By the queen's decree, His Excellency Tiberius Torston Templeton the Fifth is hereby commanded to deliver the Royal Gobble!"

The turkey obliges with a resounding call that sends the girls into delighted cheers.

"Well done, T5!" Adair calls. "This concludes our first annual turkey spectacular!"

The twins grab Adair and Stacey's hands, and everyone bows. After several encores and much applause, Stacey declares it's time for dinner.

"I had our meal set out by a caterer." She waves toward a terrace with a table covered by a red and white tablecloth. It has place settings and food covered with mesh tents. Despite being outdoors, the napkins are cloth, the plates are china, and the serving bowls and drinking glasses are crystal. The menu features mini sandwiches cut into turkey shapes, pasta and potato salads, raw vegetables, and lemonade served in a glass pitcher.

Emily pushes her slipped tiara into place as we make our way toward the table. "Wasn't T5 perfect?"

"Absolutely magnificent," Adair says. "I've never seen such natural stage presence."

"He even flew!" Evie says.

I put my arms around both girls' shoulders. "I hope I'll be able to captivate the audience as well as he did."

When we sit, T5 hops up beside Stacey and she feeds him treats from his own special bowl. She uses a miniature, lace-edged napkin to wipe a crumb from her turkey's beak. "T4 would have hated the cape," she confides to me. "He was such a pragmatist. But T5? He was born for the spotlight."`

I nod, not questioning her turkey whisperer conclusion.

Stacey redirects her focus to the twins. "Now, girls, remember— we may be eating outside, but we always use our best manners. Napkins in your laps, please, and no elbows on the table. This is what I term 'elevated casual,' darlings. We can have fun, but we never lose our elegance."

"Yes, Stacey," the girls say, sitting up straight and drinking their lemonade with practiced ease from the crystal glasses.

When we finish, we help with the twins' bedtime routine. We head to the east wing, a space Stacey transformed into a storybook fortress. The vaulted ceiling soars over a room containing a doll-house village, a miniature castle with drawbridges, and a vast herd of plush animals that look ready to stampede.

They put on their pajamas and brush their teeth at a pint-sized vanity, its surface a happy chaos of glittery hair wax, light-up hair-brushes, and a collection of fancy clips. Each has a walk-in closet stuffed with everyday clothes and dress-up costumes, from pirate gear to astronaut suits.

Adair selects an illustrated book of classic fairy tales from one of the many built-in bookcases that hold as many books as a library. He drops into a deep armchair while the girls burrow into their bed, a canopied raft adrift in a sea of toys. As he reads, he rumbles like a giant or squeaks like a mouse, bringing the tale to life.

The story does its work, and their breathing slows into the steady rhythm of sleep. A fluffy alpaca and a unicorn with a gilded horn are tucked under their arms. We tiptoe from their room and close the door.

"You should learn to stifle your huffs when princes rescue princesses," he says.

"I would prefer a story about a princess rescuing herself."

"Gee, I wonder why?"

Stacey hugs us both farewell at the door, saying, "It's time for me to tuck my darling Tiberius in and read him his goodnight story. I've done this for all my turkey companions, and it's a tradition that will continue. Thank you for coming."

When we near our cars, Adair says, "That's one dotty household, but she's great with the kids."

"So are you, but you should've left on the sash and tiara to wear home to show Jason."

"Speaking of Jason, he and Jenny have been working late, combing through the data on Eathr Bliss. I'm pretty sure I'll win the betting pool on when they get together."

"I hope you do. You need the money."

"Stop. How's your leg? As I started to tell you, I know a top neurologist in England. I found her when my mum had issues from her lengthy professional ballet career. Although Mum taught dance after Dad died instead of performing, I recognized she pushed through pain and denied her limitations. Kind of like you."

"I'm better. This injury has been on again, off again. I'll improve, even enough to go for a run, then...I return to square one."

"We can fly over and get you checked out."

"Adair..."

He stops my words by placing his lips against mine. "Think about it. And I'll see you tomorrow."

35

I button my cowboy shirt, tuck it into the black leather pants, and pull on the boots Bryce sold me when a video call from Warden flashes on my phone.

"You look ready for a rodeo, but your hair's teased high enough to scare the horses," he says.

"Ramon glamorized me this morning to fit the appearance instructions for my Valkyrie character. Salon Divine was a zoo of cowgirl wannabes."

"Like Hodge might say, yeehaw. Got your text. Did Montoya find out if Kennedy was murdered?"

"If he did, he didn't tell me. You know how he is."

"Tight-lipped. Like us. Anything on the escapee?"

"No. Hard for me to believe he could pull that off on his own, but it was also shocking to find him so involved with the hunt."

"Maybe his disciples staged a jail break."

"My guess is he's alive and on the run. If someone tried to kill him in jail, they wouldn't abduct him. They'd finish the job at the hospital."

"I agree." Warden grows sober. "Unrelated, and I can't say much for obvious reasons, but do you remember the first problem we had out there?"

"Of course."

"The network is being resurrected by someone much cleverer than the previous leadership."

A cold knot tightens in my stomach. Badger's terrorist organization was supposed to be ash.

"Do you have an ID?"

"No, but it's why Streeter wanted me to return, because of my familiarity with the operation. I didn't want to say anything until I dug deeper."

"Are you sure it's his group?"

"You recall the staged publicity events funding poor villages, then making off with people to be trafficked?"

"Of course."

"This is quieter, with many of the same overseas players involved, but I doubt it will spill over into our lives soon. It's the reason I haven't returned to watch you perform in sequins for billionaires."

"Your loss." I check the time. "I've got to go. I miss you."

"Stay frosty," Warden says with a wink.

———

"Welcome to Westworld, LT," Alex says when I join him at the riding club. He wears a pair of tight Wrangler jeans with a dark charcoal western shirt. He has the lean, watchful look of a gunslinger in another life.

"Are you the real Alex Gordon, or an android who looks like him?"

He puts a finger to the brim of his black cowboy hat. "I live to fulfill your every desire either way."

Pre-event chaos hums around us. The staff wear crisp white shirts, red bandanas, and cowboy hats, arranging booths draped in red, white, and blue bunting, with a special exhibit about "Reins of Hope." Beyond the main barn, roadies wheel massive speakers toward the covered tent where Keith Urban's crew has been setting up since dawn.

I step into some shade. "It's hot in this get-up. Guess I should've worn a cowboy hat, too."

"At least we didn't have to go on the barn tour. Doing registration will be easy."

"I'm also stuck in the horse finale, remember?"

"Be sure and make Beatrice proud."

"It's my top priority. Did you find out any more about the embezzler?"

"I have a strong suspicion. I'm waiting for one more piece of data to confirm it."

We move aside to allow caterers to hustle past. Long tables covered in checkered tablecloths sit before food stations lining the courtyard perimeter. A banner advertises "Authentic Texas BBQ" where pit masters tend smoking brisket and ribs, the sweet hickory scent perfuming the air. Another promises "Down-Home Sides" as servers arrange warming trays and chafing dishes. A bar is complete with mason jars stacked in neat pyramids beside bottles of bourbon and beer. In a separate location that will be accessible after the finale, Kyran O'Keeffe and his staff set up an array of chocolates and desserts.

"Alex, Davia!" Vivienne calls. "The vans with our barn tour guests are going to be here shortly and will need to be checked in. Please go to the registration booth and get ready."

"Yes, ma'am," Alex says with a sharp salute.

The next hour is spent on our duties, including checking off names and giving gift bags and special lanyards to the VIPs. When Bradford Kensington arrives, his dead-eyed bodyguards follow close behind. Alex tosses the items on the table before him, marks off his name, and says, "Please keep the line moving."

Bradford stiffens, then relaxes as amusement crosses his face. He puts the lanyard around his neck and picks up the gift bag as Elise hurries over to direct him to the VIP area.

Victor Hayes approaches, but lines crease his forehead as he stares after Bradford. Alex provides him with his items, and I say, "You just missed Bradford Kensington."

"I'll catch up to him later," he stammers.

Alex watches him go. "What's that about?"

"Not sure. Noticed him getting tense when Bradford arrived at the donor party, but I haven't pieced anything together. We both know Bradford enjoys hostile takeovers, but a horse farm?"

"Maybe he's decided to corner the market on hedge funds and hay."

Sherilyn and Montoya arrive together, and he wears jeans, boots, and a navy Western snap-button shirt.

"You look handsome without your detective gear," I say.

"He wanted to wear a tie, but I wouldn't let him," Sherilyn jokes, threading her arm through Montoya's. She's in a white leather, zip-front, sleeveless mini dress with tassels at the hem paired with knee-high brown cowboy boots and fancy feather earrings.

"Will you arrest anyone tonight?" Alex asks Montoya, but he shakes his head.

"I'm close, but don't have enough proof yet."

Sherilyn rolls her eyes. "His mega brain won't shut off, no matter how pretty I look."

He pulls her against him. "She exaggerates. Let's go have that thing you keep mentioning. What was it? Fun?"

"Silly," Sherilyn says. They give us a wave, then head toward the barbecue.

When Beatrice Gibbs checks in, she wears a vibrant blue outfit bedazzled in rhinestones. "It's nice to see the Ladies' League is well-represented tonight. And Davia, I hope you'll be a credit to us and not fall off your horse during the performance."

"I'll give it my all."

"You'd better," Alex says, nudging me under the table with his leg.

When the lines die down, we review our non-VIP guest list and note that Francis and Marilyn haven't checked in yet.

"You did your best, LT," Alex says. "You can't save everyone."

"She saved me," Francis says, approaching with a tall man I recognize from the hospital. He keeps a protective arm around her shoulders, and she stays close, her demeanor more fragile than before.

"Francis," I stand to greet her. "I'm so glad you're here."

"This is my husband, Elliot."

"I'm forever in your debt. Francis told me what you did."

I step around the table to give Francis a gentle hug. "How are you doing?"

"Better some days than others," she admits. "Elliot didn't want me to come tonight, but I couldn't let fear keep me home. I refuse to let what happened rule my life."

"She insisted she couldn't miss it," Elliot says.

"I knew you'd be here, Davia, and that made me braver."

Alex gives the couple their passes with a warm smile. "I'm glad you joined us. Please enjoy your evening."

Francis says, "I look forward to seeing you in the finale, Davia."

I watch the couple blend into the crowd. "I'm glad she's recovering."

"Me, too." Alex says as I retake my seat next to him. We flip through the guest list.

"Only a few people are absent," he says.

"How much longer are we supposed to stay here?"

"Adair's a no-show. Or perhaps his lordship needed a lie-down after the strenuous effort of being admired for a few hours. His barn and horses probably came in second place."

"Like Adair's right-hand man says," I mimic Jason's strong British accent. "All you'll need to succeed is for His Gorgeousness to appear."

"That's the truth." Alex stands and stretches. "Why don't we let him check himself in when and if he arrives? We should catch some of the concert before you do the Ladies' League proud."

We leave the booth, but Adair approaches with three male bodyguards positioned a distance behind him. "Sorry, I'm late. Jason wanted to talk to me, then I needed to put on this...cowboy look." He gestures to the lightweight denim shirt and jeans he wears.

"Since I know that shirt costs over a grand, I think you'll need this VIP lanyard and little gift bag to complete your outfit," Alex says. "Where's Julia?"

"Closing up after the tour, but she should arrive soon. She said she wants to be here to cheer for Davia."

Alex snorts. "Sure, she does. I'm going to get something to drink. Find me, Davia."

"I will."

When he leaves, Adair's expression shifts to one of concern. "Will you be able to ride tonight?"

Increasing the weight on my left leg, I say, "It's holding up, so yes."

"I'm glad. And before we go in, Jason found out that most of the participants in the hunt have parents who are affiliated with companies owned by Bradford."

"Is he sure?"

"The data wasn't hard to trace, but the connection to Eathr and Kennedy remains elusive."

"I meant to call you, but I'm sure you know already. Eathr either escaped or was abducted from the hospital."

"Saw that."

"Remember when Bradford said, 'I've invested wisely in the next generation.' Do you think he means through blackmail?"

"Hard to say. Until we find real proof..." Adair shrugs. "It isn't a stretch to believe he's building a network of compromised future leaders, gaining control over the next generation of executives."

"It definitely fits his style."

"Jason will stay on top of sorting this out." Adair takes my hands. "You can't be distracted tonight. I'm sure you'll ride come hell or… whatever that expression is."

He steps close and runs his hand along my cheek right as Julia comes towards us. She plasters on a smile.

"Julia," I say when she nears, "I heard the guests gushing about how remarkable Adair's barn and horses were. I'm sure it's thanks to you."

"It definitely was," Adair says. "She worked herself ragged to make sure Monroe Equine was a smash hit. I wish all my employees were as diligent."

She wears dark jeans and a burgundy silk blouse, her hair in an elegant ponytail. "Thank you."

"Were there any problems?" I ask.

"Some of the guests were unfamiliar with horses, treating them like oversized dogs, making sudden movements when they tried to pet them. The horses aren't used to crowds."

"I'm sure the people were offended." I turn to Adair. "I promised Alex I'd go with him to listen to a little of the concert before I have to get ready."

"I'll go with you," Adair offers.

"I won't make it on time if you do. I've seen how it is being with you in a crowd, getting waylaid by everyone."

"She's right," Julia says. "When we attended that donor party, we couldn't get more than a few feet before we were halted."

Adair pulls his VIP pass over his head. "Here, Julia. I forgot to get you a pass, and you earned it. Go relax. I need to talk to Davia."

Her response is automatic, professional. "Thank you, Mr. Monroe."

She gives us a slight nod and heads toward the entrance, her back rigid.

"I think you broke another heart," I say.

"I've always been plain about our employer-employee relationship. It's a recurring problem, but I can't control other people's expectations."

"Speaking of expectations, I still need that space you've given me, which has meant a lot."

A shade of a frown is there and gone. "Okay. But if your leg acts up, please don't ride."

"I won't."

"Pinky swear promise?" He extends his little finger.

"I promise." I link my little finger with his, and we touch thumbs. "See you soon."

36

When I locate Alex in the food area, he holds a glass of whiskey and chats with a couple of pretty women. Halting a few feet away, I consider leaving him to his pleasures, but the second he spots me, he excuses himself.

"LT. I see Prince Charming didn't drag you away to his castle."

"Don't worry. I'm not a fan of fairy tales."

"It might raise Julia's hopes if she learns you're not attached to his hip. Saw her surrounded by men, but her spirits were low. I think her heart beats for the Brit."

"She works for Adair, and he doesn't engage in billionaire boss romance novel behavior."

"With his looks and bank account, his bodyguards probably work double duty to keep back the hopefuls," Alex says. "Want something to drink?"

"Water. I still have to ride."

Alex retrieves a chilled bottle, and we weave through the crowd toward the concert tent. Inside, spotlights shift with hues of blue and purple light. The stage is at the far end, and Alex takes his VIP credentials out of a front pocket, shows them to security, then leads me along a deserted path. We stop at a quiet platform near a raised VIP section with seating cordoned off with velvet ropes. It offers a perfect view of the stage while providing a sense of insulation.

"Scoped this out earlier. A VIP Bradford-free zone."

"Good thinking."

Vivienne appears before a microphone at the center of the stage. "Good evening, everyone, and welcome to Hoofbeats for Heroes! I'm Vivienne Reese, and on behalf of the Ladies' League and the Rancho Riding Club, I want to thank each of you for being here tonight. Your generous support enables us to assist our veterans through the Reins of Hope program. Before tonight's spectacular equestrian finale, we're thrilled to present a world-famous country and western singer. Ladies and gentlemen, please give a warm Rancho Suprema welcome to the one and only...Keith Urban!"

The lights dim, and the crowd's energy sharpens with anticipation. A single spotlight cuts through the darkness, illuminating the singer as he strides onto the stage with his guitar slung across his shoulder. The audience erupts. Women scream, men whistle, and the applause builds to a roar that shakes the tent itself.

Urban raises his hand in acknowledgment. He approaches the microphone with the easy confidence of someone who has commanded thousands of stages, and adjusts his guitar strap. The crowd's cheers intensify when he leans into the mic.

"Rancho Suprema!" he calls out, his Australian accent carrying over the sound system. "How y'all doing tonight?"

Another wave of applause crashes over the stage. He strums a few opening chords, and the recognition sends another surge through the crowd. Guests press closer to the stage, phones appear to capture the moment, and the energy becomes electric. The bass line kicks in, followed by the drums, and the full band sound fills every corner of the tent as Urban launches into his opening number.

Alex takes my drink and sets it down, then pulls me into a two-step. The music wraps around us, a driving beat.

"How did a New Yorker like you learn country-western dancing?"

I say, surprised as he twirls me under his arm with expert ease and brings me close again.

"The steps are similar to a Foxtrot, with a quick-quick, slow-slow rhythm."

"You're always full of surprises."

He spins me into a turn where my back is against his chest and his lips are close to my ear. "I love to keep you guessing."

Flipping me around, he brings me toward him, then away again. The dance is intimate, made more sensual by his confident lead and the way he anticipates my movements.

When the song ends, we stand close. There's something different about the way he looks at me—the familiar, polished charm has evaporated, and his focus is so intense it's a tangible warmth on my skin.

His thumb caresses my hand before he releases it.

"Thank you for the dance," he says.

Neither of us moves, then I say, "I'd better go find my costume and get ready."

Alex shifts from unguarded to serious. "Don't be an idiot about the leg, LT. There's brave, and then there's stupid. You're doing this for a charity, not to save the world."

———

My stomach growls, but I skirt the food area and its noisy crowd. Glancing at my watch, I calculate I might have time to eat something if donning my outfit isn't problematic.

If I survived modeling crazy haute couture, I can endure this.

The sun has set, and the side path I take isn't well-lit. Nearing the end of a barn, I hear raised voices and peek around the corner. Victor and Bradford are in the courtyard, facing each other, while Bradford's bodyguards watch in silence.

"I'm grateful to you, I am," Victor says, tone pleading. "Crown Point was saved because of your investment."

"Investment? Let's call it what it is. I saved you from bank-ruptcy," Bradford replies. "Thanks to me, you're not auctioning off your bloodstock to pay creditors or downsizing from your estate to a rented studio apartment."

"I appreciate everything you've done, you know I do, but some of the terms..."

"You think I bailed you out from the goodness of my heart?" Bradford interrupts.

Yeah, he doesn't have one, Victor.

"No, I...but..."

"You were one missed payment away from setting fire to your property for the insurance proceeds when I found out about your financial difficulties and stepped in. And then you demanded extra insurance due to being freaked out by your debt to me, which made Samira Westbrook suspicious. That was a difficulty I didn't need."

"I took care of things before she dug too deep, okay?" Victor says. "She had concerns about whether the charity event might fold because of the rumors about my money difficulties, but once I got your investment, I thought she would drop it. She was smart, though, and wanted to know more about Meridian's stability as a company."

"You know Meridian serves multiple purposes. Tax efficiency, international transfers, operational funding for projects..."

"I got the impression it wouldn't bear up under close scrutiny."

"Oh? But you chose to do business with me, Victor, so it seems you didn't care to look too closely."

"I've done everything you asked."

"Convenient that Samira Westbrook's no longer asking ques-tions, though, isn't it?"

Should I find Montoya and tell him what I heard? I discard the idea, thinking a motive was hinted at, but there was no real confes-sion. And what about Meridian? If it's a company Bradford has an interest in, is it legitimate or possibly tied to unsavory schemes, maybe even the hunts?

A sudden fatigue hits me, a weight born from the ominous conversation. Reorienting to my original goal, I take another path. It's not far until the costume tent comes into view. The aisles are packed with others locating and donning their clothing. My name is printed on a white piece of paper attached to the top of a suit bag, and I unzip it. The costume that spills out is a red sleeveless bodysuit with intricate gold embroidery on its front. The voluminous skirt is separate, but made of endless amounts of gauzy red fabric.

The tent empties out as I strip to my undergarments and start to tug the bodysuit on.

"I hear you're the star attraction tonight," a man says, and I startle, holding the top of the garment up to cover my chest.

Bradford stands at the entrance, having drawn the curtain aside to observe me. His expression is one of cold appraisal.

"Are you looking for your costume? Maybe a fake mustache you can twirl?" I say. "This area is for the show's cast."

"Everything in Rancho Suprema is my area. I wanted to wish you luck tonight."

"I doubt that. More like you're sorry I survived your hunt and took down a few of the players."

His lips compress in a show of anger that is so fleeting I almost miss it. Then he puts on a pleasant expression. "I don't know what you're talking about."

A rush of people needing to enter causes him to step aside. He holds the curtain for them, the picture of a gracious host, but his eyes never leave me. As the last person passes, and we're alone once more, he lets the silence gather for a moment before speaking.

"Do try to make your performance tonight memorable. The audience can be... unforgiving." Bradford's eyes hold mine for a beat too long, the pleasant mask gone, leaving nothing but a flat, calculating coldness. Then he lets the curtain fall.

It's a clear warning. But is it about my role in the finale or something more?

Talia appears beside me. "Are you ready?"

"How do I mount a horse with this on?"

"Antonio is adept at fastening the Velcro once you're seated."

"Do I have shoes?"

"No. You'll be barefoot. The outfit conveys a mix of warrior and feminine energies. Your headband is at the bottom in a separate pouch." She draws it out and shows me a leather headband with an embedded gold amulet and slight, sharp golden wings on the sides. "This is to imitate the Valkyrie, Norse warrior goddesses."

Chase enters the tent. He wears tight leather trousers, and his torso is bare, except for a gold plate that crosses his chest, attached to fur draping his shoulders. "I've got the Thor six-pack abs, but I think my hair's too short for this role."

"Given your devilish personality, you need one of those historically inaccurate horned Viking helms," Talia says, bringing a huff from Chase. "Remember, be on your horses and ready in exactly one hour."

37

Astride Luciano, I wait in a shadowed chute outside the tent opening. The music's vibrations shudder through me, drums a thunder of hoofbeats, horns screaming ancient war calls. My horse shifts beneath me, a coiled spring of muscle sensing the crowd's energy. I lay a calming hand on his neck, more for my own benefit than his.

The music softens, and a deep, resonant announcement booms through the space. "Ladies and gentlemen! Welcome to Mythos Arena, where legends come to life! Tonight, witness the epic saga of Ragnar, a Viking warrior of unmatched pride, and the battle that might lead him to Valhalla!"

Spotlights sweep the tent in white and red across the mythical battlefield. Performers flood the arena, enacting elaborate combat sequences with precision. Riders hug their mounts' sides, firing blunt arrows at opponents who grab their chests and tumble from their saddles. Others stand on their horses' backs in specialized trick-riding saddles, bending over their animals' necks as they weave between obstacles. A woman stands balanced in a heart-stopping split, each booted foot on a different mount. She rides the momentum of their gallop, balanced as she guides the paired horses around the circuit.

"Behold Ragnar!" The announcer booms. "In his arrogance, he believes himself invincible. But even the mightiest warrior might fall to an opponent's blow!"

A hush falls as Chase Matthews canters into the center astride a white horse, his chest now highlighted by slick oil. His performance is flawless, a fitting portrayal of arrogant posturing that suits his Norse warrior character.

A gigantic man wielding a prop battle axe races toward him on a sorrel horse. Their choreographed combat is a dance of violence. Sound effects mimic steel grating against steel, each parry and thrust punctuated by a guttural cry from Chase or a roar from his opponent. The axe-man swings his weapon in a wide, terrifying arc, aiming for Chase's head. He ducks with an inch to spare, drawing a collective gasp from the audience.

Chase responds with a flurry of attacks, his practice sword a blur. But he leaves an opening—a deliberate, rehearsed mistake.

The axe comes down in a final, brutal swing. The blow lands with a dull thud from the padded weapon.

Chase grips his neck, prop blood spilling down his front, his mouth opening in a silent scream. He sways in his saddle for a long, dramatic moment before pitching sideways and crashing to the sand. His well-trained horse stands still above his unmoving body.

The announcer adopts a solemn, dramatic tone. "A fatal strike! The light fades from Ragnar's eyes. His journey in this world has ended."

Four women dressed in simplified versions of my costume, their skirts shorter and more practical, run forward. They lift Chase's 'lifeless' body with surprising strength and drape him across his mount.

The quiet is so profound that the jingle of my own tack and the soft snort of Chase's horse are audible. The music changes to something haunting and ethereal, which is my cue. I nudge Luciano forward, and we emerge from the darkness into the stark, sweeping spotlights.

The silence is a heavier weight than the noise had been. Each step of my horse's hooves is audible, and my gauzy red skirt flows like liquid fire around Luciano's flanks, but beneath the costume, my skin is clammy. The audience fixes on our progress, while I adopt the serene, sorrowful mask of the Valkyrie guide.

The announcer is now reverent. "But from the realm of the gods, a guide is sent. A Valkyrie, a chooser of the slain, arrives to lead our fallen hero to his eternal reward."

I take the reins from one of the Valkyrie as the announcer adds, "Weep not for Ragnar, for he is destined for the great hall of Odin!"

As I lead the horse carrying Chase, many women and a few men cover their mouths. We complete a full circuit of the ring in a funeral procession.

As we near the exit, Talia charges in on a fierce black mount, wielding a broadsword. She races toward the axe-wielding giant who killed Chase, battling him with superior skill and theatrical flair until he falls defeated. The crowd's roar is a physical wave of sound, a cathartic release after the staged tragedy.

A victory theme swells, and on cue, Chase sits up on his horse, a dramatic resurrection that makes the audience leap to their feet. Arms raised to the heavens, he's the picture of triumphant glory. Talia wheels her black mount around, her face one of fierce joy, and we converge at the center. The spotlights fix on us: the resurrected hero, the avenging goddess, and the silent guide. Then, as one, we signal our horses. Luciano rears beneath me, powerful and sure, his front legs cutting the air. The applause is deafening, and red rose petals rain down, sticking to our sweaty skin and the horses' coats.

The moment we're out of sight, the grandeur evaporates. The applause becomes muffled, replaced by the sounds of the backstage area: handlers talking, horses being walked to cool them down, and the clang of a gate.

Antonio is there, his face kind. He reaches up, finds my waist, and lifts me from the saddle with a grunt. He sets me on a patch of damp grass and takes Luciano's reins. He pats his neck, saying, "Another fine night, *bravo ragazzo*."

A few crimson rose petals remain in my hair, a stark contrast to the fake blood on my fingers. With a sigh, I gather the ridiculous skirt and throw it over my arm.

I survived another ordeal. Go home, take a bath, and rejoice in being a credit to the Ladies' League.

Chase is nearby, dabbing at the fake blood on his neck with a stained handkerchief. "You didn't do too bad for a Western rider." He gives me a slow, appraising look. "Why don't we celebrate our victory together? A Viking returned from the dead who lies with a goddess should inspire some legendary stories for us to enact."

A figure steps from the shadows behind me.

"I'm afraid that won't happen." Detective Montoya approaches Chase, two uniformed deputies flanking him. Around us, backstage conversations die away. "Chase Matthews, you're under arrest for the murder of Samira Westbrook."

Chase is disbelieving. "You can't be serious."

"We have you on video disposing of the murder weapon," Montoya says as the deputies close in. "A riding club member filming her horse's training session caught you placing an item in a rainspout behind the main barn at 6:45 that morning."

Chase gains confidence. "Videos can be doctored. And even if someone saw me throw something away, that doesn't prove anything."

"The witness hesitated to come forward because you slept with her. But when you moved on to your next conquest..."

"So you've got some bitter ex making up stories?" Chase waves away the accusation. "You'll need more than that."

"We recovered the pen you used to stab Samira Westbrook. It contained your prints."

His mouth opens, then closes. "That's, I mean, I use pens all the time at the club. My prints would be on lots of things."

"This particular pen still had Samira's blood on it," Montoya says.

Chase staggers backward a step, the deputies catching his arms. "I... she was..."

"Chase Matthews, you have the right to remain silent..." Montoya recites his rights against self-incrimination.

"She was supposed to be mine!" Chase shouts before the detective's finished. "I saw Victor leaving her office early that morning and thought she'd moved on, dating him because he's so rich. I only meant to talk to her, but she laughed at me. Said I was pathetic, that I'd never change. I didn't mean to kill her. I loved her!"

Tears cut lines through the stage blood as Chase's composure crumbles. Montoya instructs the uniforms to transport him, then comes to where I am.

"Sorry I missed your performance," he says, "but if that wasn't ironic, I don't know the definition."

38

The audience spills out of the tent and is directed by ushers toward the desserts. I wait for them to clear out, feeling deflated rather than triumphant at Chase's arrest. His jealousy destroyed a life and a future friendship in one violent stroke, and my remaining energy drains, worsened by my stupid decision not to eat.

Sherilyn's probably at the chocolate tent. I'll find her after I change.

The grass ends, and I'm barefoot, now stuck figuring out the best way to the costume tent. There's a barn across from me with a sign: "Do Not Enter-Quiet Please!" Maybe I can cut through?

Slipping inside, I pause to let my eyes adjust. There are eight stalls on each side, with horses dozing or hanging their heads out of slatted openings. The center alleyway is made of rubber and swept clean, and the smell of hay, manure, and horses fills the quiet. I keep my focus down, watching for anything sharp.

The barn door opens and closes behind me, and I expect to find a groom or an owner coming to check on their horse. It's Julia. "I saw you come in here and followed to congratulate you," she says. "That was a brilliant performance!"

"Thank you, I'm glad it's over."

She gives my arm a playful jab. "Pretty sure every man in this town wants you now."

"That's definitely not the case."

"What about Adair?" Her brown eyes hold mine.

"Our relationship's...complicated. Anyway, I appreciate your well wishes, but it's been a long day, and I need to change." I turn to walk away.

"Wait! It can't be easy to ride with an injury and be barefoot. Will you be all right?"

"I've been through worse. Are you going to get some dessert?"

"Of course. I don't want to miss out on chocolate." She falls in beside me. "You have some dangerous enemies."

"Why do you say that?"

"Bradford Kensington has an endless supply of money. I concluded he's got a vendetta against you. He didn't appear to like Adair or Alex either."

"Clever of you to figure that out."

"I watch people."

"More than most. So you know Bradford isn't a good guy. He likes to play games."

"Has he done that with you?"

"The drone attack on the horses, a flat tire on my car, and an attempt to infiltrate my home is nuisance level so far, considering."

Julia stops and lets out a short, sharp laugh like I said the funniest, stupidest thing she's ever heard. "You thought that was *Bradford*?"

"Then who was it?" But I know the answer.

She reaches behind her and brings out a combat knife. The blade is carbon steel, seven inches long, the grip worn leather. A good knife. The kind I carry front-line center on my chest during missions.

Now, all I've got is satin with sequins.

"My big regret is the idiots I hired to attack you struck when Adair and the girls were there. If they'd been hurt..."

"This seems a little overboard for jealousy." Inching backward, I scan for any improvised weapons or environmental advantages. There's nothing above me except the roof. "Was the problem I had with Wellington's bridle because of you?"

"Of course. He loves to toss his head, so I loosened it. Thought you'd break your neck or get injured enough that I could finish you off later. Then I would've been there to help Adair through the grieving process."

"Sounds like you've been reading too many novels."

"Adair extended your life by causing me to have a crisis of conscience." Her grip tightens on the knife handle, holding it in a position for a series of efficient strikes. "I fell in love with him. I mean, who wouldn't? But I could tell he thinks he's in love with you. The thought of what your death might do to him gave me pause."

She's an expert shot, has a combat knife, has cataloged my weaknesses, and is good at reading people. How deep does her training go?

Julia takes a step closer. "When James Warden showed up, I saw an opportunity. Kill you both."

She recognized Warden?

"Who do you work for?"

"Work for? I answer to no one."

"I'm missing the motivation, then." I allow my fancy skirt to fall around me. "Figured you were a paid assassin."

"I'm here because of what you did to my father."

Is this another revenge tale brought on due to collateral damage on one of our missions? We can't always know who we killed or who was impacted.

"Your father is?"

She says a name.

Badger.

"That means we also killed your brother."

"By another mother, but yes. We weren't close, but it did devastate my father enough to make him want to wipe your team off the earth."

"I guess it's you who's reviving your dad's network?"

Her forehead wrinkles. "News travels fast. Thought you were out of the loop, but since you're sleeping with your team's captain, he could have let some secrets slip."

"You're pretty efficient if you ran Adair's equine interests while also taking the reins of an international terrorist organization."

"I don't require a lot of sleep."

She lunges for my midsection with lethal focus.

I whirl away, unfasten the skirt, and throw it over her head.

The gauzy garment drops like a net, and she claws at it. I mule-kick her calf, and she loses her balance. Before I can take away her knife, she slices through the netting and is free.

Yanking the Valkyrie crown off, I swing it by the strap. The golden wings cut her cheek. She winces, then slices through the leather with her blade. I'm left holding useless scraps.

I drop the pieces and run.

A cry of frustration rips from her. The exit is too far. I grab a leather halter and lead rope hanging outside a stall. Using the lead like a whip, I snap it backward, then toward her head. She flinches, and a line of blood appears.

The horses erupt. To my left, a hoof smashes a stall wall; to my right, a shrill whinny cuts through the dust hazing the air. A wheelbarrow filled with shavings sits outside a utility stall, a rake leaning against it. I pitch a handful of the sawdust-like flakes into Julia's face. She pulls up short, coughing and wiping her eyes.

Looping the halter over my shoulder, I dive for the rake. A movement—Julia's recovered. She seizes the wheelbarrow and rams the pointed metal tip into my injured leg.

White-hot pain explodes behind my eyes, bleaching the world. A scream echoes in the barn—is it mine? The scene swims back into focus, grainy and slow. Julia leans over me, weapon poised.

The world narrows to the single, cold point of the blade descending toward my throat.

39

A surge of pure instinct overrides the paralysis. My hand shoots up and deflects the blade. A vise of molten agony clamps around my thigh, erasing everything but the need to survive. On autopilot, observations click past. Her knife technique, attack strategy, and recovery time all add up to me being the superior fighter. But my injury levels our playing field.

Julia's dark hair is no longer sleek, but full of shavings and dust. Her cheek bleeds, and her eyes are filled with a mix of fury and intent.

I flip the wheelbarrow on its side, spilling the shavings. Any space is better than none.

Julia reaches across the barrier, slashing with her blade.

A series of cuts scores my left arm. I slam the halter into her head. The blow rocks her, buying me a split second to grab the rake. Blood slicks my arm, making it hard to grip my pointed, improvised weapon.

I attack.

A jab to her midsection. A strike toward her knife arm. A blow to her leg.

I never pause, pressing forward, driving Julia away from me. She ducks whenever I near her head, and her reaction time is faster than expected.

Jab. Smack. Jab.

Lose your confidence. Lose your confidence...

But she continues to hold the knife.

Pressing my attack, I push her into a corner with no way out but through me. Julia strikes the wooden rake handle with her blade. It splinters apart. The impact jars the knife from her grip, sending it skittering away.

I punch her in the face. She wobbles, then catapults into me. I twist away, but she wraps her arms around my neck from behind. Her leg raises to sweep mine. I smash her into the wall. She counters. We crash back and forth, a tangle of grunts and loud impacts.

The knife is out of reach for both of us. It's a secondary problem or a solution, depending on who gets there first. I try for an eye strike, but miss. She stomps on my bare foot with her boot. Sharp pain almost doubles me over. I bring up an elbow to try for her chin —and miss.

With a ragged cry, Julia launches into me like a football player tackling an opponent.

My leg gives out, and I slam down onto my back.

Julia straddles me, punching my face. Her first blow is solid, but I put up my hands to block her. Trapping her leg and an arm with mine, I roll us over. Breaking away, I throw myself toward the knife. Julia lunges, driving her fingernails into the scar on my injured leg.

Another wave of white blurs my vision, but my hand closes around the hilt of the knife. I thrust it behind me.

A shrill scream tells me I've struck home.

Pulling the blade back, I strike again, and Julia falls away.

Flipping around, fiery agony shoots up my leg, but I ride the wave and raise the knife.

My opponent lies prone, her hand over a deep wound to her arm, blood streaming through her fingers.

I lower the weapon.

"That might be your brachial artery," I say. "Your choice if you want to die."

————

Blood from the burning cuts on my left arm soaks into the red fabric of my sleeveless bodysuit, the gold embroidery now sticky and dark. My left foot is swollen and throbbing from Julia's boot stomp, and my injured leg vibrates with a deep, persistent ache that promises days of limited mobility ahead. This wasn't the clean efficiency of a planned mission— it was desperate, messy, and brutal.

I can't leave Julia loose, but don't have the strength to retrieve a rope and bind her. I don't have my phone. Now what?

Julia grows paler as the blood around her spreads. A shape in her front pocket catches my eye, and I pull out her smartphone. It's locked, but FaceID is enabled. She turns away, but I persist and manage to get it open.

When I input a memorized number for my contact at Homeland Security, it rings a few times before a gruff male answers. "Agent Wills."

"This is Davia Glenn. I'm using a hostile's phone, and need an ambulance and clean-up at the Rancho Riding Club." I fill him in on the location and explain that he and his agents might encounter numerous people attending a charity event despite the waning hour.

The line goes dead. No pleasantries. Standard Wills. But I know he's already moving.

"Bradford will kill you, you know," Julia taunts.

"Oh?"

"Yes. I know his type."

"He might try, but I'm ready."

"Didn't my almost taking you out teach you anything?"

"Almost is the key word in that sentence."

A blond man in a suit opens a door on the opposite side of the barn. He speaks into an earpiece, saying, "Found her," and provides details of the location. How did Wills get here so fast? My mind is fighting to stave off the excruciating pain from my wounds and can't piece it together. The man draws closer, and I recognize one of Adair's bodyguards.

"She attacked me!" Julia whimpers.

"She's not a friendly," I tell him, wondering if he'll believe me about one of his boss's employees. "She's the daughter of a known terrorist here to kill me."

The man examines Julia's arm and launches into a running dialogue with the other bodyguards, relaying facts and calling for first aid supplies.

"An ambulance is on its way with Homeland Security agents," I say before he can call for one.

The barn door flies open. Adair bursts through, his other men spreading out behind him, and he makes straight for me.

"Davia, oh god." He drops to his knees, grimacing as he examines my bloodied arm. "What happened? Where else are you hurt?"

"Adair...she tried to kill me..."Julia says, her words faint and pleading. "Please help me."

"No." The single word cuts through her plea sharper than the blade she tried to kill me with, and his cold features are devoid of mercy.

"Adair..." she whispers, then goes silent.

One of the bodyguards has already applied a tourniquet—his belt and a splintered piece of the rake—to Julia's injury. Adair removes his costly Western shirt and wraps it around my arm.

"I owe you for an Aston-Martin, and now this?" I say. "My bill will never get paid."

"And I owe you for my life. Harry, give me your coat."

A big dark-haired guard pulls off his suit jacket, and Adair places it gently around my shoulders.

Another lance of pain runs through my leg, and I suck in a breath.

"You should...wear that. A shirtless photo of you means more magazine covers."

A different bodyguard pulls off his own coat and gives it to Adair, who dresses. Agent Wills and five team members enter and flick on the lights. The sudden brightness makes us all blink.

"Glenn," Wills says when he nears. He resembles Harrison Ford in a serious role, all-business as he takes in the situation.

"This is Adair Monroe and his bodyguards. Here's the phone." I hold it up. "It unlocks through FaceID. Contact Colonel Streeter and tell him this is Badger's daughter. I'll provide details later."

Agent Wills doesn't ask questions. He takes the phone, places it in an evidence bag, and says, "Diehl, you coordinate getting the prisoner to the ambulance out on the street. I want no eyes on this operation, got it?"

"Yes, Sir," says the young agent, who I recall from another cleanup when I first moved here. He and a second agent cuff Julia's wrists, deploy a tactical stretcher from a case, and lift her onto it. Moments later, they're gone.

While one of his other agents retrieves Julia's knife, Wills says, "Do you want hospital transport as well?"

I shake my head at Adair, who has opened his mouth to argue with me. "I'm fine."

A blonde woman in a suit kneels beside me with a first-aid case. She cleans and bandages the wounds on my leg and arm, applies cold packs to my swollen foot and thigh, and hands me prescription-strength ibuprofen for the pain, which I swallow without water.

"That should hold you until you can get proper medical attention," she says, packing up her supplies.

"You need anything else?" Wills says.

"I've got it from here."

Without another word, he and his team leave.

"No wonder you never tell me anything," Adair says. "I doubt anyone you associate with speaks more than a few words in a crisis. Explains a lot about Warden, too."

"We've pulled your car close to that entrance," Harry tells Adair, pointing at a barn door. "Most of the ticketed people have left, but there are a few performers in the area."

Adair has a bodyguard retrieve my clothing bag and purse from the costume tent, while another picks up my broken crown and the torn skirt. "What do I do with these?" he asks.

"I doubt they'll want them," I say.

"Don't worry, I'll compensate them," Adair says. "Think you can change?"

Think I can stand?

"I'll try."

Adair helps me put on my unbuttoned shirt over the bodysuit.

"Can't do the pants or boots," I say.

Not hesitating, Adair lifts me into his arms. "Let's go."

40

I wake surrounded by thousands of books. Sunlight filters through the tall windows of Adair's library, illuminating the spines. The scent of old paper and binding glue is a comfort. I'm on a leather couch where I must have fallen asleep, a cashmere throw tucked around me, and my injured leg and foot elevated on a pillow.

My phone sits on a mahogany side table next to a glass of water and a bottle of prescription pain medication. A different Elmore Leonard novel lies open on a reading chair opposite me, indicating Adair's moved on to something new. Formal gardens are outside, but the floor-to-ceiling bookshelves provide the real comfort now, their orderly presence a stark contrast to the past few days.

Adair enters carrying a tray shielded by a metal cover and places it beside the water and meds.

"I'm going to gain weight if Alain keeps plying me with treats," I say.

"We're all happy he's found a new purpose. When I hired him, I think he imagined he'd be feeding hundreds at social gatherings in my home every few days. Instead, it's been me, Jason, and occasional parties. How are you feeling?"

Weighing my answer, I say, "Better."

"Better like 'my pain levels have dipped from excruciating to extreme' or are you telling me the truth?"

"The nerve pain fluctuates, but my foot is almost healed due to your diligent alternation of ice and heat."

"And your arm?"

"Able to hold a book with no issues."

"Good. Did you remember Alex is going to stop in today?" He checks his watch as a chime sounds throughout the room. "That's probably him. Jason will fetch him."

I sit up a little straighter. "Have you ever considered a butler?"

"Only if it's Alfred Pennyworth, and he's fictional, so Jason will have to do."

There are footsteps and a rap on the doorframe. "Mr. Monroe, Alex Gordon is here to visit Ms. Glenn, and he's brought... provisions."

Jason gestures for Alex to enter. Both men are in tailored suits, but Alex carries a flimsy plastic bag full of something and wears a devilish grin. He nods at Adair, then says, "Davia, I brought you a present to help speed your recovery."

He presents the bag to me with a bow and, when I see what's inside, I release a surprised bark of laughter. It's packed with an assortment of chips, beef jerky, candy bars, energy drinks, and soda, like Alex cleaned out the nearest convenience store.

"Thank you. I'm sure this will be a truly magical cure-all."

Alex removes the lid from the tray beside me. "I figured you might need some comfort food instead of whatever seventeen-syllable French delicacies Adair's been force-feeding you,"

I pull out an Abba-Zaba bar, smiling at the thought of sweet taffy with peanut butter. "Junk food is an American cure-all that he won't understand."

Adair stabs a pretend knife through his heart. "I feel maligned."

"I'll make sure Alain doesn't find the wrappers," I say.

"If you need real-world care, I'm your man." Alex moves Adair's book and sits. "I wouldn't have hauled you out of the barn like a sack of potatoes the way this Brit did."

"You know I was careful with her," Adair protests, bringing another chair closer while Jason lingers in the door, arms crossed. "You forced one of my bodyguards aside to help hold the car door."

"Was it Bradford's henchmen who did this?" Alex asks without preamble.

"It was Julia," Adair says.

"Oh, really?" Alex presses a finger to his upper lip. "I suppose if your face can launch a thousand social media accounts, some of your employees might lose perspective. From now on, you'll need a special screening question for hiring. Maybe 'Rate your jealousy levels on a scale of one to homicidal.'"

"Make a note, Jason," Adair says.

"But she had to have been incredibly skilled to manage to hurt you, Davia," Alex continues.

"She was motivated," I say.

Alex's contemplative expression says he's not buying any of this, but he says, "If you'd like a distraction, I caught the Rancho Riding Club embezzler. Want to hear the story?"

"Sure," I say. "But if this involves talking numbers, I should take some more pain meds to forestall a headache."

"Don't worry, LT. I'll keep it simple. Someone set up a shell company named Golden State Arena Consultants. What drew my attention to it was an invoice for 'arena winterization' in May. Had my team check further, we chased ghosts for a while. The company had a P.O. box, an answering service, and directors who were paid employees."

"Sounds similar to finding out who ran the hunt," Adair says. "Guess shell companies are a trend, like pumpkin spice in the fall."

"This company had been submitting bills for years for routine stuff like monthly consultations and seasonal inspections. When

Samira took over, however, billed amounts dipped. The payments likely seemed routine as they'd gone on so long, and the money wasn't much. So I started digging and found a mistake."

Jason checks his watch. "Are you ever going to tell us who it was?"

"Hold your horses. You both know this, but Davia doesn't. When you set up a new vendor in any accounting software, you enter their payment info—the company name and the bank account number for wire transfers. But on this new, bogus winterization bill? A different bank account number was used. It was right there in the payment file. When I looked into it further, I noticed it matched a number I'd seen before, and a person."

"Who?" I say. "Was it Elise?"

"Patience. I'm almost there. I created a fake invoice from Golden State Arena Consultants for 'Emergency replacement of all piston systems in the outdoor dressage arena.'" He pauses to let the absurdity sink in. "You all know, dressage ground is flat sand. It doesn't have pistons. Marilyn approved it today."

"Marilyn?" I say. "Maybe the trauma…"

"Her trauma can explain away a lot, but not that. And, to tie this all up, when she got the manager position back, she was paying bills and transferred some money owed to Golden State into her personal account. It was the day she went to the resort, and maybe she was in a rush."

"But, isn't she well-off?" I say.

"Yes, but some rich people shoplift for the thrill. She probably got addicted to seeing how much she could get away with. It was a game."

"What was the total over the years?" Adair says.

"Around seventy grand, some from charity events, which makes it more reprehensible. It's not enough to bankrupt the club, but she stole from worthy causes to put some excitement into her life."

I pause between bites. "Did you report her?"

"Waited to see what you thought. I know she's going through a lot right now."

"It's still theft, and she'll probably resume it once she returns to work. If she does return, that is." Picking up my phone, I share Detective Rodriguez's information with Alex. "That's the detective in charge of the hunt case. Call him, and if it's not his area, I'm sure he'll know who to refer it to."

"At least you didn't disgrace the Ladies' League," Alex says. "We beat the fundraising goal for Reins of Hope, and you didn't fall off. Beatrice might deign to look in your direction at the next board meeting."

"Lucky me."

Alex reaches across to snag an energy drink from the bag and pops it open. "Switching topics, any news on who masterminded the hunts?"

Jason comes closer, standing behind Adair's chair. "It's still hard to trace, which was expected. But a logical inference is that because many of the participants who got caught in this last one have parents who hold positions in Bradford's companies, he's connected somehow."

"Bradford doing something nefarious? Say it isn't so," Alex says.

I tell Alex about what I overheard between Bradford and Victor.

"That adds an ominous layer to the reason Victor got so nervous around him," Alex says. "Nothing too far out of left field for Kensington."

"Did you find out anything more about Meridian?" Adair asks Jason.

"It seems legitimate," Jason says. "Victor probably got nervous because he's beholden to Bradford now, not because Meridian itself is problematic."

"If I see a headline that Victor Hayes has been found dead by suicide or he died in some mysterious way, I won't be surprised," Alex says. "Bradford's the type to end potential liabilities."

"Like Eathr and Kennedy," I say.

"But Eathr's still in the wind," Alex says. "Probably floating to parts unknown on an incense-scented breeze."

"Or Bradford's found and killed him," I say.

"That's likely," Adair says. "We don't have any proof, though."

Jason says, "Yet."

The conversation lulls. Alex is the first to rise. "Time to go be a responsible human. I'll call that detective once I'm at my office. And do get better soon, LT. Beatrice will expect a full report at our next meeting."

I settle into the pillows. "Not an incentive."

"I'll walk you out," Adair says.

The men leave, but Jason remains. His usual military posture softens, and he won't quite meet my eyes. "I owe you an apology."

"For what?"

"Julia Darrow got through our screening process and close to Adair and you." His words are clipped. "It's a lapse that won't occur again."

"I appreciate that."

Jason gives a curt nod and leaves.

41

"I'm considering giving up interior design and becoming a registered nurse," Sherilyn says as she changes the dressing on my arm, the disinfectant biting through her joke. "In the short time we've been friends, I could qualify for a trauma response team."

We're in my bathroom. The few days I spent at Adair's were comfortable, but here, the silence is mine. Sherilyn tapes down the new gauze with a precision Hodge would approve.

"There." She chucks the old bandages. "Try not to get stabbed again before this heals. And you said it's related to the same group that came after you when we first met? The one you gave me the minimal 'need-to-know' briefing on?"

"Want some tea?"

"Another diversion. You need to vary your playbook."

"Is that a yes?"

"Fine. But seriously." She follows me toward the kitchen. "I looked for you after your stellar performance because my man took off to arrest Chase Matthews. When I couldn't find you, I hung out with Kyran and Candy at their booth and enjoyed some of their chocolates. Ooh! And they have a new bonbon that's blue on the outside, with rum and dark chocolate on the inside. It didn't stop me from feeling lonely, though! Then Adair texts me that you've been hurt, he's taken you to a hospital where—true to form—you refuse to stay, and you're at his house."

"I told him to bring me home, but he wouldn't."

"Good. Someone needs to stand up to your insanity. And you're supposed to use crutches. Remember? I bet you stashed them in the closet and are pretending everything's fine. Now, you go sit over there." She points at the living room couch. "I'll get us a snack and drinks. And elevate your leg!"

Why did I pretend to be better than I felt? Old habits? I do as instructed.

"These trays are earning their keep!" Sherilyn brings me a glass of iced tea with a plate of sliced cheese, grapes, and crackers. "And don't pick at your food. You need to eat to recover your strength."

"Yes, Mom."

"Speaking of moms, does yours know you're hurt? I bet you give your parents the same nonsense about your life being picture perfect. Which, since they're in South Dakota, is easy to fake."

"They might visit soon with Kyle."

"Another non-answer. Did you at least tell him?"

"Not yet."

Sherilyn situates herself across from me, setting her glass on one of the pretty coasters she insisted I needed. "What about the other wounds, the kind people can't see?"

"You mean PTSD?"

"If you did everything I think you have and don't have issues, I'd be shocked. It's okay to talk about, you know. I mean, you tough it out with your social anxiety, but are you doing the same with the mental trauma brought on by your job? Let's set the before-Rancho stuff aside for a moment and focus on the hunt alone. Look at Francis and the others at the hospital. They were a wreck!"

"Francis is pushing through it best now, but she was the only one who...anyway, she came to the horse event and texted me she's started a support group for the other women, to help them remain connected and go to therapy. Marilyn got charged with embezzlement, but they're not excluding her."

"Bringing us back to my point. You were right in the middle of all that. Are you going to join Francis's group?"

"No. They're not like me."

Sherilyn sputters on her tea. "Oh, really? So you're not human?"

For a fractured second, the room vanishes. The cold metal of the cage floor, figures stumbling through the dark trees, Brittany's broken skull, Francis's glassy eyes—it all floods in at once, a single, crushing wave.

I inhale. "Part of me is...left behind. The events put away."

Sherilyn waits, not speaking.

"It's not that I don't feel it. In the moment, it's about achieving the objectives. But afterward...you can't carry that weight. It will break you. So you don't put it away like a memento in a box. You file it. Like a mission report. The data is there if you need it— lessons learned, threats identified—but the emotion is disconnected. It's a skill, Sherilyn. As deliberate as clearing a room or field-stripping a weapon. You learn to compartmentalize, or you don't survive."

"You're using 'you' instead of 'I.' That's distancing language, like how you deal with traumatic events."

"It's not that I don't have empathy for what the women went through. My job was to act. If I let what was happening—the shock, the horror—dominate my thoughts, I'd be dead, and so might the others."

"I understand your reasoning, but isn't the way you handle the trauma like being a live pressure cooker? You keep sealing all this metaphorical steam inside yourself. You might think you have it under control, but everything could explode. It might be during another life-or-death moment or when a rude driver cuts you off on the freeway. It will be a disaster—and the blowback will be on you."

"Won't happen."

"Really? You're a psychic now? Davia, you've got to realize that you have to become the priority. Take time and let yourself recover."

"Adair offered to take me to see a specialist in England about the nerve damage in my leg."

"See? Everyone around you cares and tries to help. But this brings us back to focusing solely on your physical health. What about mental?"

Do I tell her the truth? That I only feel normal fighting, surviving? That Rancho Suprema's peace feels like a movie set?

"You think the bad things haunt me. That I have nightmares about what I've done."

"Don't you?"

"Sometimes. But not the way you think." I look away, toward the window and the peaceful view beyond. "The real nightmare isn't about my previous job. It's about being *here*. It's about my team being in a firefight and me not backing them up because I'm enjoying a snack on a designer tray." I meet her eyes again. "You see a woman who should be traumatized by violence. I see a weapon that's been put in a drawer. And weapons that sit unused rust. They become useless. That's the true horror. Wondering if, when my team needs me most, I won't be able to help."

"Davia, I've met Warden. He holds you in the highest regard. He wouldn't think less of you if you couldn't work with him again."

"When I woke in the cage before the hunt, I hallucinated. But it wasn't ghosts from my past accusing me of murder. It was my team. They mocked my inadequacy." The memory is raw. "I don't want to fail the only people who understand who I am."

"Okay." Her usual effervescence fades into a grounded calm. "That makes a terrible kind of sense. The great Davia's kryptonite isn't a bullet; it's the fear of being benched. Of becoming obsolete."

"Pretty much."

"The problem is you're looking at this like you're a binary switch. You're either a perfectly functioning weapon in the armory, or you're a rusted scrap in the drawer. There's no in-between. But that's not how people work. Not even people like you. You've been living in Rancho Suprema for four months," she says. "You were injured, you inherited a fortune, moved across the country, and have taken on some dangerous people. Your body is healing. Your mind is allowed to figure things out. It's allowed to be in a third category."

"What category is that?"

"The 'on leave' category. The recalibrating category. You don't have to have all the answers today. But you do have to stop beating yourself up. Warden and the others want their teammate to be whole. And that might mean..." She picks her words. "...figuring out what 'whole' looks like if returning to the way things were isn't an option. Not because you failed, but because you evolved."

"But..."

"No buts. For now, your mission is this couch. This plate of snacks. Letting your leg heal. Letting Adair take you to that specialist. It's not a demotion, Davia, but a strategic retreat. And you're not alone."

———

The quiet that follows Sherilyn's departure presses on me. I'm in the middle of a tactical problem: How will I get back to my bedroom without the crutches?

My phone vibrates with a call from Adair.

I answer. "Tell me you're not calling to micromanage my recovery."

"I'm calling because Jason found a lead on who's behind the hunt. In London."

He has my full attention. I stop pretending I can walk and lean against the wall. "Go on."

"Jason's old contacts at MI6 supplied him with a name: Alistair Finch. He's a banker, the kind who makes complications disappear for a fee. Rumors say he's the architect for the discreet side of Bradford's finances. He could have worked on funding the hunt."

"Is Jason sure?"

"We need to verify," Adair continues. "Finch oversees a portfolio for a client looking to invest in British equestrian sports, and there's going to be a dinner party he'll be attending. It's a legitimate reason for us to be there."

"What's the plan? Ply him with stinky cheese and gin until he spills?"

Adair laughs. "I realize it's only a starting point, but it could open a door."

The coiled frustration of the last few days unlocks in my chest.

"Can you send me the file on Finch?"

"It's already in your inbox. We plan to leave in four days."

"That soon?"

"And I made an appointment with the specialist. I don't want to hear any grumbling about that, okay?"

"I've thought about it. I need answers on whether I'll ever get better, and now there's the added incentive of finding out more about who runs the hunts. I'll be ready."

———

Several hours later, I get a video call.

"Bombshell, you look like you got run over by a herd of cattle." Hodge's words are a slow drawl.

"You shoulda seen the other guy,"

"Or gal, in this case, if you're being accurate," Savant points out.

The team members drift in and out of the frame.

"Good job," K says, two rare words.

"Warden's been green with jealousy since he heard," Ned says, pulling his long hair into a man bun. "And I don't think it's because you took down a target."

"That Brit's a blessing, isn't he, Warden?" Kilburn says, his bald, scarred head glistening in the light. "Able to swoop in and be there when it counts."

Warden doesn't react. "I'm glad you're home."

Their banter is a comfort, but I can't help wondering if I'll ever be with them again on missions.

When everyone's done congratulating me and wishing me a speedy recovery, Warden and I are alone.

"Sorry, I can't come out. You took down the head, now we're shutting down the tail," Warden says, keeping his language vague on this unsecured line.

"I hope this is the end of the story, and another unknown offspring won't pop up."

"Stay alert, stay alive. Any leads on Rapunzel?"

"The commotion was caused by Eathr's Blissful Being groupies. Footage shows an unidentified person in a surgical mask wheeling him out and down a hall, at least that's what news reports say."

"It wasn't Bradford, then."

"For once. There's something I need to tell you." I hesitate.

"What?"

"I got some recent news. Jason's located a possible link to Bradford, a banker named Finch. Adair has a world-class nerve specialist contact in England who can check my leg, and we can meet Finch at some dinner party."

Warden's green eyes go flinty. "So Monroe's your ticket in. I recognize the advantage of using his contacts. But you're stepping into Bradford's world with a civilian for backup and a doctor's appointment as your cover." His voice is direct, now the team leader. "It's a high-risk play."

"Jason was with MI6, you know that."

"One professional who's not at our skill level because he's been off the job for some time and you recovering from serious injuries. Quite the team."

"My primary objective will be to find out the truth about my fitness. I would've gone on my own, but now...you know how much I want to stop whoever runs these hunts." I pause, the words feeling inadequate before I say them. "Warden, I'm sorry."

For a long moment, he's silent. He's running the same calculations I am, and we both know the mission parameters have changed in a way he can't control.

"Understood," he says at last, the word cool and professional. But his eyes hold a different story—a flash of raw heat. "Enjoy England."

The call disconnects.

THE END

ACKNOWLEDGMENTS

Thank you to all the supportive readers and fans of The Davia Glenn series. Without your reviews and social media posts, I wouldn't have achieved the level of success I have.

For advice on finances to inform Alex Gordon's character, I appreciate the input of Timothy Canty, CPFA Vice President at Wedbush, a wealth management company.

Special thanks to Candy W. for input on the equestrian world, my cover artists Cherie Foxley, and audiobook narrator, Stacey Lind.

For critique of my earlier drafts, and listening to me whine about writing, a heartfelt thanks to Collings MacCrae, Anne Lucy-Shanley, and Patrick Davis.

And a final note to Mercy P. and other sexual assault survivors whose cases I handled as a prosecutor— your strength continues to inspire me.

ABOUT THE AUTHOR

Laura Akers is a former prosecuting attorney who handled high-profile murder, rape, domestic violence, and gang trials.

She's a moderator on the Clubhouse App for the Story Sorcerers and Thriller/Crime Mystery Space rooms where writers work to improve their craft.

When not writing, Laura loves watching Korean dramas, photography, and working as an Ambassador for Mission 22 to prevent veteran suicide and help with PTSD. Find her at https://www.Laura-Akers.com